Brave N̶ ̶ ̶ ̶ ̶ ̶ ̶ ̶ ̶ain

To John
Best Wishes
from
Chris Blay
Dec 2020

To Carolyn

Brave New Woman

Copyright @ (Chris Bean 2019)

All rights reserved

•

• • ••• • • • •••• •• • •• •• ••••••• • • • • • • • • • • • • • • • • • •

ISBN: 978-178456-676-0

Perfect Bound

First published 2019 by UPFRONT PUBLISHING

Peterborough, England.

An environmentally friendly book printed and bound in England

by www.printondemand-worldwide.com

BRAVE NEW WOMAN

CHAPTER ONE

He registered her second furtive glance, this time at his lower body. The first one had taken in his robust chest and shoulders, his weather-beaten face and hands. He felt the second one had undressed him from the waist down.

She looked down at her CONSOL and checked her own personal data which was programmed to update hourly; meanwhile he continued talking to the trainees. *Yes*, she concluded, noting that her oestrogen level was crossing the amber-red line and that her body chemistry level showed an imbalance that would soon affect her work output. *Action is required in the coming hours*.

The sex column on her monitor showed no input during the previous five days. *I must do sex tonight*, she reminded herself.

Pressing the presenter's network button she drew down the profile of the male speaking next to her; one hospitalisation for a burst appendix back in 2040 (*typical man for delaying at the first symptoms*, she commented to herself) and with no other medical issue during the last ten years. The sex column showed a high sperm count and virility level with an average self-induced orgasm on alternate days. She returned to her own personal profile and confirmed that her menstrual cycle was still in hibernation mode for another two months. He would do, she concluded.

The columns relating to her body chemistry and oestrogen levels advised a three orgasm fix during the next twenty four hours. She ticked the box marked 'achievable' and pressed the button that transmitted a 'JON' on to his screen.

He paused his dissertation and posted a short video clip to the overhead projector allowing himself time to attend to the JON ...Just One Night.

Looking sideways at her he could see her moistening lips and quickly typed in 'MP19'...The shorthand for 'My Place at seven o'clock' and transmitted it to her screen.

*

At seven, hardly noticing the heaves of the North Pacific oceanic swells, she pushed open the door to his private insulated unit across the non–slip decking from the female block. He was in the shower so she shed her one-piece thermal clothing and oiled her shaven genitals. After she had plugged in the vibrating bed mat that she had brought with her, she laid herself spread-eagled on his gimbal-supported soft mattress.

'Come on. Come on,' she whispered to herself. 'Is that man drowning himself in the shower while hormones ooze out of me?'

The air dryer whined as he came through the washroom door, dragging a halo of overtly male scented perfume with him. His penis was already rampant as he straddled her. Kneeling on her vibrating mat, he pulled her pelvis to his and immediately entered her.

The hormonal flush was instantaneous and orgasm number one was not far away. She moaned to herself, when suddenly a great shudder overwhelmed her.

'Pig!' she shrieked, 'I've not come yet. I'm not that miraculously programmed! You came already?'

'No!'

'You're lying!' She spluttered as he rammed her harder while wondering about the shudder.

She was rationalising and building to her actual orgasm when a second and much more violent shudder jolted the bed off its gimbals, sprawling them both onto the carpeted floor.

'What the fuck?' he gasped, as he disentangled from her and tried to steady himself on the heaving floor. At the same moment the platform's sirens wailed into action.

*

Listening devices and satellite monitoring systems all over the planet began unveiling evidence of unprecedented seismic activity taking place on an unimaginable scale along the entire length of the Aleutian Trench.

Childlike shrieking statements came from mainland broadcasters as they poised over shaking microphones. A three hundred mile long trough in the oceanic water south of the Aleutian chain was opening up, that appeared to be several thousand feet deep. Oceanic islands of the Aleutian Chain itself were becoming a continuous land mass. New volcanoes appeared to be forming every minute and active ones were bursting into eruption.

Stunned scientists worldwide watched satellite images, numbed into disbelief as the tsunami developed. Quakes of nine and ten on the Richter scale rippled across the North American western seaboard, causing so much mass destruction that the reporting had to come from New York and London and from those that managed to scream some words into their satellite phones.

Observatories high up on clear skied mountains round the globe were recording satellite images of a tsunami of approximately two thousand metres height, travelling southwards from the Aleutian Trench at four hundred miles per hour. In a matter of minutes, commentators predicted the apoplectic and catastrophic situation that all land below two thousand meters would be swept clear of life.

Planes in the US and Canada were scrambled by elitists trying to flee to high locations such as La Paz, only to be trashed on broken runways before take-off as the whole of the west coast shuddered and new local tsunamis developed.

*

Simon English and Zack Goldsmith clung to handrails four thousand meters up in the Hawaiian observatory as the whole island shook and shuddered. Miraculously the toughened glass panel overhead and steel structure remained largely intact, as it was built to withstand severe earthquakes and frequent volcanic events. Their solar and wind powered equipment continued to document the unfolding, unprecedented, unimaginable rearrangement of the earth's tectonic plates.

G.P.S. satellite monitors showed the Pacific Plate plunging under the North American Plate, not at the rate of fifty miles in five million years but at fifteen miles in fifty minutes. The pushing forces, that produced a meter or so of movement in periodic earthquakes, had given way to an unimaginable conveyor belt of ocean crust plunging below the North American Plate at the speed of a driving car. The forces relaxed the Aleutian Island Chain allowing them to rise rapidly to create a continuous land mass.

The two scientists looked at their monitors in awe, holding their breath and expecting to die at any moment. With less than four hours before the two thousand metre tsunami would reach Hawaii, they could only pray for their relations and the people of the planet.

Zack clenched his teeth and whined to his colleague that his dire warnings, that no one had taken heed of, were manifesting themselves as they watched their screens, but on an unimaginably larger scale.

He had written to the international corporation in charge of the extraction of the enormous reserves of methyl-hydrate lying like a sausage in the bottom of the Aleutian trench. He had warned them that drilling deeply into an active subduction zone was unprecedented and might have unknown consequences. The corporation and the international community had poo-pooed his speculative comments as fantasy. 'And in any case,' they said, 'The methyl hydrate body was the last known hydrocarbon reserve on the planet and would keep the plastic industry going for at least two generations.'

During the past year, fourteen drilling platforms had been positioned equidistantly along the line of the trench, and highly sophisticated massive umbrella systems put in place, down-current of each of the rigs, to collect the methane gas as it came to the surface. Everything had been engineered to the last detail and accurately controlled by GPS technology keeping all rigs and umbrella systems correctly positioned. The harvested methane was to be polymerised on board the drilling platforms and loaded into waiting barges as slabs of plastic.

The key point that Zack had argued was that their requirement to drill a thousand feet into the bottom of the trench might be dangerous. It was to introduce heat by a complicated induction system between two adjacent bore holes on separate rigs, in order to break down the methyl-hydrate above and allow it to come to the surface as methane gas. Zack had postulated that the substrate itself was impregnated with methyl-hydrate, though be it in small quantities. This would expand enormously, fracturing the rock around it and allowing masses of sea water, under pressure from a six mile high water column, to enter the subduction zone and act as a lubricant.

'I told them!' he shouted. 'I told them if they drilled into the bottom of the trench and introduced heat, the trapped methyl-hydrate would be replaced by a rush of oceanic water under huge pressure, and that would change the dynamics of the subduction zone. They wouldn't listen. But this.....' he wailed........

His words were cut off by an enormous shock wave and the obliteration of their entire observatory by cascades of molten lava hurled out from the crater nearby.

*

Their dismembered torn-off section of tubular aluminium platform with their single insulated modular cabin was spinning like a petal on a windy pond, before it aligned itself with the front of the tsunami.   It did so because it was dragging a handful of severed, long, GPS controlled mooring cables behind it which acted as a rudder and stabiliser. The drag of the cables miraculously maintained the position of their flotsam on the crest of the mountainous wave, holding it back from crashing over the edge. If the terrified occupants of the cabin could have seen what was happening outside they would have realised that they were in possession of the world's fastest and most unconventional surf board, travelling southwards at four hundred miles an hour, heralding the mass extermination of most life forms on the planet.

Amanda and Jason were oblivious to the immensity of their precarious position as they struggled to keep out of the surging water pouring in and out from the bathroom. Finally their module settled out of its crazed spin into a tortuous list of forty five degrees. The scream of tearing metal and the cannon fire of severing bolts had ended, along with the fading sound of distant sirens. The roar of ocean water crashing around them had become deafening and only their high pitched shouts rose above the mayhem.

Their survival skills had managed the catastrophic break-up of the platform and the subsequent spinning of their module. They had wrapped their arms around the swinging gimbals of Jason's bed. Items of crockery and furniture periodically crashed into them, like attacks from aliens whose sole intention was their destruction. It was their incessant cursing that encouraged each other to cling on relentlessly in an effort to survive.

The new, merciful steadying of the unit, after its frantic spin during the earlier minutes, allowed them moments to assess what had happened. Jason's analytical mind reasoned that they had been subjected to a massive gas expulsion from far below their platform and the consequential ripping apart of their rig. He reasoned that the stand-by vessels and supporting aircraft would soon be engaged to rescue them.

Amanda was sullenly aware of her nakedness and was shivering. It was from both cold and anxiety. They had survived the terrifying break-up of the platform which had been miraculous in itself, but without clothing, without heating, and with the constant threat of imminent sinking, she was experiencing a hitherto unknown primeval sense that she took to be 'fear'. Fear was a condition she had seen once or twice in the 'psychic-state' box of her personal profile but she had never paid any attention to it. She had forgotten the routes that were recommended to mitigate it. That depressed her further.

Jason, the ever pragmatic engineer, was preoccupied with their survival. He knew that the accommodation unit, which he had considered his home while on board the rig, was designed to float in the case of a platform break-up. It had a combination of full and empty large oxygen tanks under the floor of the structure which were used partly to buoy up the module but primarily as a component in the polymerisation process that changed the captured methane into plastic. The fact that the venture had only just begun meant that most of the tanks were full and would not help with buoyancy of the module, and in fact were probably responsible for the forty five degree list they were enduring. He registered this as a planning oversight that would have to be tackled in the future.

It was the continuous roar of water rushing past them outside that he turned his main attention to. It was totally dark, and although a partly shuttered window was above the ocean outside, there was nothing to see, and they could only hear the fearsome hiss as water screamed by alongside them. There was no logical explanation. He began to develop the same sense of fear that was afflicting his companion. It was the feeling that something was out of control, and it was that something that he could not get in focus. Maybe, he thought, it was a rescue boat that was determined to tow them out of the danger area, in which case their manic speed would surely slow down soon. This idea had many flaws and he put no confidence in it.

Time went by without any noticeable changes. The incessant roar of the water outside was at such a pitch that they found that their shouting to each other was just audible at the higher octave levels, but very tiring. Amanda had managed to poke her legs behind a grab rail and hook her buttocks into the loop provided by two of the swinging gimbals from Jason's bed. The crazy hammock at least got her legs out of the water and prevented her from careering around the module each time the floor lurched.

Jason for his part had groped his way towards the shuttered window and was finally flung against it by a sudden lurch of the floor. He ended up out of the water at the higher end of the cabin with what he imagined to be his bathrobe tangled around his legs. He grappled up the robe and wrapped it round his waist, with enough slack to tie to the window opening lever. Exhausted by these antics, he let the robe support him for a while.

*

At five thousand six hundred meters above sea level in the Cerro Chajnantor Japanese observatory in the Andes, high above the Atacama Desert in Chile, an international team intensely watched their screens. They monitored the arrival of up to the minute satellite data, showing not only the progress of the monster tsunami heading southwards across the Pacific Ocean but the equally destructive threat of the ever increasing cloud of volcanic dust filling the night skies right up into the stratosphere. The infra-red detectors had listed over two hundred simultaneous eruptions down the Aleutian Island chain, with further new volcanic activity in Hawaii and the Cascade Mountains.

Frightened scientists knew only too well the destruction to be wrought by the tsunami and the violent earthquakes along the Pacific seaboard. They were enduring a constant stream of minor tremors themselves due to the catastrophic rearrangement of the Northern Pacific Plate. Their high altitude protected them from the tsunami, which in any case would have lost some of its great height by the time it reached the Chilean coast, but the effects of global atmospheric pollution and climate change would be inescapable.

The Observatory, along with half a dozen other high Andean observatories, issued the dire warnings that the Northern Pacific areas close to the Aleutian Islands, and down-wind to the south from them for three or four hundred miles, would experience little or no dawn the coming day, followed by a period of several months of cooling and virtual darkness while the masses of dust thrown into the upper atmosphere slowly settled out.

The sulphur dioxide counts within the plume of dust in the lower atmosphere near to the Aleutian Islands had gone off the scale and the condensing moisture from the sea was now bringing incessant acid rain to the region.

The observatories' communications rooms hummed with animated calls to the outside world, predicting the forthcoming devastation as the tsunami crossed the low lands of Central America and headed into the Mississippi and Amazon basins. Within ten hours of the first violent tremor that set the plates in motion, most of the Americas would be either under water or swept away. Furthermore the volcanic dust cloud was now pouring into the jet stream and within days would darken the entire planet. The whole cataclysmic sequence of events, concluded one leading scientist, was on the same scale of mass extinction that ended the Cretaceous period sixty five million years ago, with the demise of the dinosaurs and most other land creatures. In that case it was due to a massive meteorite impact in the Gulf of Mexico.

At the Cerro Chajnantor Observatory in Chile the Japanese team claimed that the Pacific plate in the area of the Aleutian Trench had moved thirty miles to the east in a period of just over an hour between 1900hrs and 2000hrs Western standard time. Their satellite images had been beamed across the globe to London, Moscow and Beijing whose populations were yet to experience the fall-out of the impending catastrophic global tsunami and the inevitable darkening of the skies by dust from more than two hundred simultaneous volcanic eruptions. Scientists commented that the plates may have juddered to a halt by 2000hrs but the damage to our living planet was done, and ominously there may be few survivors.

Animated voices screamed over the airways reinforcing their doomsday prophesy, saying the first daylight satellite images of the tsunami were coming through. A wall of water was seen to be rushing across the Isthmus of Panama while at the same time it was burying the Galapagos Islands completely with the exception of its highest peak, Wolf Volcano, which stood at one thousand seven hundred metres above sea level, an exact marker of the true height of the wave. Flotsam on the crest of the wave brought down from the Aleutians beached itself near the crater and could be seen hanging from its rim as the giant wave passed by. The stark reality could now be seen in the broad daylight images. The lush vegetation of the Western seaboard, the cities and the island communities were no more. Where the sea level had returned to its normal height, the land had been scoured of all physical surface features.

CHAPTER TWO

Dawn was breaking over the eastern horizon of the Pacific as Jason, both terrified and exhausted, managed to get his first glimpses of their dire predicament through the partly shuttered window. At first he was unable to grasp the situation. He could only see the clear sky with a diminishing bright star which he knew to be Venus as it faded in the gathering light of day. Water was rushing past the lower frame of the window like a jet stream from a pressure washer. Stiff from the exertion of clinging to the window lever for the duration of the nine hour night, he just managed to hoist himself further up the sloping floor for a better view through the glass.

Amanda, jammed in her crazy hammock, had managed to alternate the foot that was tucked through the grab rail during the period of darkness. Her cries of pain had just been audible to Jason each time the floor lurched as were her occasional outbursts of loud sobbing. She was clearly as terrified as he was. Ironically she was no longer cold in her naked state and pondered the reason for it. Without heating in their respective heating blocks, the Aleutian island air at five degree Celsius would have killed them both with hypothermia by then but it hadn't happened. There was no internal heating in the individual modules as heating was centralised throughout the platform. Where the heat was coming from mystified her scientific mind. Those thoughts were suddenly interrupted by a shriek from Jason.

'Fucking impossible!' he cried out above the roar of the water. He had long since dismissed the idea that they were under

tow, and his logical mind had evolved a tsunami scenario resulting from the forces that broke up the platform but he was totally unprepared for what he could now see in the early morning light. Their accommodation module was perched on the edge of an abyss. It was tearing along at hundreds of miles an hour on the crest of the monster wave. The white hissing water at the side of the accommodation neither broke nor receded, but just continued along with them. In his blind panic he tried to imagine what was going to happen when the tsunami made a landfall.

As if on cue, he suddenly noticed something sticking up out of the ocean some tens of miles away. He shouted as loudly as he could to Amanda that they were riding a tsunami and it was about to crash into something, islands he thought. All Amanda could do was to groan and grip the gimbals of the makeshift hammock even tighter.

'It's a group of islands,' he yelled. 'Volcanoes! They're miles down below us. We're going over the top of them.' Then he finally screamed, 'No! Maybe not! Hold tight like Hell!'

*

The international community at the high Japanese observatory of Cerro Chanjantor in Chile had continuously transmitted pictures and data from their satellite images. Their animated commentaries of the incalculable devastation being wreaked throughout the plains and lowlands of Canada, America and now the northern parts of Japan and China, became more and more desperate and hysterical. It had become clear that the global tsunami was scouring the planet of all life forms below the one thousand five hundred meters contour. All the major cities had disappeared leaving only a ribbon of flotsam along the fifteen hundred meter line of the mountainous areas. Bare bedrock was showing where important agriculture areas had previously existed.

A French meteorologist and American cosmologist were intensely monitoring the spreading cloud of volcanic dust that had spewed into the upper atmosphere from the multitude of eruptions along the Aleutian Island chain. The plumes had reached up into the jet stream in several places and were beginning to blanket large areas of the northern tundra, stopping much of the sun's light from reaching ground level.

One scientist miserably remarked to another that such a situation was unprecedented in the history of mankind. The only evidence for an event of this scale came from the geological record and the sequence that marked the sudden end of the Cretaceous period, when dust from a meteorite impact caused an extended period of darkness.

Hysterically, the American scientist skipped from one monitor to another, proclaiming that they were witness to the end of a geological era. Shrieking loudly into the transmitting microphones he broadcast to the listeners in London, Paris and Moscow that cooling of the planet would follow in a few days, together with a period of darkness that might extent into months, or even years.

As evening fell in Europe, petrified listeners abandoned their daily routines in panic and started a mass scramble to high ground. Ticket counters and normal channels of commercial transport became chaotic and ceased to function as elitists and bully boys surged to take up the prime positions, creating total gridlock in all the transportation links heading towards the Alps. Violence and anarchy became widespread as the general public perceived the threat to all life.

CHAPTER THREE

No sooner had Jason screamed out to hold on like hell, than massive g-forces hurled them both flat against the front window and submerged them in water as it rushed forwards from the flooded bathroom. Mercifully the surge retreated to the bathroom again after a few seconds and they spluttered for air shouting each other's names. Reassured that their lives remained intact, Amanda coughed out, 'Jesus we are still here.'

Jason heard her clearly for the first time in nine hours and realised that the roar of water rushing past their module had died down, although at the same time a nasty shuddering had begun shaking their whole structure. There was a high pitched squeak of a wire under tension, together with a succession of violent jerks, until the squeal of the wire relaxed briefly before the sequence started again. This happened half a dozen times before subsiding to an uncanny quiet. They peered out of the window unable to understand the sudden changes.

Facing them were screes of volcanic rock debris, leading up to a sheer face of black bedrock with cascades of water running down every available gully from the top. Their module was resting on the loose material with the bathroom end half submerged in the ocean. As they watched, the ocean water dropped further and further down the mountain side, taking with it tons of loose material, leaving them stranded at the same forty-five degrees as before.

Staring up at the rock face, they could just see a tangle of GPS mooring cables. These had once held their section of the drilling platform in place. The cables had apparently dragged across the mountain side until they had slowed the accommodation module enough to pull it back from the crest of the tsunami and eventually bring it to rest.

Within minutes the ocean level was several hundred meters below them and receding rapidly from a vast plain of lava. There was volcanic debris everywhere and gullies filled with water. One area was covered in a large grey film of fabric which Jason recognised as one of the giant 'umbrellas' from their methyl hydrate operation.

Amanda swivelled herself uneasily to face him while clinging to the window lever handle and punched him lightly on the arm and stuttered a statement in shaking jest.

'Well Engineer, we have survived the break-up of the platform, the world's biggest tsunami, hypothermia and now a crash landing on an unknown mountainside. What other thrills have you got in mind for my night out?'

He looked down at her slender naked body and reminded himself that she was not just a model woman but a person hand-picked for her scientific brain, tenacity and communication skills by the methyl hydrate cooperation. She was no one-nighter from downtown Vancouver or LA but a brilliant innovator and hardy veteran of rig technology.

There was a little shudder and he held the window lever more tightly and uttered the words, 'There may be many.'

The moment he spoke the module was overtaken by a mud and debris avalanche from above and started to move downhill. It careered down the mountainside, trailing the cables behind it but stayed aloft of a sea of moving stones and sodden ash particles, like a ship on a tempestuous sea, until it finally came to rest at the bottom of the slope near the water's edge. This time in an almost horizontal position bedded nicely into ash and sand.

'Holy shit!' she exclaimed. 'Is there no limit to the thrills you have to offer? By the way you need to sort out the shower over-flow. There is nearly a foot of water in the bedroom!'

He took a long look out of the window before splashing round the now horizontal floor to investigate.

'Wassal,' he stated in a sigh of relief. He used the Arabic word which had a ring of finality unmatched by any western equivalent. It crudely meant, 'It has arrived at its destination.'

'Can we open the door? I need to go outside for a pee,' she said in a voice that could have been part of a casual weekend camping trip.

He managed a quick smile at her and grinned, 'You are so well controlled! I've had two already.'

'Urgh. You're disgusting,' she whined, while examining the foot of water sloshing round her legs. With that she yanked the window catch upwards and opened up the frame. There was a rush of warm moist fresh air into the room. Furtively she glanced up the mountainside, not sure whether it was fear of further mud slides or hosts of men keen to avail themselves of her nakedness, a ridiculous thought she conceded afterwards. Without further ado, she swung a leg up and over the window ledge to let herself out. Her personal CONSOL would have surely directed her to perform this antic with knickers on, she reflected, as she caught the engineer's eyes following her exit.

She dropped lightly onto the clinker outside and squealed in pain shouting back, 'Find some frigging sandals while you are fixing the overflow! You can't walk on this stuff. I know now why it's called frigging 'aa aa' Lava!' The silence following was only punctuated by the sound of her ablutions. Shortly afterwards she was scrabbling outside the door clearing stones, lava, ash and sand until she could prize the door open and walk in freely. Water from inside the cabin rushed out past her into the bed of sand and rocks, disappearing almost instantly. Sodden items of clothing and papers came with it and lay outside in a heap while the water filtered away. She recognised her knickers and recovered them from the pile and wrung them out. She yanked them on back to front without noticing.

Standing in the doorway with one hand on a hip she demanded, 'What now?' half expecting Jason to produce logical solutions.

'As an engineer I'd say we've survived miraculously so far, but also as an engineer I would say we're still in deep shit.'

She grunted and after a pause said, 'I didn't find the street too busy outside.'

'Busy enough for you to put your knickers back on,' he teased. 'Were you afraid of catching cold or did you think you would start a new fashion trend?'

She looked down at herself and, realising her mistake, peeled them off and hurled them at him. He ducked and followed them into the bathroom and kitchen area, where he began an investigation of what was left of his trashed apartment. She came in after him and sat on the built-in wooden bench seat, which was minus its soft cover but otherwise intact.

'You asked me if I was afraid of catching cold. Well, I want you to know it's bloody hot out there, maybe thirty degrees and it's still early morning! The sun is only just creeping up over the mountain we tobogganed down a few minutes ago. We must be in the tropics somewhere for the night time temperature to be so pleasantly warm.'

Jason stopped searching for useful objects and sat down at the other end of the bench considering her words.

After a while he broke into her thoughts saying that Venus, the morning star, had been obliquely on their left hand side before they grounded. It was in the north-east and therefore by simple deduction they had been travelling south-eastwards at day break.

'At four hundred miles an hour for the average tsunami,' she interposed, 'that means we are probably four thousand miles from the epicentre.' She whistled at the thought of it.

'Which would take us way past Hawaii, to where?' His question hung in the air for a few seconds. 'I could definitely see a small group of volcanic islands before we crashed into the highest peak,' he added.

'The highest peak,' she reiterated. 'How high?'

'Hard to say. Over a thousand meters I guess, maybe two.'

She whistled again. 'This is unprecedented, the planet is finished, or at least most of life on it. Your family, my contacts, friends, our organisation, our civilisation will vanish from the face of the earth.....' Her face was stricken with terror. Their own survival suddenly seemed pointless. 'No place can be unaffected by a five thousand foot tsunami.'

Jason was sullen but remained convinced that logically there must be whole areas unaffected by the massive wave. He said as much and argued that many communities will have had a chance to scramble to higher ground.

Amanda found some comfort in those words and re-addressed her thoughts to where they might be.

'The Galapagos Islands?' She suggested. 'They would be about the right range and right height, wouldn't they?'

Jason shrugged his shoulders, unwilling to speculate.

To Jason, their immediate survival was more to the point. What remained of the contents of his cabin? Closets and cupboards had catches but no safety locks and had burst open with the water surges. He could see a shoe locker remaining shut as it had a sliding bolt at its front. He remembered that he had always bolted it as he tended to overload it and the contents would have otherwise spilled onto the floor. He recalled the pile of soggy clothes outside the door as the water drained away. All the contents of his cabin were there somewhere. Piled up in the corner, he could see his fishing rod and tackle bag, some vac-packed soups and dried fruits plus a host of battered oranges, squashed bananas and papayas. Mops and brushes were tangled together with clothing, broken drawers and bedding. Surveying it more carefully, he could imagine being able to restore some things to a useful state.

His eyes alighted on fragments of his own communication equipment; radios, smart phones and his personal CONSOL, totally ruined, smashed and pouring water from their shattered screens. It was no more than he expected but depressing nevertheless.

His assessment was suddenly interrupted by Amanda, who had been reading his thoughts, suddenly leaping to her feet.

'The fridge,' she exclaimed as she picked her way through the debris.

They had both forgotten the sanctuary of the fridge-freezer. All the units on the platform had their own fridges, customised to cope with the heaving swells of the North Pacific They were fitted with self-locking devices which activated once the doors had been shut. They could only be opened by a manually operated latch on the outside. She slid the bolt and lifted the latch.

Alerted to the sound of items rolling around inside, she barricaded moving objects as she opened the door. It appeared that the only casualty was a ketchup bottle whose contents now rested with the potatoes in the bottom drawer.

They both peered in as if discovering Aladdin's cave. There was an array of litre water bottles, a dozen or so cans of beer and two bottles of red wine plus some mixers, all held securely behind bars in the door.

Amanda was elated. Her own cabin was much less stocked as she was a social bird who preferred to eat in the rig's communal canteen.

On the shelves were vac-packs of smoked hams, Alaska smoked sockeye salmon, the best part of a whole salami and numerous packs of burgers. The stash began to look like a fine shopping mall in LA. Even the battered granary loaf had its appeal.

Suddenly their short term survival was within their grasp, commented Jason, but added cautiously, 'That is if there are no more tsunamis.'

'Or volcanoes springing into eruption,' Amanda added.

He hauled out a litre and a half bottle of water and handed it to her. She closed her eyes and threw her head back while she guzzled down half a litre without coming up for air.

He watched her patiently, taking in the form of her pert little breasts with well-formed nipples. It was the first time he had surveyed her as a girl, as a woman, as a companion and not just a lustful fulfilment of his body urges, since her visit to his cabin and the break-up of the rig.

He thought that perhaps he should be disappointed at the size of her breasts but somehow he knew he wasn't. She was the tough, sexy, skinny woman that maybe would be the perfect survivor in what was certainly going to be a challenging time ahead, he mused.

She handed him the remaining half bottle and wiped the sweat off her brow and chest and then instantly set about the task of clearing up the cabin.

'There's no point in living in a shambles, not knowing what's good and what's beyond redemption,' she uttered.

Jason could see that this was the way it was going to be with her and was thankful for her initiatives.

He opened the locker containing his boots and shoes and located the only pair of plastic sandals. Clearly they would only fit his feet so he put them on. They would have been hopelessly too big for her but he suggested she could look through what remained, and so saying he went outside.

There was a little breeze wafting over the lava fields but it was still inescapably hot. Picking up his hard hat with caption 'Senior Rig Technician' inscribed on it, he rammed it defiantly on his head in defence of the sun's rays. As he did so, sea water trapped under the rim trickled down over his face and shoulders. He snorted in disgust and after casting a few furtive glances up at the volcano decided it was safe enough to do a bit of exploring.

He noted that the ocean was no more than a hundred metres down the slope from where the cabin had come to rest. It was surprisingly tranquil and he could see by the off-shore breeze they were on the lee side of the mountain. After clambering up the slope through the washed bare aa aa lava, he stopped and took a long look around him. There was an uncanny silence; no birds, no bushes to house buzzing insects and definitely no ships or aircraft from horizon to horizon. It was no more than he expected but he found the confirmation of their situation profoundly depressing.

His sense of utter hopelessness was lifted by the sound of his companion scurrying round outside the cabin, rounding up items of clothing that had washed out through the doorway. He caught himself actually grinning as he watched that naked skinny form clutching one item and then another and spreading them out on nearby rocks to dry. She was wearing nothing but his heavy work boots and what looked to be several pairs of socks to pad them out. She reminded him of the iconic cartoon figure from last century, Olive Oil, the lover of Popeye the Sailor man and smiled to himself in jest with the thought he would ask for his spinach later on.

Climbing up the slope for another five minutes, he broke out in a heavy sweat. It was hot, very hot, he pondered. The sun had climbed also and, although he reckoned it was no later than ten o'clock, it was already very high in the sky above the volcano. As he judged the elevation of the sun he noticed a thin, wispy column of smoke rising from behind the top of the mountain.

'Active,' he quietly noted to himself. Worrying, he considered whether the volcano had smoke rising from it during his previous glances. He didn't remember any smoke and his depression returned.

Although his previous outdoor activities had allowed him to develop a reasonable tan, he was now aware of the powerful sun on his shoulders and hoped that 'Olive Oil' had located one of his t-shirts.

As he turned to come back down, he caught sight of the big grey area off to the south which he confirmed as one of the huge methane collection umbrellas. It must have made the same journey as them. It had spread itself over the lava, covering an area the size of at least a couple of football pitches. He filed the information away in his brain without any ides of a future use for it.

Amanda had found the foam cover to the kitchen bench seat. She had it rolled up and was standing on it to squeeze out the water as he arrived back at the cabin. He grinned at her, shooting glances at her footwear without saying anything.

She caught his glance and fired a crackly comment in his direction.

'You don't look so frigging wonderful yourself with your 'senior rig technician's white hard hat on your head and jelly sandals on your feet with your precious tool swinging in the breeze!'

'Hmm,' conceded Jason and went into the cabin to see what he could do next.

'The volcano is smoking,' he stated as she came back inside.

'So?' she said curtly. 'Isn't that what volcanoes do?'

Her mood was definitely testy. She was clearly missing her CONSOL, thought Jason. Today's high-flyers had become twinned to their CONSOLS and now he was going to be subjected to her withdrawal symptoms.

'Did you see smoke before?' he offered.

'Not particularly.'

'Not particularly? What does that mean - yes or no?' Jason was irritated now.

'Well no then – I didn't notice any smoke,' she conceded and looked up concernedly at the mountain top. 'What does that mean? Is it about to explode or something?'

Picking up the mop, she began furiously cleaning the floor spaces that were cleared of debris.

He didn't answer her and assumed her vigorous actions were a ploy to disguise her underlying panic. She was better educated than he was and Jason knew he had no need to explain the relationship between plate tectonics and volcanicity. It almost went without saying that a violent movement of the earth's plates would trigger volcanic eruptions.

He looked again at the mountain top.

'Maybe its steam,' he suggested, 'just drying out.'

'My arse,' she snorted without looking up from her mopping. 'Since when did steam have yellow curls in it?'

They continued in silence sorting out the cabin until it began to have the homely look about it that it had while part of the platform four thousand miles away. It lacked an electricity supply, a water supply, any form of communication linkage, and looked totally incongruous resting on a lava field somewhere in the tropics, yet nevertheless Jason conceded it represented a home and a shelter.

As the sun went down he opened a tin of sockeye salmon and sliced up the battered loaf of wholemeal bread. They sat together at the kitchen table, now with its restored soft foam seat. They ate hungrily and shared a can of beer plus half a bottle of water. A sense of civility returned and the previous tensions began to melt away. They had spoken little for most of the day, each being preoccupied with the outfacing dilemma they had found themselves in. As the light faded, they each knew that it was only their joint resolve and resourcefulness that offered any hope.

He apologetically put his arm round her shoulder and gave her a reassuring hug.

'Sorry I fucked up on your evening out.'

She relaxed and gave his hand a tight squeeze and giggled.

'It was a little different I suppose. If that frigging volcano keeps quiet maybe there will be other nights.'

CHAPTER FOUR

They slept together on the floor on top of his mattress, now no longer in gimbals. It was still wet, as was the carpet, and with the atmosphere hovering round dew point they admitted it was far from ideal. However their tiredness soon overcame those issues and they slept for several hours.

She had put her knickers back on, this time the right way round, and he slept in the shorts and t-shirt he had worn that afternoon. There had been an unaccountable restoration of their previous relationship, the considered norm between one colleague and another. The lust and desire of the 'JON' had been eclipsed by the traumas of the past twenty four hours. Amanda had not put on a bra for her visit and, now naked, her pert little breasts seemed normal and natural. Those features could have been part of a sculpture or freeze round a Roman temple.

On the mattress they spooned, turning together from time to time. Jason had removed his t-shirt soon after they lay down but their sweaty contacts became so unpleasant that they mostly remained apart.

It must have been the early hours, Jason calculated, when he rolled off the mattress, slid into his sandals and went outside for a pee. He spent some time looking up at the volcano. Nothing was different except he thought he could detect a very faint glow on the underside of the smoke clouds that silhouetted themselves against the starry sky. The air was still. The smoke rose up into the atmosphere in an almost vertical column.

His mind tried to focus on what must have happened to the

rest of the planet. He could not help thinking that the present situation of tranquillity was anything else but the calm before the storm, figuratively speaking.

What could be left after a fifteen hundred metre high tsunami swept across the surface of the earth? he asked himself. *Would it just have affected the Pacific? Not possible,* he concluded. What of his family? What survivors would there be on the higher ground? What industrial base could survive? How could they themselves possibly survive with no more than a week's supply of food and even less of water?

Jason had a passion for living and at that depth of depression the animal instinct kicked in.

They would survive!

He firmly convinced himself. He would draw on all his skills to make water, to make fire, and to find food. Maybe species of fish would have survived as the giant ripple crossed the ocean's depths.

They would have risen to the surface ahead of tsunami and dropped back to their normal depth after it had passed, wouldn't they? These thoughts were unconvincing. They could distil sea water or make a solar still, he reassured himself. At least they would not die of thirst.

His last thoughts were disturbed by Amanda coming out from the cabin and shuffling across the clinker in her oversized boots.

'What's new?' she demanded.

'Nothing. Just thinking. The volcano is quiet anyway.'

'Then what is that glow on the underside of the smoke clouds?'

'Hot lava I guess,' he suggested, knowing it actually needed no explanation.

'Let's hope it stays within the caldera,' she commented nonchalantly. 'It's hot enough as it is and by the way, when are you going to fix the AC?'

'When you provide me with some electricity,' he quipped.

They both knew the answer to that and no more was said as they made their way back inside for what was only broken sleep until dawn.

*

They were both up, with footwear on, by the time it was light enough to see. It was the coolest part of the day and probably the right time for exploration. Retracing his footsteps up to the vantage point of the previous day, he allowed Amanda to take in what he had observed. There were still no traces of life to be seen. In the direction of the sea there were no birds, no fish shoals, no dolphins or anything. Neither was there anything on the island, no bushes, no insects, and no lichens; nothing but clean washed lava fields.

They clambered up the rocks for half an hour, hoping that a view round the corner of the mountain might bring them more encouragement. Their route was impeded by a deep gulley leading up into a dark cavern-like hole in the side of the mountain.

Amanda, who seemed to have some knowledge of volcanoes, declared it to be a lava tube, where periodically fresh lava would rush out, once the caldera level had reached a certain height. This was usually just before an eruption.

With some trepidation they climbed down into the gulley, intending to climb up the other side and continue their way round the mountain, when suddenly they both got a whiff of an obnoxious gas emanating from the hole where the gulley entered the mountain. They were on the point of arguing as to whether it was sulphur dioxide or hydrogen sulphide or a mixture of both, when a deep reverberating hollow sound, followed by a rushing noise like moving gravel, caused them to grab each other in panic. They rapidly scrambled back up the gulley side in great haste.

The experience was so intense that they kept running for a further five minutes, until they regrouped, totally out of breath, a safe distance from the gulley. They waited a while, expecting a rush of molten lava to pour out of the mountainside. It didn't happen. Convinced that it might do soon, they made their way back across the lava fields and over to the cabin and then continued down to the water's edge.

Being completely downwind of the mountain, the effects of the oceanic swells were negligible. Only small wavelets lapped the shore, rattling the freshly deposited volcanic debris that had washed off the mountain. Here and there were white battered coral heads that had been ground down by the abrasive clinker as it surged to and fro at the water's edge.

For Jason, coral was synonymous with fish, but this battered and destroyed coral would provide no habitat for fish anymore so, disappointingly, another source of food looked unlikely. The tsunami had certainly taken its toll of life. They both became very despondent and trudged back to the cabin in a state of misery.

Sitting down on the kitchen bench seat again, they evaluated their options. Number one, they concluded, rescue seemed very unlikely for an indefinite period; number two, since they only had three days water, they had better prioritise making or finding more; and number three, their most likely source of food was probably fish that may have survived the tsunami. They should surely devise methods of attracting and catching them as a food source.

'Fourthly,' Amanda piped up, 'we shall need to make fire in order to cook whatever we might get from the sea.' She then offered, 'I could make a solar oven by scavenging through the trashed items piled up in the corner over there.'

Jason took some heart from these enthusiastic remarks. He knew that the brain of his companion was not just wasted by lecturing the newcomers on the rig. The depth of her knowledge was far greater than that.

'What about a solar still?' he enquired.

'You will have to dismantle the AC to give us some copper pipes,' she responded, and added as an afterthought, 'The bathroom mirror will have to go to enhance the heat flow on the sea water unit. You have several pots and pans........It could be done.'

She paused, her mind racing on. 'We best do it down by the sea, where there is plenty of water for cooling, to make the condensate.'

He was considering dismantling the AC and the engineering issues involved, when his eyes suddenly alighted on the two metal pipes alongside the skirting board, that had conveyed the hot and cold water to his cabin from the centralised distribution system in the heart of the rig. The pipes had been severed somewhere beneath the floor of the cabin. Without too much difficulty, he could recover some lengths of these pipes and they would be ideal for the still they had in mind. Amanda followed his eyes and gave a nod of approval.

An hour later they were down by the water's edge, equipped with a five gallon metal drum, which had contained cooking oil, the bathroom mirror, a couple of metres of copper pipe and a large saucepan. After some difficulty, Jason had affected a seal between the can and the water pipe, using tape and chewing gum. After selecting a rock shelf some distance away from the water's edge, the equipment was set up. Amanda wedged the mirror up in such a position that it reflected the sun's rays onto the side of the drum, which had been partly filled with seawater.

Jason's task was to fetch sea water to pour on the copper pipe, to cool it and condense the water vapour. The operation was so labour intensive that they reckoned more water was sweated out than they were producing. 'Clearly something better needs to be done,' commented Amanda, as she scurried off along the shoreline to find a better site.

Looking up from his task, Jason followed her lithe figure as she hopped from one rock to another and allowed himself a private smile. *What a spectacle she made*, he mused. She was wearing his oversized work boots, a tea towel round her waist and a hand towel over her head, which she had fashioned into a hat that trailed down over the back of her neck, in the way typified by the legendary French Foreign Legion of history books. The sight of her small breasts had become so normal to him now, that they no longer held his gaze; rather they symbolised a pleasant acceptance of their shared existence.

Some moments later his thoughts were interrupted by a shout from her direction. He could see her head-dress peeping up from behind a rock promontory and a flaying arm beckoning him to come over to her. His first thoughts were that she had hurt herself on the aa aa lava, and he prepared himself for bad news. Soon he realised it was something in the water that she was waving about.

He joined her and followed her finger to a white object bobbing about in the waves some fifty metres out.

It was a bizarre shape and appeared to reflect light from a scaly, almost reptilian surface. Jason, not in the mood to let anything slip from his grasp, peeled off his t-shirt and hard hat and waded in. Soon he had to swim, at which point he lost sight of his target. Amanda wailed directions from her vantage point and soon he could see the shape again. It appeared to be the upturned body of a scaly reptile of perhaps a meter in length.

'Urgh!' snorted Jason in horror and stopped swimming. He was unprepared to do business with a crocodile, alligator or any other such beast and retreated cautiously back towards the shore, where he could tread water and survey the creature from relative safety.

'Is it dead?' demanded Amanda from the shore.

'Can't tell. It's a crocodile I think. It's on its back and not moving.'

Amanda was on her way, not wanting to hold a biology lesson over forty metres of water. She had slipped her boots off on the shoreline and made an impressive swim to his side.

'It is not a crocodile,' she said with authority. 'Look at its feet. It is, or was, a land animal.'

She approached the corpse cautiously, with Jason a couple of lengths behind. It was big when they got closer. *More than a meter*, thought Jason, revising his former estimate. Its tiny short legs and clawed feet were tucked in against its body and were just awash.

Jason's bravado had returned so he gave it a substantial prod. To their surprise the reptile gave a flicker of response. The slight tail movement caused them to back off.

'Not quite dead; injured maybe,' suggested Amanda. 'I don't think it is well enough to be dangerous. Let's try pushing it ashore.'

The scaly object showed no further signs of life, so they gingerly grasped a leg each and glided it slowly to the shore, keeping well away from its head.

Once in the shallows, they beached it on a smooth coral head and studied it in amazement.

It was heavy out of the water. 'Maybe twenty kilos,' commented Jason, as he rolled the dead weight over. The poor creature's nostrils and mouth drained of water and bubbled. The whole body was armoured in large green scales. It had a prominent dorsal spine that made it look like the stereotype dragon of fairy stories. Amanda claimed it to be an iguana, one of the giant lizards of the Galapagos Islands.

Jason shook his head in amazement. Amanda kept nodding her head, as if to acknowledge the correctness of her guess of the day before.

'We better haul it up the beach so it can't escape if it recovers', he remarked, thinking of their dwindling food supply.

Amanda gave it another nudge without effect. She said it was probably brain-dead as a result of total submergence under a thousand metres or more of water and would never recover. Jason agreed but remembering an old Arab proverb, *Trust in God but tie up your camel*, he proceeded to build a rudimentary corral out lava rock and then dragged the reptile up the beach and into it. With some finality, he placed a couple of big stones across the entrance.

'So!' she said emphatically, 'The Galapagos! It was a guess but it seems I'm right. These creatures are only found there I think. Ten degrees north and a thousand miles from the Ecuadorian coast.......' she paused, while desperately trying to recall her oceanographic knowledge. Like most academics, engineers and even lay persons of 2050, she had become heavily reliant on her CONSOL for accurate information and now felt lost without it.

'Does it rain here?' she mused.

'I think they have rainy seasons. Surely it must rain near the top of the high mountain,' he added hopefully.

'Frigging engineers,' retorted Amanda, disgusted. 'They only know about nuts and bolts and the strength of materials!'

Jason, a little downcast, choked out something that seemed intelligent. 'There must be strong sea currents and predictable winds. After all, Darwin found the place without any help, didn't he?'

Without further discussion, Amanda announced that she had found a better location for the still, where sea water spray frequently plopped on the rocks adjacent to a suitable site. This would save the arduous task performed by Jason with the saucepan.

They quickly moved their rudimentary equipment to the new location but were depressed by the small amount of water they had so far collected. He suggested that the collection vessel needed insulating and trotted off back to the cabin.

Shortly afterwards he returned with a kettle and soft clothing, and proceeded to arrange the copper pipe so it flowed into the spout of the kettle, wrapping the soft clothing round the outside for insulation.

'That happens to be my elegant one-piece thermal underwear,' she whined in dismay. 'What if I need it?' The fake hurt in her voice faded into a grin as she wiped beads of sweat from her face.

'Anyway, Regina blew out more bubbles.'

'Regina?' enquired Jason, raising his eyebrows. 'Why Regina? Maybe it's a male.'

'Jason, I used to think you were intelligent. My CONSOL indicated that you had a brain! Vagina. You know what that is I suppose, so I thought that as the name rhymed with that word you would remember. Regina has an anatomical feature I thought you might have recognised!'

'Ah!' chirped up Jason, 'we have an engineer's song about that......

There once was a girl called Regina,
By gum she had an enormous.......

'All right. All right!' interrupted Amanda. 'There is no need to descend into boy's locker-room drivel in the presence of a lady.'

'Some lady,' muttered Jason under his breath, as he followed her naked form back to the cabin and the shade they so badly needed.

The cabin had become a centre of refuge against the heat of the day. It was both insulated and level, unlike any of their outside world. The sky was an unbroken relentless blue. The little breeze there was had come round the mountain and had heated up over the black lava. Jason had commented earlier that, judging by the position of Venus at night, the steady direction of the wind was westerly.

The presence of a steady westerly wind inspired them into discussions about reaching South America by wind power, if only they could build a vessel of some sort. These discussions always ended in depression once they took stock of their present precarious position. Unless the still did brilliantly, they had only two days of water and not much more than that of food provisions, plus the fact there were no materials to build any sort of raft or boat.

'Doesn't the Ecuadorian current run counter to the wind?' Jason enquired, thinking back to his oceanography briefing prior to working on rigs.

She had lost her enthusiasm for conversation and gave no answer. She felt it only led into deeper realisation of their desperate situation. She was hot and sweaty and having peeled off her head and waist wrap, lay spread eagled on the floor mattress with her eyes closed.

Jason allowed himself an unashamed contemplation of her body. In any normal situation he would have lowered himself on top of her and made love but somehow at this point in time it seemed inappropriate and almost a violation of each other's space so he refrained.

Lifting himself wearily off the bench, he sauntered over to the fridge. It didn't smell too good anymore, so he assessed the various products in their vac-packs and made a mental note of their eating priorities. The vac-packed ham would have to be eaten before it went rotten or became dangerous to eat. He hauled it out and evaluated it as four portions. The dilemma was the half not eaten that day would spoil by the next. *What to do?* he pondered. Wasting their precious food supplies was not an option.

Thinking about the sailors of old, who used to cross the Atlantic with only pork and biscuits, he suddenly seized upon the idea of salting the half they were not going to eat straight away. Before his enthusiasm waned, he grabbed a bowl and took off to one of the nearby gullies, where he had seen crusted salt deposited following the receding waters of the tsunami.

On his return, he cut open the ham vac-pack and sliced it up, salting half for the next day. Satisfied that they could eat well the following day, he then set about laying out a supper.

Amanda roused herself shortly afterwards and they ate hungrily. 'Warm pork and warm beer,' remarked Jason, 'but preferable to eating raw Regina!'

Amanda let out a groan of agonised disgust but enjoyed the feast.

CHAPTER FIVE

They arose from their slumbers as the heat went out of the day. Amanda was the first out of the cabin, anxious to look at the still. She had paused and was staring up at the volcano when Jason came out.

'Wow! Look at the sunset!' exclaimed Jason as he shuffled into his sandals and then hesitantly looked up a second time with a more serious look on his face.

The sun was an orange disc with areas of red, purple and green above and below it. The streaks finally disappeared behind the summit of the volcano.

'Well?' demanded Amanda.

'Dust in the atmosphere,' said Jason cautiously.

'Not from this volcano?' stuttered Amanda, with a definite tremble in her voice. 'What does it mean? Volcanoes far away, nuclear explosions or what?'

'Nuclear?' muttered Jason, 'I hadn't considered that. I suppose many nuclear installations will have been wiped out by the tsunami. It doesn't bear thinking about.'

'They have shut down procedures taking less than an hour these days,' she stated. 'Only their plutonium stockpiles would have been affected. The tsunami warning would have been broadcast efficiently, allowing shut down procedures to have taken place. They all have multiple earthquake provisions. There would be no dust. In my opinion this is volcanic dust.'

They looked at the sky a while longer before going down to the shore. The still had produced about a cupful of fresh water, much to their surprise.

'So!' exclaimed Amanda enthusiastically, 'Mathematically we can capture enough fresh water to stay alive if we build more stills.' She took some comfort from that and without saying more, went over to the corral to check on Regina.

The reptile had blown a few more bubbles from her nostrils and moved her tail from the earlier position and they agreed she was definitely alive, and hopefully would remain that way until they needed to eat her. They were Jason's words.

By the time they reached the cabin, it was almost totally dark and they expressed surprise at how rapidly darkness had arrived that day and that no stars could be seen through the hazy sky. Groping their way over to the bench seat, they realised that the starlight of the previous night had been enough to see the basic shapes in the cabin but not tonight. The only light was the uncanny orange glow on the underside of the volcano's smoke.

'This dust in the upper atmosphere: is it global do you think?' enquired Jason thoughtfully. 'Do you think it will last for long?'

'Depends how much volcanicity resulted from what we assume were drastic plate movements in the Aleutian area.'

'There are dozens, if not hundreds of volcanoes in that chain. I saw them several times when flying out to the rigs,' he said.

'It's unlikely that they kept quiet when so much tectonic activity was going on right on their doorstep,' she concluded. 'The tsunami was unprecedented. I assume the plate movement must have been massive and I can only believe that dozens of volcanoes in the Aleutian chain will have been triggered into eruption. The plumes of dust would have entered the stratosphere and the circulation will have gradually become global. That is what we are seeing now, I reckon.'

'Holy shit!' Jason exclaimed. 'Could last for days then.'

'More likely weeks,' responded Amanda, miserably thinking about her solar still.

'Holy shit!' repeated Jason. 'I remember reading about the event that ended the Cretaceous period. The author talked about two years of darkness following the meteor impact and the dust in the atmosphere. How are we going to cope with that?'

'I can't imagine it is going to be anything like as long as that,' she said sullenly. 'After all, it has taken two days to reach us here and the dust will be settling out all the time.'

Jason remained unconvinced and totally depressed. He recalled, from the account he had read, how the blocked sunlight had allegedly prevented photosynthesis taking place, and that all green plants had vanished from the face of the Earth.

They had a long discussion about making water should the solar still fail and concluded that the simplest method would be to boil sea water and condense the steam. There were two problems however, they conceded, one being they had no fuel and the other was that they had not yet devised a way to make fire.

Jason, playing out his engineer's role, went into a dozen or more possibilities of creating sparks using various electrical motors, coils and magnets from the AC, fridge and other gadgets, and a hand cranking mechanism to get them going. The long technical talk made Amanda sleepy but she finally pitched in the remark that dismantling her vibrating mat was only to be the last resort!

Hope was all they had left, she thought, and went to sleep.

The night was oppressively humid and they slept badly. Jason got up off the floor and headed outside for a pee. Something had awoken him other than his bladder and he instantly realised what it was as he headed outside. It was raining.

'Amanda it's raining!' he shouted and tripped over her as he groped for saucepans, buckets and bowls to put outside.

She was instantly awake and pushed her way outside to experience the event. That night one of her recurrent dreams had plagued her. It was to do with dying of dehydration. Now this was a salvation.

It wasn't heavy rain but it seemed to be getting more persistent all the time. Jason commented that the saucepans were tinkling with each heavy drop and it would not be long before their production overtook the solar still. He gave her a little hug which needed no explanation and they crawled back to their sleeping positions with renewed hope.

The night seemed endless and they dozed fitfully for some hours expecting it to get light. The rain had become incessant and rivulets could be heard tracking off the cabin's flat roof. Jason slid his sandals on and ventured outside to assess the situation, quite happy to get a shower and wash the saltiness off his body, which had bothered him since his afternoon swim.

There was enough light to see the outline of the cabin, the volcano and adjacent rocks, so he stood under a cascade coming off the roof and showered. The rain and the run-off water were pleasantly cool after the stifling humidity of the night. He called to Amanda inviting her to luxuriate in a tropical shower. She needed no prompting and was soon under a cascade coming off the roof. She took an exaggerated sniff at the air and wrinkled her nose.

'Sulphurous a little bit I think.' Licking her lips she added, 'Definitely sulphurous, like the hot springs in Yellowstone. We at least know it's not nuclear dust,' she said with relief, 'just acid rain from the sulphur dioxide spewed out by volcanic eruptions. We can cope with that.'

'Is it okay to drink?' enquired Jason with a worried voice, from the rim of an upturned saucepan. 'It tastes like a chem-lab smells.'

'You won't die. When it gets light we can bash up a piece of coral rock and filter the water through it,' she said wisely. 'That should zap the acidity.'

'When it gets light? You know I don't think it's going to happen. The light has not increased during the whole time we have been outside and also it hasn't got any warmer has it?' he reflected seriously.

She shot a concerned glance in his direction.

'You mean this is it? The two years of darkness, the nuclear winter they mentioned followed by the mass extinctions of dinosaurs and eighty percent of all life forms?' She sounded distraught. 'Will it get colder?'

'Almost certainly so, at least according to the geological records,' he paused. 'I think the evidence is that after some years it gets hotter as the greenhouse effect kicks in. No green plants, no photosynthesis and no carbon dioxide absorption.'

He painted a very gloomy picture much to the distress and annoyance of Amanda.

She knew only too well that what he was saying was reflected in the geological record, yet she was not prepared to accept that the current scenario was anything on that scale.

'For one thing,' she insisted again, 'it took more than two full days for this curtain of dust debris to reach us and it could be just local to the Eastern Pacific. I cannot believe that this is the catastrophic global wipe-out you would have me believe! I cannot imagine this place getting cold either.' She was testy, her words covering a thin veil of fear. 'You must surely realise we are surrounded by ocean which has an incalculable amount of heat energy stored up in it. A few degrees cooler would be quite pleasant. In any case we have the volcano.'

Jason thought better than to argue with her. He also did not believe that the darkness could be anything but temporary, a week at the most. He said as much to Amanda who seemed unsure whether to believe him.

'Inshallah,' she muttered as she struggled on with her boots and took off down towards the sea avoiding any further disagreement.

'Where are you going?' demanded Jason.

'Checking on Regina.' Then over her shoulder, 'and recovering my thermals!'

He sploshed off after her in the half light. They recovered the components of the still and while she was prodding Regina for signs of life, he located a cobble of coral rock and carried it back to the cabin. Her silhouette soon appeared beside him and he could just make out the shape of her sodden one-piece thermals tied round her neck. By this time the incessant rain had made them both cold enough to be grateful for the sanctuary of the cabin's interior.

In another development they had both started coughing as a result of the sulphurous air whenever they exerted themselves.

They shared a beer and washed the salt out of Jason's ham left from the day before. They ate hungrily and finally downed another bottle of water.

'Four left,' remarked Jason, as he fumbled his way back to the bench. 'I suppose we should store up as many bowls and buckets of water as we can in case the rain suddenly stops.' He then added sullenly, 'There seems no urgency,' as the rain pounded on the cabin roof. Rivers of water were running off the mountain in all directions.

'The ham didn't taste too bad did it?' he said trying to cheer up and then without waiting for an answer, 'I guess we don't find salt so easily now. Good job I kept what was in the bowl. Do you think Regina would be nice salted?'

'Ugh!' she responded in the dark. 'She might revive now it's raining and escape. You never know.'

There was almost a note of optimism in her voice as she could be heard ringing out her thermals in the doorway of the cabin.

'Can we not make light of some sort, if we are to be here through days of darkness, so we can at least see what we are doing?'

Jason thought long on the subject before answering. He knew he had a small pencil laser torch somewhere in his possessions but could not imagine where it could be or whether it would still work after being swamped. He needed light to search for it in the first place, so chose not to mention it.

'Wait!' she said enthusiastically. 'You have a door key? There is a light attachment on it if it is the same as mine. Where is the key?' She groped the obvious place and there it was on the inside of the door. She let out a little cheer and pressed the button. A small light beam illuminated the cabin.

'Ah. We are lucky the door never got submerged like the rest of the cabin. Now engineer, can we use the little light to make a bigger light?'

'We have a couple of gallons of cooking oil and some string to make a wick', he chirped up in a positive manner.

'A spark to light it?' she queried, always seeming to hold the stopping card.

'Hmm,' he considered, thinking of the various totally wet electrical items around the cabin and in any case, sparks needed a flammable gas or liquid to generate a flame and they had neither. It would take more than a spark to ignite cooking oil unless there was loads of oxygen, he suggested to Amanda.

'I know where there is loads of oxygen,' she suddenly exclaimed. 'It's right under your feet.'

'Halleluiah!' he shouted. 'I had forgotten all about that. This could be a life saver!' He jumped to his feet.

'If we make a light with a flame, we can also cook and ultimately we could control the air that we breathe!' With that he deliberately coughed to emphasise the sulphurous air they had been putting up with.

'Shine the key again. I need to locate some items in my tool bag.'

They went over to the closet, which thankfully had safety catches on it and had retained the contents inside, though not keeping them dry, during their exodus from the Aleutians. Knowing he would have to work outside the cabin to fix a small bleed pipe from the oxygen storage tanks, he surveyed his small personal tool kit very critically. There would have to be improvisations.

'What's this?' Amanda demanded, pointing to a plastic bundle.

'My wet weather gear which I put over my working clothes. Well spotted. I may need it ,' he said with a chuckle.

'Someone has to look after you,' she quipped, 'and since it's raining.......' So saying she unrolled the plastic overall and something heavy fell on the floor.

'Maybe this will be useful too,' she said, guiding his hand to the small laser pencil torch she had picked up off the floor.

'Are you some sort of magician?' he exclaimed, while clicking the 'on' switch. It worked. 'Modern technology,' he sighed, 'completely waterproof.'

The beam illuminated everything in its direction.

*

After more than an hour of awkward engineering, Jason had a length of flexible washing machine pipe connected to the central manifold of the oxygen storage tanks. This fed up through the bathroom waste water outlet into the cabin living room. He then cracked open the main valve to allow the smallest possible leak of oxygen up into their living area. The flow was just a faint draught where it came out of the hose. Jason assured Amanda that at that rate the cylinders would last for months.

She seemed satisfied at the progress and the improvement in the cabin's atmosphere, but remained sceptical about their ability to make fire. In vain Jason struck his hammer on various rocks over a tray of cooking oil and enhanced oxygen supply without success. Although there was the very occasional spark it died instantly before igniting the cooking oil. Meanwhile the laser torch seemed to be running out of power.

They returned to their bench seat in darkness and assessed their failures, both thoroughly depressed.

After a long silence Jason stated, 'Well at least we have stopped coughing, that's something. We seem to have modified the cabin atmosphere for the better!'

'You know something?' Amanda replied philosophically, 'In the old days people used to light tobacco and inhale the smoke into their lungs and had devices called cigarette lighters; a flint against steel with an inflammable gas. Simple device, everybody had them. Sometimes I think we have gone backwards.'

He reflected on the concept and fell back on his thoughts again.

Finally he conceded, 'I have concluded that without fire we can do nothing. We cannot cook, we cannot have light, we cannot distil water and we cannot fabricate many things..... We have to succeed somehow. Making fire is the key to our chances of survival.'

CHAPTER SIX

Amanda was up early the next day. Well, that was what she presumed was the next day by the eerie twilight coming through the doorway. There had been no change in the rain pattern which continued steadily without any wind at all. The sound of the water cascading from the roof had become the normal accompaniment to the chatter of streamlets running off the mountain.

One thing Amanda had concluded was that there was thankfully little danger of avalanches or mud slides, since the sheer force of the tsunami had removed every loose item from the mountainside.

She put on her boots and, without further clothing, made her way carefully down to the corral to see how Regina was faring. The shower, she reasoned, would smarten up her senses and do her good. She finally fumbled her way to the reptile's compound. At first she thought the unbelievable had happened and the creature had gone. She traced the perimeter of clinker rocks with her fingertips until she suddenly touched a scaly surface and withdrew her hand abruptly, letting out a shriek.

'The little bugger is alive alright,' she whispered to herself. 'Its hiding under the rocks....doesn't like the rain!' With that she made her way back to the cabin to give the news to Jason.

She felt a few shivers before getting back, and also the need to cough several times from the effect of the sulphurous air. It had definitely got colder, she acknowledged, and she made up her mind to hijack some of his clothes before venturing out again.

Jason welcomed the news of Regina's improving health, but then went on to claim he had hardly slept all night due to the worrying issue of creating fire. 'Even primitive man had fire,' he whined.

'Can't we rub sticks together or something?' He was angered at his failures the day before and thought Amanda should spend her day rubbing sticks together as her contribution. He was testy.

'We must have tinder of some sort; dry leaves or something like that,' she said miserably, 'and everything in here is soggy and wouldn't burn anyway.'

Something caught Jason's eye, just visible in the half-light over the door. He jumped up and ripped it down and gave it to Amanda who, even in her depressed state, uttered a small laugh. The first words read 'IN CASE OF FIRE'. It was dry and made of paper.

'Do you have any more posters?' she enquired, as she put it away in the kitchen drawer to keep it dry. 'A couple more would be enough to start a fire.'

He thought about it.

'There was one in the bathroom. It's gone now.'

'What did that one say?"

'Conserve water!' he said with a laugh.
During the day, he dismantled the motor and evaporator from the fridge, using periodic bursts of light from the laser

torch. He claimed that there might be a capacitor somewhere in the electrical system that might have retained enough energy to make sparks between two connecting wires. The theory was correct, Amanda accepted optimistically.

When Jason had finally extracted a capacitor, they found it to be totally discharged. 'I'm not surprised,' he commented, 'considering it's been submerged in water several times.'

They opened the vac-pack of Alaska sockeye salmon and ate half of it, washing it down with water collected from outside and stored in a bucket of crushed coral. It was foul and Amanda commented that the acidity was preferable to the taste of decomposing organisms from the coral rock. They needed to collect older, inert limestone and so, with nothing else to do, they wandered back down to the shore to find older white rocks.

Back in the cabin in a state of miserable depression they assessed their survival chances again. Jason stacked up the odds.

'Acid water, three days max of food stuffs and next to no light.'

'I don't think water is a big problem,' Amanda said thoughtfully. 'We can overcome those issues and we still have three full bottles of mineral water left, and if we starve ourselves we could eke out our food supplies for a week, I guess......and then there is Regina.......What are the chances do you think of finding more food supplies?'

Jason was despondent.

'Depends on how long this ash cloud keeps us dark. We have

to be able to see to identify other Reginas and maybe other survivors. Which way does the jet stream operate.....west to east I suppose, so maybe we will get clearer air from Russia or Africa soon?'

Amanda considered.

'Other volcanic dust plumes have only lasted a day or two during my lifetime,' she replied.

'And how many five thousand foot tsunamis have you encountered?' He retorted sarcastically.

She was irritated and replied sullenly, 'You don't know which or how many volcanoes are responsible either, do you?'

Jason did not reply immediately and looked out into the night air, as if expecting to find the answers there.

'Look,' she said thoughtfully. 'Our volcano has not erupted has it? Surely if it was going to it would have done so by now. If the plates have settled down, so will the volcanic activity presumably, so the dust is not ad infinitum and may not last for many more days. We have to think positively.'

Jason took some heart from what she said and they both looked up vacantly at their volcano. Suddenly she leapt up and pointed. Jason half expected an eruption to be taking place.

'The red glow!' she exclaimed, 'The glow we see each night reflected in the clouds is from molten lava, right?' How close do you think we could get to that in order to capture fire?'

'I see,' he joked. 'I abseil down the neck of a volcano and bring back a chunk of molten rock! Be realistic.'

'No, but we could maybe lower something down to catch fire and then retrieve it, contain it and bring it down here to the cabin.'

'Desperate situations require desperate solutions,' Jason replied flatly as he considered the possibilities. They both fell silent for a while.

'What about the canvas methane umbrella? Amanda suddenly interposed. 'It's not far from here. Could we not cut great long strips from it and make some sort of rope to lower down into the caldera?'

'Maybe. That is a possibility,' replied Jason in a much more positive voice. 'The canvas would burn slowly, more like a smoulder. Also,' he said much more cheerfully, 'there is tons of the stuff which we could use as a slow burning fuel.'

They chose to avoid the practicalities of getting close to the red hot lava, and concentrated their thoughts instead on planning the recovery of the canvas.

CHAPTER SEVEN

The following day, as the half-light extended into the cabin, they set off towards the site of the canvas umbrella. Amanda had commandeered a soggy overall from Jason's pile of clothing and he clad himself only in the plastic overall he had worn while sorting out the oxygen supply.

Moving carefully across the old lava flows and clinker in the semi-darkness for half an hour, they eventually came to the massive sheet of canvas that had hitched itself on the aa aa lava and beached itself. They painfully negotiated their way up the edge of the sheet. Finally they reached the top corner. Jason, ignoring the thick hemmed border, pushed his knife through the material and cut along the top edge for about a metre. Before long he had a strip of canvas with parallel sides running down the mountain.

The fabric tore down the line of the fibres quite easily and before long they had a roll several metres long.

Then Amanda turned to Jason, 'Why are we doing this?'

'To make a rope with three such long strips, as I suggested yesterday!' he responded, slightly irritated.

'If we want to make a rope, why don't we just use the hemmed up edge. It already is like a rope.'

He looked at the hem and then back at her and grinned, conceding his oversight. Shaking the rain off his face, he declared, 'You are right,' and then clambered back up the slope to the corner and hacked through the thick hem.

They proceeded slowly down the mountain, with her cutting the canvas and him coiling up the heavy hem.

It was halfway through the day when they finally got back to the cabin, exhausted but happy with their achievements. Both had chest pains from their continuous coughing due to the acrid air. They lay down on the floor close to the oxygen supply from the bleed pipe for a long time, until they reached equilibrium. They then devoured the remainder of the vac packed sock-eye salmon and downed one of Jason's precious beers, while they formulated what Jason referred to as Plan A.

They concluded that there were many dangers, whichever way they got close enough to the red hot rocks to capture fire, but what else could they do?

'How do you think we should contain the fire once we've captured it in all this pouring rain?' she enquired miserably.

'The only waterproof thing we have is a large saucepan,' pronounced Jason. 'We could keep feeding dry material into that from a dry bin-bag, to keep the fire alive while we get down from the mountain.'

'Plan A sounds a bit optimistic,' Amanda said and then added, 'Also we need shelter and fuel to keep the fire going in an area outside the cabin. We cannot have toxic smoke in here.'

'Another trip to the canvas umbrella then,' replied Jason, trying not to be so negative. 'Tomorrow we'll carry back as much canvas as we can, like the Incas used to do, in bundles on our backs with straps across our foreheads. You never know, the weather might change by then.'

His last sentence carried little conviction.

Tomorrow never came.

The darkness intensified, as did the acridity of the atmosphere outside the cabin. They dared not venture out for the whole day in case the polluted air irreparably damaged their lungs. Instead they passed a totally desperate and disagreeable day inside, drinking only rain water and nibbling at the few vac-packed dried apricots that had survived inside their packet. Much of the time they lay down close to the oxygen bleed pipe in order to breathe properly. Their moods were very sombre, both believing that they had underestimated the extent of the damage to the planet's atmosphere and that the 'nuclear winter' had set in.

When it became totally dark, they estimated that night had arrived and made preparations to sleep. With empty stomachs and fading hope, they each tried to go to sleep, without much success. Nightmarish scenarios kept flashing before them, of the many different ways they were to die as slow starvation set in.

When an eerie light penetrated the closed cabin through the one window, Amanda claimed another day had arrived and she would check on Regina, admitting to herself that even that poor scaly creature would have to be on the menu before too much longer. Because they had slept so poorly, they found themselves cold for the first time.

'Regina is either dead or in deep hibernation,' reported Amanda on her return. She had given her a series of prods that had produced no movement whatsoever. She also reported that it had become distinctly cooler outside and she fumbled round for some of Jason's clothing to put on. Bits of it had been spread round the cabin for a couple of days and were basically dry by then.

'I detected a slight wind today, coming round the side of the mountain,' she announced, 'and I don't think the rain is so heavy.'

'Any change is for the better,' uttered Jason in a pitiful and depressed voice. 'I think we should try to get the canvas we need for fuel and shelter today, and make an attempt to put step one of Plan A into effect. What do you think?'

He was quite shocked and almost disappointed that she grunted in the affirmative, so they set off again in the direction of the canvas umbrella, this time at a slow pace, aware of the coughing that followed exertion. There wasn't much light but Amanda commented that it was noticeably lighter than the previous day, which had been oppressively dark all the time, and they found the journey quicker than expected.

They peeled off two parallel strips of canvas and simultaneously rolled them up as they went down the hill. In half an hour they had two bundles, which they tied up in the manner Jason had suggested. He then cut out a big square of canvas, folded it up and lashed it to his bundle. He staggered as he humped it up onto his back.

After several rest stops, they regained the sanctuary of the cabin. Amanda was soaking wet from the rain and Jason from the sweat he had generated inside his plastic coverall. They ate one of the three tins of beans and slowly recuperated from their exertions and coughing, by lying down beside the oxygen bleed tube again.

'How much of this sulphurous air can we breathe without permanent lung damage? 'Amanda asked after finishing a coughing fit and gulping great inhalations of pure oxygen.

'The secret is not to breathe too deeply,' coughed Jason, following her actions with the bleed tube. 'I want you to stand on my shoulders and climb onto the cabin roof on the front side when you feel fit again.'

She knew what was expected and shortly afterwards he got her up onto the roof and passed her up the square of canvas. After tossing up a number of lava stones, she had secured the leading edge of what was to be their awning.

It was the body contact of his nubile companion that threw him off guard, as she slithered down off the roof over his waiting torso. It sent sensual messages reverberating through his body that he was totally unprepared for. He could hardly see her in the gloom but her form sliding down his back ignited primeval senses he found difficult to ignore. The heat of the moment passed, but its memory lingered, while he continued with the task of stretching out the canvas up the slope away from the cabin, to make their awning.

Once the top end was secured with more rocks, they had a respectable sized area, free from rain and big enough to build a fire under and to store and dry fuel. The rolls of canvas that they had gathered that day were spread out to dry off, but they had started coughing again and so, with little else to do, they retreated back into the cabin and closed the door.

*

Having got accustomed to endless nights, the increasing definition of features in the cabin, as the following day's dawn got underway, came as a complete surprise. Jason leapt up off the floor mattress and inspected the lightening sky. He opened the door and stood outside. Not only had the rain eased to a drizzle, the outline of the mountain could be determined for the first time and the ruggedness of the nearby lava flows were quite visible.

A light breeze made it feel colder than before but Amanda, who was already by his side, was quick to point out in an excited voice that the sun would now penetrate the dust and rain clouds and the temperature would rise again.

They enthusiastically ate another tin of beans, but it did little to alleviate their hunger. The meagre rations of food, that they had allowed themselves over the last days, had not kept up with their canvas gathering activities, and Jason claimed he felt weak and was losing weight. Amanda's only reply to that was a sarcastic, 'Not before time!'

'Come on!' she said, trying to cheer him up. 'This is the big day. We go searching for fire!'

The way she put it was as if they were about to go on a mushroom finding expedition, not the possible descent into the crater of an active volcano.

Armed with a coil of canvas hem rope each and a saucepan,

lidded down with dry paper inside, the laser torch with its diminishing battery and wearing as many of Jason's clothes as possible, they set off up the mountain.

The rivulets of water running off the mountain were now little more than trickles. 'The heavy rain must have finished hours ago,' commented Amanda. The eerie gloom of the past days had been replaced by a sort of twilight, quite adequate to see their footing.

During the previous evening, they had worked out a number of actions for Plan A. The first one was to investigate the lava tube, in the hope that it came out into the caldera close enough for them to dangle their rope onto the hot lava below, so that it might catch fire. At the same time, they could retreat to the relative safety of the entrance. The plan was simplistic, but although they both knew it was inherently dangerous, it was still preferable to the idea of scaling down into the caldera from the rim at the top of the mountain.

Jason was losing conviction with every upward step and weakly argued that it would all be easier another day, once the rain stopped and it became properly light. It was only the thought of his empty belly that made him press on.

They soon arrived at the lava tube and descended to the entrance. There had been no changes since they had fled the area nearly a week ago; no lava outpouring and no noises this time. As they cautiously went into the entrance of the tube, they again caught a whiff of the same obnoxious smell as before.

Pausing with his nose in the air, Jason said thoughtfully, 'It's not exactly sulphurous is it? It's not like volcano gasses at all; more organic maybe.'

Amanda was sniffing like a cat. 'You're right. It is not hydrogen sulphide. Even so we have to take care in case it is poisonous. No rushing and no deep breathing. I can't afford for you to drop dead on me.....and even if you did, I'm not ready for cannibalising!'

'I should take some comfort in that I suppose,' Jason replied miserably over his shoulder, as they entered the tube. It was about two meters high and a similar width. They were soon in darkness. Jason produced the laser torch and, as previously agreed, he would flick it on and off at regular intervals, so as to conserve the battery.

Amanda remarked that it was already hotter than outside and also that the smell had intensified and, although it was obnoxious, it did not feel dangerous to breathe. They stopped a minute into the cave while he fumbled for the 'ON' switch of the torch.

Suddenly they froze, clutching each other in terror. There was the sound of moving gravel not far away. At the moment Jason got the torch to work, it was pointing downwards and illuminated only their feet, and at the same instant a louder sound of horrible scraping and the rush of moving gravel came reverberating down the tube.

Their first reaction was to hare-tail back to the entrance but, remembering their previous encounter with the same noise, they held on to each other, while Jason directed the light beam up the tunnel. Some fifty meters away there appeared to be a rock the size of a fridge blocking the tube. To their horror it seemed to move slightly, as if it was about to roll down onto them.

At the point when he was about to lose his nerve, Jason suddenly cried out.

'Holy fuck! It's not a rock. It's something alive!'

'It's a frigging giant tortoise!' yelled Amanda, with an air of both relief and excitement.

With that they moved cautiously up the tube until they were near to the beast. The dung all round their feet explained the obnoxious smell.

'The animal must have been thrown into the tunnel by the tsunami,' commented Amanda. 'They don't live in such places. It's trapped up here.'

'It's massive; couple of hundred kilos,' Jason said thoughtfully and added, 'Will keep us in food for a month!'

Amanda chose to ignore his last remark and instead followed the torch beam round the creature's body. She tried to avoid the sad beady eyes that begrudgingly flickered in the light beam. It made a movement with a leg and dislodged a small group of round objects, from under its giant carapace.

'Eggs!' exclaimed Amanda excitedly. 'She has been laying eggs! It's her way of trying to preserve the species. She is probably injured and dying, like Regina.'

Jason could only shake his head in disbelief. 'She is not going anywhere from here then?'

'No! Look at her head. She has no strength left to hold it up.'

Jason agreed, relieved somewhat that he may not after all have to slaughter an angry animal at some time in the near future. Cautiously, they stepped round the great shell of the tortoise and proceeded up the tunnel, flicking the light on and off so as to pick their way round obstacles. There was a slight air flow towards them and they quickly lost the stench of the dung but it became increasingly hot.

After ten minutes they conceded defeat. The rock wall was almost too hot to touch and the air was stifling. They almost ran back to the tortoise, grazing knees and knuckles as they went.

'Phew!' gasped Amanda as they climbed round the hulk of the stranded animal. 'I didn't think we would make it. I thought we might die of heat stroke!'

As they drew close to the entrance, they realised that the sky had cleared some more, so much so that they could pick out the shape of their tiny cabin, far below and off to the side.

'We might as well leave the hem ropes here where they will keep dry in the tunnel, Jason suggested, as he considered Plan B for the next day and the climb up to the rim. 'At least the ropes will be half way up the mountain.'

'Yes,' she conceded, 'and we know we won't immediately starve now and also on the bright side, the drizzle has nearly stopped. It's getting brighter and also warmer!'

'We will be able to explore more of the island now and possibly find more survivors,' Jason chirped in a much more positive voice.

CHAPTER EIGHT

The drizzle became intermittent by evening. They both had agreed that the climb to the top of the volcano should be postponed for another day, and instead they should concentrate their efforts into storing up as much fresh water as possible, just in case the rain did not return.

Their thoughts dwelt on where their next decent meal should come from. 'Logically it has to be Regina,' insisted Jason. 'She's close by; she's probably dead by now and should be eaten before going rotten. Regina fresh or salted would be infinitely better than Regina decomposed,' he argued.

With that threat hanging in the air, Amanda immediately shot off down to the corral to establish the status of the reptile. Jason with more bravado than true conviction, took the big knife out of the drawer, located the sharpening steel and was busy honing a keen edge when she returned.

Amanda scowled at the sight of the knife sharpening exercise and issued the report on Regina, in the way a hospital medic would hand routine information to a consultant surgeon.

'Moved one metre, passed some droppings and appears to be on the road to recovery.'

'Shit!' exclaimed Jason.

'Yes. I smelt it before I got to the corral.'

'Shit!' he repeated, 'I suppose this is postponing our evening meal?'

'She might be the only surviving iguana on the planet. We can't just eat her!'

'If she is the ONLY surviving iguana then we best eat her. Iguanas are finished without a male survivor somewhere.'

'She may have eggs inside her,' pleaded Amanda.

'Eggs or no eggs, if we don't do something soon about eating, the last two surviving humans will be no more.'

'You think we might be the last two surviving humans?' she echoed. 'I'll have to think about that, meanwhile you will have to postpone the day of execution a day or two longer. My gut feeling is that life is now so precious that preservation should be a first priority.'

Jason reluctantly put his knife and steel back in the drawer and muttered something about his stomach and Darwinism.....the survival of the fittest.

Amanda heard him and snapped, 'Survival of the fittest is the ruling between individuals of the same species not between reckless carnivores and unsuspecting herbivores.'

'I'm not a reckless carnivore,' whined Jason, and then added in his defence, 'If that Regina creature is a herbivore then what hope is there for her without a blade of vegetation on the island?'

Amanda could offer no further argument and they reluctantly called a truce and decided to wait and see what the next day would bring.

They lay down on the same mattress together, maintaining a distance between each other and tried not to think about their empty stomachs.

*

At dawn they were awake and allowed themselves to be excited for a moment about the improving weather. It looked as if the sun might even break through the haze, yet all the while they remained depressed and hungry.

The column of wispy smoke could be seen coming from the top of the volcano, as it had done before the period of darkness had set in.

Jason opened their last tin of beans and they ate aggressively. This time it was on a bed of uncooked rice that had been soaked overnight in fresh water. Jason conceded that it was enough to keep them going another day, as they set off up the mountain in the direction of the lava tube. It was their intention to round up their store of hem rope and the saucepan of dry paper, before climbing up to the rim of the volcano.

On arrival at the lava tube, and on Amanda's insistence, they went inside to check on the status of the giant tortoise. With the help of the weak laser torch light, they just managed to inspect the reptile.

Amanda rolled its drooping head out from underneath its great shell. It was lifeless and its beady eyes were shut. An unpleasant smelling dribble issued from its beak.

'Dead!' said Amanda with finality.

'I'm not surprised,' said Jason. 'I thought it looked on the way out yesterday.'

Amanda rocked the carapace as if to encourage any sign of life to manifest itself. She then caught sight of the eggs.

'Right!' she said. 'There is no time for sentimentality; we have to do something straight away.'

'Sentimentality!' Jason huffed, remembering Regina's stay of execution.

'There are probably loads more of these eggs underneath her,' Amanda said positively. 'They will hatch under the right conditions and might by some miracle preserve the species.'

Jason showed no enthusiasm on hearing the last comment as he had mistakenly thought she was going to suggest they ate the eggs.

'If we attempt to drag the beast out, the eggs will probably get crushed in the process. Shine the torch down here and I will dig out as many as I can,' she instructed.

After some time, with sporadic aid from the torch, she dragged aside a dozen or more eggs and buried them carefully under the gravel behind them, marking the spot with a small stone. She then directed Jason to fetch the hem rope from the entrance of the lava tube.

It took them over an hour of heaving and straining to manoeuvre and drag the giant tortoise corpse out into the open air and roll it over on to its back. They had agreed by this time to abandon Plan B temporally, in full knowledge of the urgency to get their new food supply under control.

To their amazement, a hazy sun had appeared through the murky sky and it was already much warmer but oppressively humid. Jason, following his exertions and driven by pangs of hunger, became quite animated. He could only think about preserving the flesh of the tortoise and filling his belly as soon as possible. Plan B had gone completely out of focus and all his energies and expertise were directed into getting the carcase to the shore as quickly as he could.

He fastened the rope to the front legs, and for security's sake round the creature's neck, and within minutes had it tobogganing down the gully on its back towards the sea. They both held on to the two restraining ropes like reigns and controlled its descent to within a few metres of the shoreline.

Sweating profusely, it was agreed that she would go back up to the cave and recover the saucepan which they would need, while he returned to the cabin and rounded up a big knife and some utensils.

The sky continued to clear and it became oppressively hot. As luck would have it, by the time Jason returned from the cabin, a breeze had developed from round the side of the mountain. It cleared the last of the murk from the atmosphere and made his butchering task more bearable. Not wishing to witness the event, Amanda returned to the cabin, intending to gather up items for storing the salted meat.

Jason nervously cut the throat of the dead reptile in the halal fashion, being fully aware that the liberation of blood was essential, otherwise it would lead to the quick and unavoidable spoilage of the meat.

It bled profusely, much to his surprise and relief, indicating it had not been dead for very long. The blood quickly drained away, turning the seawater red over a large area. After washing the carcase down, he quickly gained confidence and cut through the muscles holding the body to the scaly upper-side and separated off the heavy shell. The meat was red, like fresh beef. 'It looks very tasty,' he muttered to himself.

He was constantly aware of the heat of the sun and aggressively quickened his pace. Finally the whole beast had been butchered into thin long strips of red meat and washed thoroughly in seawater. He then laid them out on clean lava rock to dry. He stood back, stretched his back and with a degree of satisfaction, surveyed his work. Not perfect, but considering it was a whole step up from his previous experiences in his younger years, of preparing fish and small game in the outdoors, this was OK. That lady over there somewhere should be well pleased with him.

Finally, he dragged the entrails and rubbished parts into the sea and washed out the scaly shell, leaving it to dry in the sun. Glancing up at the mountainside and across in the direction of the cabin, and seeing no sign of Amanda returning, he became concerned about her welfare. They had not done anything separately up until then and she had been gone for two to three hours. His thoughts dwelt on the dangers of crossing the rugged aa aa lava fields in loose fitting footwear, and so he decided to cross the mile or so of volcanic rocks to find out what had happened to her. A 'missing Amanda' was a consideration he had never made and he felt acutely uncomfortable. He skipped across the lava in a mild panic despite the heat. Only one objective was on in his mind and that was to find his companion.

As he approached the cabin, he became fearful of her possible fate and became sullenly aware of the inexplicable bonding that had taken place between them since the rig break-up. His worries intensified as he climbed over the last few lava ridges with still no sight of her, either up the trail to the lava tube or down towards Regina's corral. He suddenly felt dreadfully irresponsible to have let her go off on her own.

He was preoccupied with these thoughts when he heard a shriek from the direction of the cabin and the nymph-like naked figure of Amanda, dancing about outside beckoning him to come quickly. Jason wasted no time in leaping over the last bits of lava to get there.

'Look!' she cried out. 'Look!'

There was no need for explanation. A curl of blue smoke came billowing out from the gully near the cabin.

'How the fuck did you manage that?' Jason cried out, while grabbing her arm and giving her a massive hug.

'Urgh!' she blurted out. 'You stink of blood!'

'Never mind the stink! And by the way you stink of burning canvas!'

She laughed.

'How did you do it?'

'Secret!'

'Secret, my arse! What magic did you perform this time?'

'A woman looks in the mirror as normal routine several times a day. During the days when there was no light, I never had the urge to do so, but when the sun came out.........'

'The mirror,' he interrupted. 'Why didn't we think of it before?'

'I thought about it when coming back down the mountain carrying the saucepan full of dry paper. By the time I got back to the cabin, the saucepan was almost too hot to hold and then I remembered your convex shaving mirror. I put the underside of the saucepan lid and the shaving mirror at the side of the gully, both reflecting the sun's rays onto the dry paper, and within a minute it was smouldering. By the time I got some strips of canvas ready, the paper burst into flames....Not magic!'

'I can't believe it. You're brilliant! Can you keep the fire going while I recover some of the tortoise meat? I've laid it out in strips to sun-dry?'

'Go! I will establish the fire more permanently under the awning, in case of more rain and where we can keep an eye on it,' she then added, jubilantly throwing him a kiss. 'We are going to survive, partner! We are going to survive!'

CHAPTER NINE

My name is Amanda, she reflected silently to herself. *I'm a designer baby, now twenty five years old. I was born from a surrogate mother, implanted with a foetus constructed of specially selected stem cells taken from three different male donors, each known for their academic and physical brilliance: Ahmed, Andrew and Alexander, hence the three 'A's in my name. I was never told about the female stem cells implanted, only that the ovum was from a woman of Balkan descent.*

I have no relatives waiting or watching for me, and my genetic designers have long since concluded their program of monitoring and follow-up. I am alone now and have been for several years. I was given a designer vagina as pretty as the petals of any flower, designed perhaps to attract the most elegant and eloquent of the males that showed up on my CONSOL. I have a brilliant brain, or at least that is what I was told, yet I am programmed to fit into a 2050 environment, a technically engineered bubble of existence. Now I find myself here, lost and stranded, sitting on a smooth black lava rock in an unknown, devastated world, where no CONSOL or any norms of modern life exist. Whatever do I do next?

She got up from her resting position and carried another saucepan of seawater up to a dried out rock pool, in order to start another evaporation cycle for their salt, much needed to preserve their precious meat supply.

Now look at me, a naked woman carrying water like an African bush girl of history books. I know nothing of this existence. I have only the survival instinct to overcome pain and feed myself, no matter on what, no matter how. She stopped and shuddered, putting down the saucepan and sat on a smooth lava rock by the sea shore.

Survival, she reiterated to herself. *I don't think it's an issue anymore, for the time being. We have water, we have salt, we have meat, and that man said he saw a 'swish' in the water yesterday, where the blood of the giant tortoise had run into the sea. He said it could have been a shark or some other marine creature that had survived the tsunami. Today he's gone off to the site with his fishing tackle to investigate. At least,* she mused, *Jason has retained some hunter-gatherer genes in his modern day make-up.*

There must surely be other life forms that survived, she reasoned. *After all, the dust cloud only lasted a week or so, not months, although,* she concluded, *we could not have survived those toxic and horrible days without the oxygen supply into our cabin. Others may not have been so lucky perhaps, and died, their lungs saturated in sulphurous fumes and acid water.* She gave another shudder and stood up, shrugging her shoulders.

The sun was hot, and although her skin had darkened considerably over the last few days and needed much less protection, she still indulged herself in a quick dip into the blissful shallow waters to cool down.

Shaking herself dry, she paused, trying to estimate the time since the rig broke up. *Must be close to two weeks now. My daily trips to gather canvas strips and salt have merged into one*, she mused. *These days have become one long uncomplicated episode. Meanwhile that man is scouring the land for life, like an Inuit in the high Arctic on ice-flows looking for seals. Although he's found nothing, he is preoccupied with hope and extending his horizons. He comes home and eats grilled tortoise like a wolf and sleeps soundly until the next morning. Now he is excited about a 'swish'. I wish I could summon up such enthusiasm.*

She lapsed into deep thoughts about their first encounter while delivering lectures to new-comers on the rig. She recalled the 'JON' and how nothing, just nothing had happened in a sexual context since that night. Primarily it had been their concern to survive against the odds that had out-weighed other desires. It had been too hot and too sweaty to spoon for more than a few moments at night and they had respected each other's space.

She shuffled her bottom uneasily on the smooth black basaltic rock by the water's edge, until she straddled it like riding on a horse's back. Smiling to herself, she felt the warmness of the smooth rock drying her splayed legs and heating the softness of her inner thighs. It was intensely comforting and seductive. As if there might have been crowds of passing onlookers, she cast glances around her, before almost secretly allowing a hand to rest on her pubic bone.

'Designer vagina,' she huffed to herself, while feeling the prickles of what was becoming a conspicuous, black pubic mound. 'They did say that the donor of the egg had Balkan ancestry,' she mused, in an unconditional acceptance of what her new body would soon look like. 'And,' she chuckled to herself, 'you know what?...I don't care! No more plucking, no more shaving to think about and maybe I'll adapt to being a stone age girl after all!'

Do you think that away back in the Stone Age, women had orgasms? she taunted herself, *or is that an awareness thing of the modern era?* She dwelt on those thoughts for a few moments, until the heat from the black basaltic rock made its presence felt on the petals of her labia minora.

'Fuck it,' she said out loud, and casting her eyes again furtively around, placed her index finger firmly on her pulsating clitoris. 'I want to fly high, high......It is over a week!' she screamed and threw her head back.

At the moment of closing her eyes, Amanda's whole world became green. For a second or two she allowed the imagery to become a fantasy, of rolling over in green fields and summer flowers......then she shook herself into wide awareness. The micro second before her eyes shut she really had seen nothing but green.

She stood up straight, shaking off her intimate thoughts and stared at the open ocean. There was a huge raft of green stretching from horizon to horizon, a mile or so off-shore. All her private fantasies of the previous moments drained away in a flash, as she strained her eyes in the direction of the flotsam.

It had to be algae, or some sort of foliage, she reasoned excitedly. Organic material of any description had to be useful. Yanking on her boots she set off along the shore to where Jason had butchered the tortoise and where he had claimed to have seen his famous 'swish'.

Sweating heavily in the midday sun, she finally caught sight of her companion, bent low over the lava and intent on something. Getting closer, she shouted to him. In acknowledgement he shouted back in animated tones while waving vigorously. She could soon see he was preoccupied in dragging something.

'Holy shit!' she cried out loud as she got nearer, 'He has caught something! He has caught the 'swish' maybe. I had a secret feeling that someday he would come home with dinner!'

'Look! Look!' He was jumping up and down and punching the air. 'I caught the bugger that was sniffing round where the tortoise blood was going into the sea. Now we can eat more than just tortoise and beans!'

'Brilliant!' she beamed, bouncing over to him, her body glistening in the sun like a shining bronze statuette from a Greek museum. He looked up at her and grinned.

'It gave a hell of a fight.'

She laughed. His boyish indulgencies had come to the surface. It mattered not for that moment that he had procured a great deal of food; more importantly it was the thrill of the fight that any fisherman would experience. He could have butchered it there and then but no, he had to drag it over a mile of lava to show off to his tribe what a hunter he was. Amanda gave him a little pat on the head, as if he were her cat that had presented her with a mouse, and at the same moment she experienced a new emotion that rocked her whole body. Had she got her CONSOL with her it would have explained that she had fallen in love for the first time.

She then flashed him a devastating smile, that conveyed both her approval and a hint of her newly found virility. Without diminishing his achievements, she drew his attention to her own discoveries and suggested that they should stand together on the nearby rock and look seaward. They could clearly see the green mat a mile or so away.

'I saw it just now and rushed over here to find you. What do you think?'

Letting go of the shark's tail, Jason climbed up onto a higher rock and took a long look, shading his eyes.

'Jesus! It's floating vegetation,' he shouted back. 'Remember I said ages ago that, if we had any luck, the westerly current coming away from the Ecuadorian coast at three knots might bring us something sometime? It seems that our luck is in today.'

'There could be any number of useful things in that green mat, if it has come all the way from South America. Will it come ashore or pass us by?' she added cautiously.

'Surely some will come ashore,' he stated confidently. 'South

America is a big place. The tsunami must have washed out millions of hectares of forests, harbours, houses and all sorts, so surely something will come our way. Look, there are miles of flotsam in that green area going right out to the horizon.'

Finally, after taking turns to drag the shark back to the beach below the cabin, Jason went off to fetch the big knife, while Amanda, in a new, very buoyant mood, went over to the corral, where an almost lifeless Regina lay motionless, in the same position she had adopted for a week.

'I'll bring you some nice leaves and roots tomorrow,' she told the reptile with some conviction, hardly daring to believe it herself.

Then she returned and helped Jason cut up the shark into steaks, and collected a bowl of salt to preserve everything they could not immediately eat.

*

As the evening light faded and drew a close to their outdoor activities, the green mat of flotsam was still tantalising too far from the shore to swim out to, or even identify anything of its composition. Yet at the same time it was nudging closer to the land and, with the offshore wind dropping, they remained hopeful that by morning it would be nearby. Jason said that because of the eddy current created by the island, the raft could even consolidate on their doorstep.

They barbequed the shark steaks on the hot stones, up wind of the burning canvas, laced them with hot chilli sauce and finally cracked open one of the remaining precious cans of beer. It was pleasantly cool in the light evening breeze and, as they sat by the glowing embers, they each knew that a turning point in their existence had been reached. No longer was it a case of whether they would survive. It was more of a case of how their survival would pan out.

As Jason pointed out, they now knew that there were live creatures in the sea. The tortoise had staved off starvation and Regina might help out at some point, though hopefully she would not be needed. They had enough fresh water for a month or two, plus the solar still for back up. Now materials were arriving on the sea current from South America, which they would surely be able to utilise.

Although they both knew their existence was pretty precarious, they were infinitely better positioned now than they had been previously.

For the first time in two weeks they did not go to bed as it became dark. Instead they stayed up by the fire side and talked at length. They had come to recognise the fire as their beacon of hope.

'So, do you think there are more fish to catch?' she started off.

'In the deep water. Yes. Probably. Surely there can't be just one.'

'Why the deep water? What is your reasoning?'

'All I can say is that the corals and habitat of the near-shore are trashed. I cannot imagine that any shallow water species can have survived. They would have been swept away into deep water to God knows where. With no habitat they would have been eaten by the deep water and oceanic predators, I imagine.'

'Hmm,' she responded out loud. 'Sharks have a reputation for survival, don't they? Some species have not evolved significantly for hundreds of millions of years, taking them through several mass extinctions.'

'Talking of mass extinctions, how many of us do you think are left?' he asked cautiously, not wishing to sound too depressed. This was a subject he had painfully avoided, as he had privately concluded that his whole extended family, which collectively lived close to the ocean on the West Coast, must surely have been wiped out.

Feeling a sense of the crushing pain he would be going through by just mentioning the subject, she reached out for his hand and held it sensitively.

'We don't know Jason,' she said quietly. 'There may be many survivors.....'

It was the first time she had used his name, and the tender tone in her voice came from an undiscovered inner Amanda. He was unprepared for that, and turned his head away in case she saw him wipe away the tears that were welling up. An awkward silence followed. Then, clearing his throat, Jason put the question to her.

'What about your folks? Where were they at the time of the tsunami?'

'I don't have any.'

'What none? No cousins, not one...?' Jason sounded worried, perturbed and little doubtful. He wondered if she was covering up for reasons of fear and anxiety.

'Jason,' she used his name for a second time, but this time by the light of the fire he looked at her straight in the eyes, awaiting an explanation. 'I am a designer baby. I have no relatives.'

'In 2025 I was created in a test tube, incubated on a petri dish and implanted into a surrogate mother. My genes come from two scientists, an Arab donor and an egg of a Balkan athlete. That's what my medical team told me when I was old enough to understand, at the end of my monitoring programme. So I have no relatives.'

Jason swallowed hard. He had heard of the designer baby experiments back in the twenties, and understood modern stem cell techniques to avoid genetic diseases, but thought that ethics committees had outlawed the sheer construction of a human from donor cells. He whistled and did his best to hide his discomfort.

'You are a miracle of science then!' and he hesitantly added, as if to soften the worrying concept, 'and not just a pretty face!'

She snorted.

'I've not disclosed these facts to anyone before, but it doesn't seem to matter anymore now.'

'My team were acting illegally, apparently, and the surrogate mother was whisked off to Switzerland for my birth in a private clinic. She departed soon afterwards, in order to prevent any bonding I suppose. The team of geneticists and child doctors were paid by the Arab donor, who had no further dealings with us, other than to know the experiment was succeeding. I was constantly monitored until I reached puberty, and privately taught by a number of highly specialised professors, mainly in science and technology. A foundation was set up to fund my way up through mainstream education, until I entered full time work, as a technical advisor in hydrocarbon capture from the oceans.'

'Wow! That's quite a CV. I guess I feel honoured to work with you and to be the first person to be told of your origins. My own CV is so conventional, I won't bore you with it.....'

She cut him short, 'Forget the bullshit about being honoured. We are here together every day fighting for survival and you, my intrepid great big hunter, brought us home a shark today, and by the way, I downloaded your CV on my CONSOL while you were lecturing on the rig, and it also said you had a high sperm count and a self-induced orgasm every two days!'

Jason snorted this time and a sense of déjà vu returned.

'My brain was manipulated to work in conjunction with my CONSOL, and without it I am almost lost. Even my body chemistry is programmed to take advice from my CONSOL, hence my rush to balance oestrogen levels during my visit to your cabin....' and then laughingly corrected, 'our cabin. I have never had a relationship before that was based on anything other than the management of my body chemistry, in order to maximise and enhance my work output.'

Jason stared at her in utter disbelief. Could there be any more twists and turns to their exodus from the Aleutian Trench?

As if to defuse his fears she continued, 'I realised while we were being hurled about in the cabin after the rig break-up, that I was way outside of my comfort zone, and that certain emotions were unknown to me. Normally my CONSOL would immediately direct me how to mitigate the impact of emotions.'

'You are amazing,' he uttered. 'What sort of emotions? I want to understand you better.'

'The ones normal to you, I suppose...fear, hate, hunger, love' ....she broke off suddenly, realising that she was in unchartered waters and turned her face away.

'Hmm,' he smiled and reached for her hand. 'Why couldn't I be cast away with a normal person!'

'We are not in a normal world anymore Jason. I have to start again from the beginning.' She paused and repeated the statement, emphasising the 'start again'.

'I *want* to start again. I want to understand emotions and want to learn how to cope with them. I want to know how to fight them, how to cruise along with them and how to enjoy them. This is new territory for me and you may find me difficult for a while, but I am determined to arrive at the same position you are in somehow.

I have no CONSOL now and years of catching up to do. My professors and lecturers always lead me down scientific paths, and although I occasionally skim-read classical novels, I tended to dismiss them as irrational over-sensitive crap. I have decided now that I want to go back to being a teenager. I want to have the innocence that frees me to appreciate the horrors and joys of adulthood.'

Jason coughed and cleared his throat.

'You know something? We are not so very different. Your emotions seemed to have been *programmed* out of you, whereas mine have been *deliberately avoided,* in as much as I ran away from situations that would have demanded my attention or commitment. I've never allowed myself to be at the mercy of another. I've simply moved on.'

'In our life here, I suspect we'll have plenty of time to go back to our adolescence and play our cards differently. In fact, the more I think about it, the more I believe we have to learn to absorb stuff from each other. You're right Amanda. We'll both start again. Just like the boy and girl who live next door to each other and meet only on the way to school.'

They both laughed, and looked up into the night and then down at the smouldering embers of burning canvas, and tried to think what it would be like to meet only on the way to school.

'Tomorrow we'll open a new chapter,' Amanda said, throwing her arms to the sky and silhouetting her pert little breasts against the stars. We can comb the sea and shoreline for whatever gifts the sea currents have delivered to us from

South America. The day that two school kids find treasures on the tide line!'

Jason, for the first time in two weeks, felt a genuine uplift. He smiled at her and felt he was prepared to surrender himself to this new fantasy and follow Amanda's desires. His thoughts suddenly returned to the afternoon's episode, where she had met up with him on the lava fields as he had been dragging the shark back. She had patted him on the head and shown sensitivity he had not encountered before. There had been moisture in her eyes that betrayed an emotion she had fought unsuccessfully to control. He had felt it also when she proudly made him scramble up on a high rock to point out her discovery of a green ocean full of hope.

They climbed onto their mattress a few minutes later and he noticed, with some amusement, that she had made up a roll of clothing, stretching the full length of their bed. She had intentionally separated their bodies. The mutual respect that they had previously held for each other's space had somehow melted away following their confessions and revelations of the evening. Amanda was determined to keep the lid on their desires for the time being. The barricade was symbolic of the control she now felt the need to exercise.

It's a funny thing, Jason conceded to himself, *that after two weeks of abstinence and a lack of concern over my own state of celibacy, that this night of all nights she has put up a barrier, when I have a burning desire to make love with her.*

Remembering his new role as schoolboy, he folded his arms behind his head and lay on his back, trying to recall the feelings he had had as a fourteen year old, who fancied the neighbourhood girl that caught the bus with him each morning. These thoughts were at times eclipsed by speculative ideas as to what might arrive on the beach for them when first light came. He hoped fervently that no wind would develop that might shift the mass of debris off shore.

As if on cue, he heard a rustle and the sound of air moving. He was instantly awake and alert. He quickly realised that the sound of air moving was merely that of Amanda's steady exhalations and not an unfriendly wind outside. He lay still so as not to disturb her dreams but then he detected a slight movement of the mattress, accompanied by even more audible exhalations.

'Christ!' Jason exclaimed silently. 'That bloody woman is masturbating!' With that his member unravelled and went rock hard. He was half in mind to jump on top of her and finish the job, but remembering their plan, he chose to quietly turn away from her as if in sleep and pretend he had heard nothing. Shortly afterwards the sound of her exhalations started again, at first softly and barely audible but gradually quickening pace.

Jason started to sweat and felt for his penis. It was wet. He knew that two weeks of semen build-up would be uncontrollable, and so slowly manoeuvred his body to the edge of the mattress. He dared not masturbate one tiny stroke; he must contain himself. He could imagine her index finger running down over the darkening mons pubis that he had noticed developing recently, at the same speed as his own facial hair. The image drove him mad, yet he managed to remain still while his heartbeat climbed another ten beats a minute.

On the other side of the barrier, the breathing of his companion had become even more audible and was deep and throaty. She was trying desperately to conceal it....but too late. Her body was about to go into orbit and her efforts to hide it were futile. Jason felt a dribble of clear fluid run off his penis onto the thigh he was lying on. 'For fuck's sake Amanda, come! I can't hold on to this much longer!' he gritted through his teeth and silently choked his words down.

Suddenly there was a whirlwind of body movement from the other side of the bed, together with a stifled guttural moan, followed by a series of fake coughs, during which time Jason launched his own orgasm with just a few swift flicks of the wrist. It shot off into the darkness to rest somewhere on the cabin floor. He cared not where, and hoped he had not drawn blood from his lips where his teeth had bitten hard, in order to gag his own mutterings.

The two would-be school kids lay silently on their respective sides of the bed in deep and satisfied sleep for several hours.

CHAPTER TEN

It was the sound of Amanda scurrying round the cabin in the half light of dawn that brought Jason to his senses. He caught sight of her tugging on a pair of his shorts and a short sleeved shirt from his stock of clothes at the end of the cabin. At first he thought it must be cold outside. Then he realised this was to be the new Amanda. She was no longer bare skinned from head to toe, but an intelligent unavailable young woman, fully dressed, about to start her day's work. At first he conceded that he preferred the other version of his companion and then accepted the charade with a grin and leapt up excitedly to investigate the beach.

Amanda was already outside putting on a third pair of socks and Jason's over-sized boots. The gloom of the night was already turning into the murkiness of early dawn.

'Listen!' commanded Jason. The normal silence had been displaced by a distant rumble, similar to that of a bough of a tree rubbing another in the wind. It came from the seashore. Without hesitation they picked their way down as fast as they could over the lava, until clearly what they heard could be identified as trunks of trees and smashed timber, rising and falling with the slight swells as they grounded on the rocky shoreline.

Their dreams had been answered. Here was fuel, construction material and possibly food sources right on their doorstep. Amanda skipped along the water's edge, shrieking with glee as she tossed coconut after coconut up onto the dry land. In the strengthening light, they could see an endless ribbon of coconuts, cocooned in their green outer husks, bobbing up and down in the shallows in both directions. The bigger trees were grounded some ten or fifteen meters further out. Many of them still had leaves on, as if they had just fallen off a river bank. Caught up in their branches were tangles of vegetation, ranging from small thorny bushes to the long dark green leaves of banana plants. There were also pieces of the ubiquitous prickly pear cactus, found so frequently near shorelines in the tropics.

Jason busied himself pulling a sodden, sawn plank ashore and what looked to be fragments of wooden boxes, but then longing for a change of diet, he picked up a coconut from amongst the ones she had tossed ashore and set about opening it. From previous excursions into the tropics, he felt he was fully competent in the procedure, one which he knew baffled most people.

After dropping a large rock several times on to the pointed end of the coconut's outer husk it split into several segments, whereupon he attacked it like a man possessed. By this time Amanda had joined him, also eager to have a change of diet. After removing the hairy fibres, Jason hurled the nut at a rock and it broke open into several pieces, spilling all the milk.

They shared the fragments and gnawed hungrily at the white tasty meat inside, before he had a go at several more nuts in their husks, until he had perfected his technique. Remembering thai women opening them in a way that preserved the milk, he located a sharp stone and experimented. Finally he found that a sharp blow, at right angles to the line which went around the nut, caused it to crack exactly round its equator. He then prized the coconut open, retaining most of the milk.

Amanda was elated and made many cheers of 'Bravo,' her eyes beaming in respect for her schoolboy lover. He gave her the first one and then cracked several more which they drunk with gusto, and marvelled at the prospect of having mountains of food and drink at their disposal, that needed neither refrigeration nor cooking.

Without further ado, she gathered up all the husks and pieces of shell, bundled them loosely in the front of Jason's baggy shirt and traipsed back to the awning, to store them for fuel. On the way back she remembered Regina and the promise she had made. Feeling a duty towards her, she quickly rounded up a banana leaf, some other green leaves and a few prickly pear segments, and by wrapping the long banana leaf round everything, she plodded off to the corral, where she found the motionless reptile just in the sunshine, away from the shelter of the lava rock wall where she had been the last few days. *She's still alive*, thought Amanda optimistically.

She spoke kindly towards her and offered the bundle to her nose. Amanda waited patiently for some recognition but there was none. Refusing to believe the animal to be dead, she poked it and dragged the foliage right up under its head and coaxed her again to eat. Nothing happened, so she went back to join Jason in scouring the shoreline for useful items.

Like Amanda, he was tossing every coconut he found way up onto the rocks above the tide. As he said to her later, there was no point in allowing these gifts to drift away on an off-shore wind or change of sea current. They must have rescued several hundred coconuts before changing their priorities to cover longer stretches of the coast, in the hope of finding other items.

By midday, they had hunted through a couple of miles of matted debris, throwing ashore the odd piece of sawn timber and a tyre. They came across several pallets, which were well encrusted with goose barnacles, that obviously pre-dated the tsunami, but had been caught up in the debris. Nevertheless, they represented a food source and Jason secured them in shallow water, by tethering them with vines and odd pieces of rope that he had collected, in order to keep the crustaceans alive.

By this time, the heat of the day was quite intense, so they clambered down into a crevice that had a small overhang and shade from the sun, and had a further impromptu lunch of coconut milk, and gnawed once again on the succulent white meat inside the shells.

Following Jason's finger, it was agreed that they would go a few hundred meters further, to see what lay beyond the nearby headland, so as to have an idea of what they might find on a further day's exploration.

On arriving at the headland, they noticed that, by being slightly more exposed to the wind, the next section's gullies were jammed tight with debris that had been driven in harder by the oceanic swells. There were more spoils to pick through in these gullies, but they could now wait another day as it did not seem that they would go anywhere.

On the way back, Jason scraped off a couple of handfuls of goose barnacles from one of the tethered pallets and wrapped them in a scrap of plastic sheeting that had been washed up.

'You know these are incredibly expensive and only available in a few very exclusive restaurants,' he claimed. She looked askance at him, partly through disbelief and partly with apprehension born of the idea that he intended making the miserable looking tubes of slime their next *piece de resistance* at supper time.

When they were near the cabin again, they jointly dragged ashore small trees and branches and piled them up on the lava field, to dry out for fuel. Jason, in his usual analytical way, commented on the huge variety of species in the flotsam.

It had also not gone unnoticed by Amanda who, with her deeper scientific knowledge, placed the flora as coastal tropical; estuarine, but definitely not rain forest, hence the presence of the prickly pear cactus segments. She noted also that there was a lack of any human or animal traces amongst the debris, apart from the tyre and a few pieces of sawn timber. To her mind, it looked like this particular swath of flotsam had its origins in a remote and un-populated part of the Americas.

She inwardly cursed the fact that her missing CONSOL would have prompted her to identify likely regions, and that now her own memory could only visualise the pockets of the South American coast with large cities and make crude guesses at the rest.

Jason boiled up the goose barnacles on a fire, much more robust and sweeter smelling than before, because of her copra and coconut shells. He even extracted a shelf of stainless steel mesh from the unused electric oven in the cabin, to make a platform over the fire, so that their steaks of tortoise and shark meat could be cooked without the odour of burnt canvas sheeting. They gulped down another batch of coconut milk and acknowledged life to be generally improving.

She had pulled a few monkey faces at the serving of goose barnacles Jason put in front of her, but after chewing a few of the tender succulent tubes, proclaimed them a culinary success, and congratulated her schoolboy friend on his profound knowledge of all things marine.

He felt adequately commended and stole a sneaky view at her limpet breasts with extended nipples, which poked up under the fabric of his shirt that she was wearing. The midday heat, together with the fire had caused her to sweat profusely, causing the dark aureoles to identify themselves and Jason felt suddenly horny again.

She caught sight of his lingering glace and reading his mind, decided that attack was her best line of defence.

'Why did you throw away the water you boiled up the barnacles in?' she chastised.

'Why?' He responded puzzled, while at the same time trying to dismantle his thought of seducing her.

'Why?' she continued, 'Because we should try to make some sort of soups now, to get vegetables back into our diet, if we're to remain healthy. Surely you must be missing something green. You can't just tear away at raw protein day after day. You're not a tiger or a wolf.'

'You're right,' he conceded, somewhat subdued after her onslaught, which he realised had been designed to deflect any sexual intentions he might have had. 'What greens have you spotted today then that might be useful?'

'The prickly pears are full of sugar. We could make alcohol.'

They both laughed wholeheartedly and the previous incident melted away.

'Great! We can both get pissed as rats every day and lie quietly awaiting a UN evacuation I suppose!'

'No, but I spotted vine leaves and more importantly there is, caught up in one of the big tree's branches, what I think is a Meringa bush or horse radish tree. Its few remaining white flowers caught my attention. I've seen it many times in Mexico and also down on the coast in Peru, when I was there for the company's investigations of the ocean trench. It was growing wild and cultivated also. In Peru the tree is much revered for all its nutritious properties. In fact it's translated into 'the tree of life' in English. I remember having it served up as a broth of flowers and stems. It was delicious.

When I researched it out of interest, it had the amazing properties, as I remember them, of having something like seven times the vitamin C quantity of oranges, four times the vitamin A content of carrots and four times the calcium content of milk.'

'If you are that sure about it,' Jason said excitedly, 'let's find it again and rescue it. Maybe we could establish it somehow.'

Buoyed up with renewed enthusiasm after their meal, they set off back to the area she had seen the bush and it was quickly located, caught up as she had described in branches of a much bigger tree that had no foliage. They sploshed through the shallows and climbed up onto the bobbing trunk of the bigger tree, and finally pulled the bush free, careful not to break off any of its twigs or roots.

It certainly did not look that impressive but, as Amanda remarked, it was virtually intact and, unlike most of the debris, had none of the signs of a violent tsunami impact.

'I reckon this little tree must have slithered down an unstable slope after the tsunami had passed, and has since ridden piggy back on the rest of the vegetation mass until it arrived here. That is why it is caught up in the top of the tree.'

Jason marvelled at her logic, but agreed that this scenario was the most probable one, and he would in further searches look out for similar beached erratics.

'What now?' He enquired of his schoolgirl companion, now turned chief botanist and gardening advisor.

'Let's return it to a site near the cabin and plant it.'

'Plant it!' he exclaimed. 'What in lava rocks? I thought you said we could eat it.' He sounded disappointed.

'If we select a suitable gully, put foliage in it that is washing up everywhere, cover its roots over and give it water and fertiliser, it should grow. As soon as new leaves start to appear, we can harvest them. If nothing happens and it dies, we will have to be content to eating what is there now.'

Jason was a bit concerned over using their precious water supply for irrigation purposes and, trying to remain enthusiastic, raised the question of fertiliser.

'Fertiliser?' She smiled back at him. 'I suppose you can at least pee!' He looked back at her a bit embarrassed before responding.

'And you likewise I suppose!'

'No. Actually I am using my wee for other things.'

'Like what?' he exclaimed puzzled.

'My sandals.'

'What sandals?' he demanded.

'My sharkskin sandals,' she said hesitantly. 'It is part of the hide preparation used by primitive peoples in ancient times. I shall be starting work on them this evening.'

'Really! He spluttered, barely able to believe what he was hearing. 'Does that mean I shall soon get my boots back?

You're not planning to wear them as carpet slippers in the cabin are you?'

'No, but I need half a litre of your washing up liquid for the next stage of the preparation.'

'Ancient peoples had access to washing up liquid?' he asked quizzically.

'No, but since it is available here, I thought I should short cut this stage, as I'm fed up with wearing your old boots everywhere.'

'Hmm', he concluded, and they set off back to the cabin carrying the tree of life as if it were a hunting trophy.

*

Later in the evening, by the light of the camp fire, she appeared out of the darkness smelling strongly of washing up liquid and carrying parts of the shark hide. By using Jason's fish scissors, she had already fashioned the lower sections of sole-heel, and was trying to introduce a series of holes along their edges with point of the scissors when, without saying a word, Jason disappeared into the cabin and remerged with a bradawl from his tool kit.

Handing her the instrument, he said quietly, 'Can't have you in casualty tonight with a gash in your thigh, and here is a cutting board to rest on.'

She looked up at him appreciatively, thankful for his help, without either comment or interference. Afterwards he stoked up the fire to give her more light and shortly turned in and left her to continue with her dubious inventions. He located the mattress, still with its dividing barrier down the middle and gave a little snort, saying under his breath that he had better devise some sort of schoolboy dreams to sleep with, as that girl is determined not to let him take liberties.

Strange, he thought as he was drifting away into sleep, he could recall such emotions and desires when he was fourteen. His hand drifted down into his pubic hair as he pictured his girl neighbour's fine legs as she stepped up into the bus in the mornings. He was sound asleep before Amanda climbed onto the mattress on the other side of the barrier.

CHAPTER ELEVEN

For the next three days they laboured endlessly, hauling wood and trees ashore and piling them up on the lava to dry out. The high point of their discoveries was a raft of banana ferns, complete with the vital corms that form the roots of the plants and enable them to produce more stems each year. Again their find was tangled up in the branches of a broken tree and had probably arrived there like the tree of life, by sliding down an unstable slope after the tsunami had passed.

Amanda located an ash filled gully close by and they dragged the raft of banana debris to it, and scraped out enough of a depression to bury the roots in ash and small stones of pumice and coral rock, until the plants at least looked established. They then covered the area with a carpet of decaying leafy material from the tide line and hoped that there would be enough nutrients to get the plants going.

From time to time they both looked up at the heavens and wondered if it would ever rain again. They knew that volcanic soils were famously rich but that water was essential also.

Something had been on Jason's mind for a while and, after they had woofed down their late afternoon meal of tortoise and shark steaks and imbibed copious quantities of coconut milk, he sat in the shade with Amanda and suggested they had some sort of conference. They had hardly spoken about their plight during the past days, such was their rush to secure wood, fuel and plants from the seashore. They had been exhausted by their efforts by evening and had no energies to plan for the future.

Amanda feared the conference was going to lead to a disagreement about the sexual activity status and was prepared to protect her position. She was relieved to hear that the two topics Jason wanted to discuss were nothing to do with their domestic arrangements, a charade which she inwardly acknowledged was hard enough to keep a grip on.

'Firstly it's water and secondly it's the rest of this island. It needs looking at. These are my main concerns.' He said it in a tone that was a flat statement, as if he were addressing a congress of engineers.

Amanda nodded and would have started to take notes, had it been in her former life. This was how things moved forward, how things got done when she worked with the Ocean Drilling company.

She urged him to go on, feeling a sense of pride that her boy from next door, the same one that she was secretly in love with, was taking charge and planning them through the next stage of survival.

'We can't rely on rain for our continued existence. It might be months away and our captured water is finite. Even Regina is now on the drinking list.' He paused while Amanda made an apologetic cough before he continued again. 'What we need is a well. There must be a water table some distance down in the soft ash layers. Not all that fresh water run-off reaches the sea.'

'A well,' she echoed, looking up from her invisible note pad.

'And secondly,' he continued, 'we need to know exactly what

our resources are on this island. This means a hike right around it which could take several days. There's no point in doing all kinds of stuff here if it's much simpler somewhere else. What do you think?'

She was reluctant to intervene when it was obvious that he had hatched a plan already.

'The moon is up at night now,' she observed, 'so maybe we could cover the ground we know about in the last hours of the night, and then do a full day's hike and sleep outside somewhere, before returning the next day. That way we could carry enough water and food without danger of running out. We could do the same thing in the opposite direction from the cabin and then judge what the length of the un-surveyed gap might be.'

He looked across the fire at her and grinned. He knew that domestic arrangements like food and water were safest in her hands and felt comforted by her unqualified support for his plan. 'Have you any idea how big this island is?'

"If it's the highest island in the Galapagos group, the one that has the Wolf volcano on it, which if I remember correctly erupted back in twenty fifteen, then it's about fifteen miles long, I vaguely remember, and called Isabella. There is, or was, a largish town at the southern end, which had berthing facilities for cruise ships. I don't remember any other significant active volcanoes in the group, only that the active ones were at the northern end of the group, due to the plate moving over a hot mantle plume. I can't remember any other geographical features.'

It was Jason's turn to wish he had a note pad. He tried to remember if he had had any general maps of the Pacific amongst the papers in the cabin, and then sadly recalled the heap of pulped and mashed paper and books that washed out from their cabin door into the ash the day they arrived. There was nothing at all salvageable, so it was on Amanda's memory and intuition now that they solely depended.

'I'll leave the task of digging a well until we've looked around a bit in case we miraculously come across a fresh water lake or a spring or something. The fresh water we have stored and the production of the still is enough for what?...A month?' he suggested.

Amanda nodded. 'With the coconut milk, a little more maybe. I think it would be prudent though, if we keep throwing coconuts up above the tide line during our exploration. It would be horrible if they all drifted away again. I'm worried about the fire if we go for two days.'

'Ah. I never thought about that.' He paused and then said, 'What if we heap it up with canvas sheeting and cover the whole thing with rocks? It should keep smouldering for a couple of days, don't you think?'

'Maybe. Anyway, I could probably make another if the sun continues to shine.'

Jason regarded her again and softened his leadership stance, realising how much he counted on her intelligence and skills and tried to hide his growing love for her, and just stopped himself from saying the words.

'I'll empty out my tool bag and we can carry supplies in that. You could take your thermals to sleep in and I'll make do with what I have on. What about your footwear?' he asked hesitantly, having noticed she had at least two pairs of his socks on inside her newly made sharkskin sandals.

'Hmm,' she snorted, 'Mark One sandals need some modifications before a long hike. I had better go back to your boots.' She sounded a little broken, having realised that efficient 'cave woman' was a long way off yet, and that twenty five years of having her feet pampered to in snug fitting footwear had done little to prepare them for aa aa lava and sloppy sharkskin slippers.

'I thought they looked pretty darn good I must say. All they need is a little breaking in and they will be fine,' he replied encouragingly.

'Yes, but it would be better if the alpha male came back with another shark or a wild buffalo or something, so I can improve the design with Mark Two!'

He laughed, 'Yes it would be nice to go fishing again.'

She snorted again with incredulity. It was the way he said it. There was a nonchalance that expressed nothing to do with providing vital food or leather, but more to do with seeking again the thrill of a big fish on his line and the fight to get it ashore. She sighed with resignation. If only she could remove herself from the immediate reality of survival enough to become excited about a possible future success.

She reflected a moment and then remembered Regina. She

smiled silently and thought about all the prickly pear succulents the creature had devoured in the last two days and how she was moving around and restored to life. That was a success surely, maybe of monumental proportion and then there was the banana plantation and the tree of life. These were little things, but yes, she was excited about them. She would tend them with passion.

'So,' he interrupted the pause in their reflections, 'shall we go tomorrow and aim, by first light, to make the distant headland we saw yesterday?'

*

The moon was setting over the western sea horizon just as the sun's first chinks of orange light captured the rocky outline of the rugged lava flows that had punctuated their route ahead, round the far side of the headland. They could see that the mountain side was at its steepest; the caldera being closer to the sea there and in the miles that lay ahead.

The lava flows had periodically reached the sea in quite recent years. There were no platforms of ash anymore, like the one their cabin sat on. Altogether, the scenery was somehow much more hostile and unforgiving. What loose material the tsunami had not removed was scoured away by the onshore wind and ocean swells.

They found the gullies difficult to negotiate, with lengthy diversions inland. Jason commented that there was great thickness of rotting vegetation driven hard up into the heads of these gullies, some of it high above the reach of the current swells. They could only suppose that the wind and sea state would change as the sun got higher.

They did not have to wait long for the confirmation of his theory as, no sooner had he spoken, a gently waft of sea breeze drove small rafts of foam towards the shore, trapping them amongst the grounded big trees. The breeze soon picked up into a steady trade wind, that rumbled the trees agonisingly against the broken corals and aa aa lava. Fragmented bits washed ashore occasionally looking like pieces of white polished ivory.

It became intolerably hot as the morning went on and their scrambling up and down near vertically sided gullies made their progress very slow. It was in one of the deepest gullies, that fingered well into the mountainside, that a shady overhang offered a little relief and they decided to take a rest.

Here they spotted a round log no more than six feet long and sawn at both ends, a clear reminder of South American man's activities prior to the tsunami, and sat themselves on it in comfort. Jason dragged out a bottle of water and some of their remaining precious dried apricots and they breakfasted in silence.

Jason didn't like to say it, but he was depressed about the futility of the day's mission. They had found nothing of any use, covered hardly any distance and had had to negotiate some pretty hazardous climbs with inappropriate footwear.

While he was preparing a speech for Amanda, justifying their early return to the cabin, she was rummaging round through the debris at the head of the gully. It was already beginning to stink of mulching vegetation and was unpleasant to clamber across. Nevertheless she was determined to use the rest period resourcefully and dragged out a few miscellaneous fragments of plastic sheet and tossed Jason the leg of a plastic chair before continuing her search.

She had her back to Jason and was squatting on her haunches intent on extracting anything that attracted her attention from the matted vegetation. Jason's mischievous thoughts, contemplating her upturned bottom and sneaky waistline, were suddenly interrupted by a howl of delight, as she yanked a plastic sandal from amongst bent banana leaves and placed it beside her left foot, which was half buried in Jason's oversized boot.

'Perfect size! Now where is the right one?'

Jason leapt up and joined in another ten minutes of fruitless search. Finally Amanda stumbled right up to the head of the gully, because she had spotted an unusual spike of very pale green material. She beckoned to him and together they examined her find. It was not an uncommon sight anywhere in the tropics. In fact it was quite normal at the head of any windswept beach, but here, in a post tsunami environment, it had huge implications. What Amanda had partially uncovered was a germinating coconut, with its husk split open and rotting but with a vibrant green shoot reaching skyward and a root feasting on the rotting vegetation around it.

She said the nut must have been on the point of germination before the tsunami struck and now it had found itself in the perfect growing conditions. It would be some years before it bore coconuts, but to Amanda it signified a recovering world. A world of the future, and what is more there would be a host of other seeds and seedlings in that vegetation mulch that would establish themselves when fresh water arrived.

She discussed this breakthrough find with Jason. He could follow the exciting logic and imagined a lush tropical environment in these creeks in ten year's time, but the images were tarnished with the looming famine and lack of identifiable food in the intervening years. However, it gave him a huge boost of morale to realise that his Eve would be the gardener, the cultivator, the agronomist, while he could do his best to maintain their intermediate food supply as Adam the hunter. It seemed simplistic, yet it provided their ultimate solution.

Without any further discussion, Jason declared that there was little point in going on that afternoon and covering so little ground and that 'enough was enough.' They had better make it back home while all their limbs were intact and hope that tomorrow's venture in the opposite direction would be more eventful.

She conceded, having thought as much herself, and by the time they arrived back at the cabin with enough scrapes and grazes to be sore all over and feeling truly dehydrated, she was extremely grateful for the way Jason aborted the trip.

They had gathered some more of the goose barnacles on the way back, together with a few twigs and leaves from the tree of life so, after re-establishing the fire with coconut husk, she set about making a broth.

An hour later Jason looked up from his tilted bowl, and licking his now well-formed whiskers, beamed a smile of approval at her.

'Not bad. Not bad at all! Is there any more?'

She felt it again; the pang of outstretched love, the dawning of appreciation for one another. She wanted to say some words but nothing appropriate would come out.

She imitated his whisker licking and stuttered out, 'I think I like your beard. It sort of gives you a look of congenial authority. It's taken me a while to get used to it, but yes...it's okay.'

'That's a relief,' he replied in jest, 'because there's not a lot I can do about it. I haven't come across many barber shops on the island yet, and as a matter of fact, while we're on the subject,' he hesitated and wondered if he dared voice his next sentence and then continued, casting fate to the wind and giving her a devastating smile, 'and your pussy is not doing too badly either.'

'Huh!' she huffed in an attempt to be embarrassed, 'I can't imagine how you can know that. I've been wearing your shorts the last few days, and in any case to quote you, 'there is nothing I can do about it either.'

There was an intimate silence, while each considered their boy-girl relationship and the sweetness of anticipation. Amanda symbolically crossed her legs, while Jason just wished he could jump into bed with her there and then.

She rose to her feet.

'I suppose I better get his lord and master his second bowl of soup,' she said sarcastically and then stretched over him to take his empty dish and, in so doing, made sure that he got a fleeting glance down the loose fitting shirt she had been wearing lately.

The pert, pyramidal breasts, that he had become so used to seeing during their first two weeks, had suddenly become symbols of desire. Now they were cloaked in mystique under the light cotton of his shirt and he could only imagine their softness brushing against his lips. He only had a towel draped over his lap and the power of his erection was forcing it up into an unnatural ridge.

She returned with the soup and, giving him a wicked smile, said, 'Would you like me to find you a flat surface to put this on sir!'

'That won't be necessary. Thanks. I'll manage thank you.'

'Manage!' he muttered under his breath. 'If I don't manage under this towel, I will certainly manage when she is not looking after supper!' he thought.

The evening was pleasantly charged, though they each kept to their vowed independence and feigned sleep on each side of the barrier. It was Jason's turn this time to fake a need to cough, in order to stifle his body heaves and intense orgasm. He had 'managed it' poorly apparently, for a guttural moan came from the other side of the barrier. The attempt to drown out her murmurs of extreme pleasure failed to synchronise with the theatrical coughing drama, and her sighs relayed the message that the ultimate expressions of their love could now only be days away.

*

It was not quite light when they arose, gathered up some supplies and headed off along the shoreline, in the opposite direction to the previous day. It was still today. Hardly a wavelet rustled the floating vegetation. If anything, the raft of trees and bushes was denser than the day before. It seemingly stretched to the horizon.

'Don't you think it's strange that there are no birds or animals clinging to it or perched on the branches?' Jason enquired, after the daylight fully came. 'Shouldn't there be creatures that slid down the unstable slopes above the reach of the tsunami, like the banana trees and tree of life? Couldn't they also have hitch-hiked a ride here?'

'You would think so. Perhaps we've underestimated the devastation caused by the sulphurous air and acid rain. We were lucky that it didn't linger long here, but without the oxygen supply we also might have perished.'

'No. I still cannot believe that life has been more or less wiped out,' Jason said in his pragmatic voice. 'There must be caves, sheltered enclaves and even man-made structures where atmospheric controls could have been put in place, in highland areas above the reach of the tsunami.'

'I admire your hope,' she replied, as they stumbled on along the shoreline. 'Assuming you're right, it'll take years for the surviving human beings to set up a civilisation, without any industrial base to fall back on. Even food supplies will make progress intolerably slowly for years to come, especially if most wildlife and domesticated animals have been wiped out.'

She pondered for a moment. 'One aspect that might jump start civilisation is the mountainous regions' generation of hydro-electricity. There must surely be scientists and technicians high in the mountains that can keep this going. There is hope with an energy source Jason. You're right. With an energy supply you can do most things. We just have to keep alive until someone rescues us with a boat!'

She threw her head back and laughed. It was all too simplistic and she knew it, and they walked on in silence, peering into the mass of flotsam, wishing to see something to raise their spirits.

Finally Jason broke the depressed silence, 'I could build a boat of some sort with all these trees and wood around. But then we need food to keep going, so it is not possible in the short term.'

'You could build a boat?' She responded over her shoulder sounding a little dubious. 'Isn't that impossible without tools and plans?'

It was Jason's turn to derail her programmed concepts of normality, 'I don't see why not, with the basic tools I have and a choice of sawn timber and trees. Some of the sawn timbers we have chucked ashore have nails in them, so do the pallets. It's the food I'm worried about. We only have enough for two or three weeks at the most.........' His voice tailed off into a slur of words.

'What the fuck's that! He shouted pointing to a shiny object, two or three hundred meters out, glinting in the sunlight.

She jumped with excitement, crying out while leaping up onto the highest nearby rock.

'It's massive and it's metallic, smooth and floating high in the water. Could be an upturned boat or a tank or something.'

Jason jumped up beside her and, shading his eyes, claimed it could not be a boat hull, as it was too shiny.

'Will it come in any closer do you think?' Amanda demanded.

'Can't see how it can. It's jammed up amongst all these trees. It could be useful to us if it is metal, especially if it's aluminium.' He leapt down and rushed to the shore. We have to beach it somehow. You know, I think it's part of a plane.'

'Don't tell me,' she shouted down to him, 'you are going to build a plane if we can find the rest of it,' she jested with a chuckle.

'No, but an aluminium boat might be a possibility. That hem rope we dragged the tortoise with. Where is it?' He shouted excitedly.

'Back where you butchered it.'

'I'll go and fetch it while you check the shoreline ahead for other treasures.'

With that said, Jason set off back towards the cabin with renewed enthusiasm, without paying attention to her stream of questions as to how he would reach the metal object.

Amanda shook her head and stared vacantly back out to sea. That man's enthusiasm never ceased to amaze her. Her own mind was programmed to analyse facts and build up solutions to problems as they arose, yet his approach was an uncontrolled dash into the unknown, based only on a wish or a whim. She recalled the 'swish' scenario but then two days later he had appeared with a shark. Whatever will he attempt to do with the rope and his treasured metal trophy, once he manages to get it ashore? She looked again at the tangled mass of trees and debris separating whatever-it-was and the shoreline, and shook her head again.

For another half hour she continued picking her way along the water's edge, throwing every coconut and all pieces of sawn timber up above wave's reach. She tethered another goose barnacled old pallet to a rock on the shore, using a vine, and congratulated herself on her ingenuity before wandering back.

Jason arrived at the site nearest to the floating metal object just after she did. He was sweating profusely and draped in coils of the hem rope. After he had slid into the shallow water to cool off and despite his feeble protestations she made him sit down and forced him to drink a large share of their day's water rations. It was obvious he had a plan and she was not going to be able to stop him putting it into action.

Without further discussion he announced he would first do a recce to see what it was and determine how to drag it ashore, and with that he waded in until he was forced to swim, nosing his way through the sticks and leaves like an otter. She looked on with great apprehension, rehearsing in her mind all the survival and rescue methods and techniques, in which she had been so well trained when working on rigs. Few were relevant here, she concluded.

Meanwhile, Jason had reached the first grounded tree, hauled himself up onto its semi-submerged trunk and scrambled along its length into the extensive branch system, disappearing at times amongst the remaining foliage.

Amanda kept skipping backwards and forwards along the shore, trying desperately to keep him in view. She registered an abnormal quickening of her pulse and realised that the new mixture of fear and concern that she was experiencing had to be part of an uncontrolled pattern. It had to be the developing love for that man out there. She started shaking unexpectedly. What possessed him to take on such risky tasks without good reason?

He was negotiating his fifth or sixth tree and was only in sight from the shore intermittently. Amanda's pulse started to race as she considered all the possibilities of his non-return. How could she endure the loneliness never mind survive on her own? The intimacies of each other's company, which she had taken all too much for granted, all flashed before her and she gnashed her teeth, then sat on a rock and cried. The tears ran down her cheeks like a baby. She knew a new chapter in her life was about to open.

CHAPTER TWELVE

'It's a plane wing,' he shouted excitedly as he waded ashore.

Amanda had regained her composure since she saw his tiny figure standing on top of the shiny object twenty minutes earlier, and concluded that if he could make it out there, he could probably make it back.

'I thought as much. What can we do with it and what of the people who were in it? And what have you got in your hand?' She was looking at the tassels of soggy vegetation he had dragged back with him.

The questions were coming thick and fast from the excited girl off the school bus. Meanwhile Jason was still trying to fully regain his breath.

'It's maize. It's a stem of maize with two cobs still intact. This is brilliant Jason. I'll sort out the good kernels and plant them in composting vegetation, and we might have a crop in a couple of months!' Her eyes were glistening with emotion and she hugged his wet shining hairy chest until the oversized shirt she was wearing stuck to her breasts.

He stood back from her admiring what he saw and grinned and then burst out laughing, handing her the stem of maize. 'I knew you'd get excited about this bit of old vegetation. I should have hidden it from you so it didn't eclipse my discovery of half a plane!'

'Tell me! Tell me!' she danced around him, like a six year old girl who is being denied the end of a fairy story. 'You were really, really brave to swim all the way out there. I am so proud of you....' She faltered, knowing again she was in unknown emotional territory and after a pause continued on safer ground, 'but what of the people in the plane?'

'It's hard to say. It may not even have been flying; just sitting on the ground when the tsunami struck. I couldn't see any other parts or personal effects in the area. I had a good look when I stood up on the wing. It's not off a very big aircraft, a company jet, a twelve-seater or something like that. Where it was ripped from the fuselage, there are internal struts and braces which would be perfect to attach our rope to.'

'Our rope is not long enough to reach there,' Amanda stated quite confidently, hoping that he would not put it to the test by making an even more hazardous swim out there dragging the hem rope behind him.

To her relief he nodded in agreement and conceded that they would have to find more rope material, or wait until the wreckage jogged in a little closer. He looked intensely at her tanned arms and legs, her puckered nipples probing the inner material of his shirt, her messed up hair and girlish smile and impulsively put his arm over her shoulder. He was about to say, 'I love you,' when a wave of fear or embarrassment, he knew not which, overtook him and he pulled away.

'Let's go baby. Let's see what else we can find!' He dared not look behind in case she saw in his eyes what he had nearly said.

She was ecstatic and skipped along in his wake, her mind cocooned in a reoccurring dream.

It was well past noon and intensely hot when they came across the find of their lives. Amanda saw it first as she raised her head to toss a coconut up the beach.

'What's that?' she exclaimed waving her arm ahead of them, while at the same time bounding into an ungainly skip , with her sandaled foot leading the one in Jason's oversized boot. She was determined to reach her prize before he did, and sat down panting by an inflatable dingy, as a breathless Jason plonked down beside her. If it had been manna from heaven there could not have been a greater moment of excitement shared by the exhausted couple.

'Holy Jesus,' muttered Jason, as he probed it, testing its rigidity. 'Must have been caught up with the trees when it left South America. On its own, the wind would have held it close to the continent, whereas the current brought it here, hijacked by the floating vegetation. What luck! This is miraculous! Now we have a means of catching fish, once we can clear a way through the flotsam to deeper water.'

Amanda knew instantly that this is what he had had at the back of his mind for several days, since he caught the shark. This was the way he planned their survival. As he had said many times, 'Where there was one shark, there would be others.' She shuddered at the thought of him setting off to sea in a flimsy inflatable.

They hauled it clear of the water and up the beach some distance, before tethering it to a boulder of lava rock by its short anchor rope. Jason was quick to suggest he could make paddles from their sawn timber. Amanda chuckled at his never ending enthusiasm and made up her mind to find or make the longest piece of rope in history so that she could always haul him back to the shore. With that they set off back to their home with spirits uplifted, collecting the maize cobs on the way, along with another meal of goose barnacles from Amanda's pallet and some prickly pear cactus for Regina.

It may not have been the perfect meal that evening, with their rations of salted turtle meat, salted shark meat and the delicious chowder made from the goose barnacles, fragments off the tree of life and bulked up with coconut milk, but the finds of the day had been so inspiring that Amanda thought it fit to open one of the sacrosanct bottles of wine. She marched out from the cabin in her sharkskin slippers to where Jason sat on a log in the light of the glowing embers of the fire. She carried the bottle in one hand and a couple of beakers in the other. Before leaving the cabin she had deliberately left the top button of his oversized shirt undone in full knowledge that her breasts would be exposed when she leant forward. The provocation, she argued, would be lessened by the darkening of the evening sky and would hide the deliberate nature of the seduction.

Jason paused and looked up from his task of shaving away slithers of wood from a spar he had brought back, which was now beginning to take the shape of a rudimentary paddle.

'Just a small glass,' she spoke sheepishly, as if it were to taste the forbidden fruit. 'I thought that since we've found a plane and a boat on the same day, we should mark the occasion with some sort of toast.'

She handed him a beaker and unscrewed the cap of the bottle. She poured a little out for herself and then, with a trembling hand, leaned forward and poured out a similar measure for him.

There was an electric silence while Jason did what he was supposed to do, and that was to gaze down the front of her shirt, taking in the details of her firm little breasts. At the same time he had to wrestle with the instantaneous surge of adrenaline and regain control over the desires that caused his penis to erupt into an erection.

It wasn't that he had never seen those breasts before, of course he had, for days on end in fact, but the newness of them peeping out from secrecy was both seductive and wild.

She turned around and squeezed up beside him on the log so that the points of their hip bones were touching. She nervously raised her beaker to his and gently enquired, 'Did you see anything different about your shaving mirror?'

He hesitated and chuckled, 'I did. It had a little heart on it with an arrow through it.' He chuckled again. 'The initials on the arrow were a mystery to me and I planned to ask you about it. BSG and MF. What's all that about?'

'Did you not ever have read to you as a boy Robinson Crusoe?' she laughed back spiritedly.

'Yes,' he conceded. 'Everyone did, and watched the video. That is a clue I suppose?' He groaned and took a sip of the wine.

'Wait!' she commanded, 'We have not had a toast yet'.

He withdrew the beaker from his lips and paused in thought, before stamping his foot on the ground causing the fire to flicker and put up a new flame.

'MF........of course 'Man Friday'. Now I realise what to search for.' He rubbed his hairy forearm against her skin.

It was like a warm shock of electricity and, for the first time in her life, she felt the race of her heartbeat and the flush to her face, the feeling of uncontrolled longing, heat and affection for the man of her daily dreams.

'You will not know the BSG and I will not allow you to have any crude or ungainly efforts to guess, so I will have to stoop to telling you of my adolescent dreams.'

Jason laughed and made and animated, 'Whoop!'

'I am listening. I like the way this is going. Come on tell me of your adolescent dreams!'

'They are not the sort you imagine!' she cautioned, while being aware of his arm rubbing hers again. He withdrew his arm and allowed her to continue after a brief silence.

'No need to stop rubbing my arm. It's nice...... Anyway, when I was a young teenager, my tutors saw fit for me to have some interaction with the outside world. I was driven to a nearby bus stop where I boarded the local bus, which happened to be a school bus. After a fifteen minute ride, I alone got off at the academy where I was privately taught. Other young people continued on to their day schools. This routine continued for a few weeks. Thereafter, I was driven directly to my place of study by one of my monitors or tutors, and the experiment in interaction was considered over.'

'I realise now why the communal bus journey experiment was terminated. It was observed by my monitors that I was developing affection for a boy that waited at the same bus stop. He was nothing special, nor was there any more than a few words exchanged. It was just that he was a boy and I was experiencing my first hormone flushes and it was considered by my monitors, possibly wrongly, to be a risky intrusion to my programming.

When I reached adulthood, this early denial of love and suppressed affection for males manifested itself in my lack of ability to form loving relationships. Yet at the same time, my programmed athletically built body, with sky high oestrogen levels, demanded regular sexual satisfaction....'

'I was aware of that on the rig,' he interposed, giving her a friendly nudge, 'but what of the BSG?'

'Well since the whole situation of my life... our lives,' she corrected herself, 'has now changed, then I thought I had better turn the clocks back and learn how to love....'

She stuttered and choked on the last few words. He put an arm around her and gave a reassuring hug, before springing to his feet and giving the fire a kick so that it burst into flames, lighting up their faces.

'I got it!' he exclaimed. You are the bus stop girl! You are BSG and you love Man Friday. Wow! Now all we have to do is work out who Man Friday is! If he is my competition I'll kill him!

She cheered and rose to her feet. Joining him by the fire, she clunked her beaker against his, raising it to the stars and shouted into the night, 'Shall we start a new chapter?'

He echoed, 'A new chapter.'

CHAPTER THIRTEEN

At five and a half thousand metres above sea level, high above the Atacama desert in Chile, the Japanese observatory of Cerro Chajnantor had been in total shut-down for over a week, when Yoshi Yeversan nudged his fellow technician Janet O'Harrah, the English language radio operator, to see if she still had any heat in her body.

She moaned and grunted back before breaking into a bout of coughing.

Dragging a blanket round him, Yoshi staggered to his feet and stumbled slowly towards the tiny vented window that had been their only contact with the outside world. From here he had been shouting for help daily since the darkness and the sulphurous cloud had overwhelmed the facility seven days earlier.

It had been their fate that the Head of Operations at the observatory had sent them down into the storeroom, to bring food supplies up to the canteen, when a series of successive sharp tremors knocked out the station's power supply, together with its back-up generators. It had plunged them into darkness.

Yoshi and Janet had clung on to the metal framework of the storeroom's central aisle for the duration of the tremors. Coming from their respective homelands of Japan and New Zealand, they were quite familiar with earthquakes. In any case, their whole team had been anticipating seismic activity since the monitors unveiled the catastrophic events happening in the Northern Pacific earlier that day. This had triggered the order to shut-down. The tremors had been a series of very sharp jerks, quite unfamiliar to the pair, and the crashing of concrete and glass, above and beside the basement storeroom, had raised their fear to panic level. They realised that the sudden jolts were more powerful than anything they had previously experienced.

By the time the shaking had stopped and the cascading and repositioning of concrete and steel slabs had ceased, only dust and absolute darkness prevailed. The dust had partially settled after an hour or so and the frightened couple were only experiencing a series of minor tremors. Despite the darkness and choking dust, they had made efforts to extricate themselves from the storeroom, to discover what if anything remained of the observatory and their fellow scientists.

Those efforts to escape had been thwarted by the masses of concrete slabs and first floor debris that had fallen down the stairwell, completely blocking their exit. In the fading light of that first afternoon, they had simply hung on, expecting to hear sounds of a rescue party. The silence had only been broken by the hiss coming from the oxygen pipe that provided the enhanced atmosphere to every room at the high altitude observatory. Yoshi knew that the storage tank for the oxygen was located in a shock proof vault adjacent to the basement store, and assumed that their storeroom was the first in line on the distribution network. He had remarked to his companion that they should be thankful for that.

A week later, Yoshi reported back through the darkness to his companion, who remained curled up under a heap of blankets, the unwelcome news that the world outside remained black and starless and reeked of sulphur. Her responding moan was more of despair than pain and only the continuing hiss from the oxygen pipe broke the silence.

It was bitterly cold and, according to Yoshi, a grey snow was incessantly falling onto the sill of the small vented window. If only they had more light, he had muttered many times to his companion, who he suspected was developing pneumonia and in all probability would die in the coming days.

Stricken by this depressing thought, he groped his way along the shelves of biscuit tins and canned foods, in the hope of feeling something useful. He turned the corner of the aisle and fumbled along a section unfamiliar to him. It felt like brooms, mops and brushes and he could smell soaps and detergents. He assumed he had arrived at a janitor section. Continuing further, his fingers fell upon what felt like hammers and screwdrivers and other basic tools, and then there was a break in the shelving. His feet contacted metal and the familiar rattle of an aluminium step ladder met his ears.

Janet called out in a husky, broken voice, 'What are you doing?'

'Kicking a step ladder I think,' he replied reassuringly, glad that she was still alert enough to hear something.

The shelving had continued again and his fingers contacted small cardboard cartons stacked one upon another. He remembered such boxes in their living quarters and quickly persuaded his stiff, cold fingers to prize a box open. As he suspected, inside he felt the small oblong shapes of a layer of lithium batteries.

Excited by this initial find, he groped further along the shelf, half expecting to find empty torches. He was disappointed, for his hands came into contact with flat plastic bags that seemed to have towels or bed sheets inside. Not to be beaten, and knowing he was racing against time now for both of their lives, he knew he had to continue his search. The intense cold was getting to him as well, and while they had been relatively warm during the first few days, they had missed opportunities. They had just camped in the dark, living on biscuits and bottled water, hoping to be rescued. This seemed not to be happening and he was angry with himself for not investigating earlier.

He shuffled back to the where he had located the boxes of batteries. Resting his hand briefly on the opened box was significant. He could feel hope. Stretching up to the shelf above, he could feel packs of what seemed like plastic plates and beakers, and other picnic items such as bundles of spoons. He stood on tip-toe to find out what was at the back of the shelf, and concluded that it was much of the same. While his chest was close against the ice cold metal framework, his toes came into contact with something softer and warmer. A cardboard carton, he concluded, and immediately ducked down to investigate.

If it had been the captain's treasure chest from a sunken Spanish galleon, it could not have been more welcome. Yoshi dived into it and fumbled round, locating hand torches and elasticated head lamps. Within a minute or two, he had a lithium battery in a torch and engaged the switch. He yelped with delight as their underground prison leapt into a circus of silvery light and shapes and pools of total darkness, together with undiscovered material riches.

Janet became animated and shouted to him to rescue her and get medicines and fire. Her croaky voice defied the gravity of her situation but conveyed her determination to live.

Within an hour, Yoshi had hammered open the locked medicine cabinet, and fed Janet substantial doses of the latest highly effective antibiotics, to clear her chest infection. He had located a pallet of emergency oil heaters and fired up two of them, placing them near to where she was lying on the floor. He then supplemented the stale, cold blankets with a heap more and finally located high energy drinks and food for them both.

Yoshi remarked that their rescue might be weeks away and, although the stores were for the benefit of the entire team, they could not be criticised for using what they needed to keep alive in the interim. He propped Janet up against the wall while he made her take the antibiotics and high energy drinks. The oil heaters were quickly warming the room so, armed with two more torches, he set about investigating the remaining area.

Five days ago, he kept reminding himself, he could have done all this, and they would not have arrived at the low state they presently found themselves in. If only he had not put faith in the belief that they would soon be rescued. This belief had slowly melted away after the first few days, when the tremors had been replaced by silence. He now believed that the rest of the team above ground had either been killed by masonry collapse during the severe quakes, or had booted it downhill to safer locations, without realising they were entombed in the basement. They were on their own now, he decided.

The anger that welled up inside him for the delay in his actions, made him even more determined to get them out of their prison and down the mountain to warmth and civilisation. There had to be a fire escape or emergency door or something, he decided, after a more detailed inspection of the choked stairwell. There was no hope of gaining a passageway up through the slabs of concrete and masonry there. That was not an option. The tiny window vent, through which he had gained knowledge of the conditions outside, was too narrow for a person to squeeze through, and in any case, there was an unknown drop to the sloping ground below.

Janet called out to him, so he retraced his steps to the place where she was propped up against the wall and immediately realised the problem. The oil heaters were producing not just heat but fumes, and also gobbling up the air around them. The atmosphere had become sticky and oppressive so he reluctantly turned them off.

The issue was one of lack of good air, Yoshi reckoned, and turned his attention to the oxygen supply pipe, that hissed in the back corner of the room. He remembered that in the gym, at least, there was a control valve which could be adjusted to allow more oxygen into the room when people were exercising. He located the one in the store room but, unlike the gym, it was high up on the wall and needed a tool to adjust it. He reported back to Janet, who by this time was bravely making a recovery.

Yoshi was not a practical person. He had spent his days in the observatory in front of a computer, analysing data and transferring information about the outer universe to the senior astronomers. Anything to do with tools and engineering or practical applications scared him, to the point he would find another person to carry out the task.

Janet egged him on. 'Can't you fix it?' Her voice was so weak and pathetic, he felt compelled to try and shuffled off in the direction of the step ladder.

As he remembered while groping for torches, the tools were close by. The aluminium of the step ladder was icy cold, as were the tools.

Twenty minutes later, he had prized open the valve sufficiently for the oxygen flow to be fast enough to raise the dust from the area nearby.

Delighted with his success, he hugged the blanket closer to his body and climbed back down the ladder. Part of the way down, his progress was impeded by the hem of the blanket hitching up on some obstacle. He freed it and regained the floor. Casting his eyes back up, curious to know what had hitched him up, he could see a small lever inset into the wall, and with the swirling flow of oxygen from the valve blowing the dust away, he could just make out the sign saying: EMERGENCY EXIT.

CHAPTER FOURTEEN

Jason, aware of her nervousness, gently put his arm round her. He had slid it slowly and deliberately under her shirt so that his rough hand scalloped out her tiny waist and came to rest on her pelvic bone. It seemed so delicate and feminine and almost fragile to his touch that he imagined she might recoil in self-preservation.

The fire gave a little crackle while the burning wood rearranged itself. The ensuing tongue of flame lit up Amanda's face so that he could see clearly that her eyes were shut. There could be little doubt, Jason imagined, that she was setting her clock back to the bus stop days. She was allowing those whirlwind emotions to set her body on fire. He was caressing her hip bone softly with the tip of his forefinger without any resistance and he contemplated what an Amanda on the loose might be like.

He had admitted to himself earlier that the charade could be coming to an end sooner rather than later and that his own self indulgencies, his own desire to love and be loved might unleash an energy he had never before experienced. He certainly hoped so because he could imagine what that athletic whiz-kid and Balkan queen of oestrogen would demand of him, both physically and mentally, once the brakes had been taken off.

With his free hand he gulped down the rest of the wine and put the beaker to one side.

'More?' she enquired.

'No,' he replied, but symbolically nodded his head up and down.

'What does that mean?' she asked with a chuckle but his hand had already undone the remaining buttons of her shirt.

'Need you ask?' He took her half drained beaker and offered it to her lips. Before she swallowed, he turned and placed his own lips on hers, allowing the red wine to flow freely between them in an act of pure intimacy and bonding. She turned also so that her open shirt allowed her breasts to nuzzle into his hairy chest.

'Jesus wept!' gasped Jason as he finally pulled away, 'I have wanted to do that for an awful long time. I hope I have not upset your programme. Where do we go from here?' he asked hesitantly while wiping the red wine off his whiskers with a sheepish grin.

Amanda had already slid her shirt off and stepped out of his baggy shorts and was prancing round the other side of the fire, wearing only her sharkskin slippers and every now and then pouting her new pubic mound in his direction.

'If you don't know, Mr. Senior Rig Technician, you are about to find out,' she said in a guttural voice that defied any explanation, and with that she placed both hands on her naked hips and thrust them out provocatively in his direction across the fire and then skipped off into the darkness.

'Jeesus,' wheezed Jason under his breath, 'I hope I'm up to this,' and then thoughtfully reflected, 'In any case, dying in the process shouldn't be too bad!' He looked down at the wet state of his member and concluded he could give her a run for her money, at least.

He was about to chase after her when she came back into view, dragging their mattress behind her.

There was no barrier to go between them this time and when she had finished placing it comfortably up-wind of the fire, she tugged him over to it and told him to lie on his back and keep still.

Any thoughts he might have had about a quick satisfaction of his desires to start with, were quickly dissolved when she disappeared again into the cabin and returned with two hefty cushions. Jason thought again that she was preparing a perfect nest for them to initiate their love making and she would settle down beside him.

Amanda had her own programme, it seemed, based on the reconstruction of every bit of fantasy from her adolescence to the man that hunted down the 'swish'. She wished to savour all the build-ups and crescendos that had washed through her brain over the last ten years, and particularly the last week, but this time with the reality of the man she loved and wanted more than ever and was now at her mercy.

She was not going to let him dismantle her in a flash. She was going to devise every possible ploy to engage his longing before she surrendered to him. She chuckled to herself and thought of her CONSOL. Had it been there, she giggled, it would have probably blown up, with her sexual desire column completely off the scale!

For his part, Jason just lay there with his eyes half shut,

waiting for the moment when she lowered her raunchy hips on to his. His excitement raced into top gear when she raised his buttocks and stuffed the two cushions underneath. By the light of the fire his member resembled a beacon atop a hillside. It shone with anticipation and he knew that if she just lowered herself gently on to it nature would take its course very rapidly.

He opened his eyes expectantly and found her prowling around the mattress like a cat about to spring onto its prey.

His phallus gave a series of small involuntary jerks, allowing a little more seminal fluid to trickle down its trunk.

'For Christ's sake fuck me!' he muttered under his breath. He tried to entice her down onto him but she ordered him not to move. She continued to prowl around him and finally bent over and put a finger and thumb at the base of his penis and gave it a little reassuring fondle, before letting go almost immediately.

'It's beautiful Jason,' she said softly.

He groaned in desperation as she again commanded him not to move.

Amanda on her next prowl got between him and the fire and he could clearly see the shining wetness of her inner thighs and he began to wonder who would crack first in this antagonising game. The wildest thoughts flashed through his brain about her being a superwoman and he half wondered if he was now going to be subjected to something way out of his comfort zone. He felt another dribble run down his shaft, followed by another command telling him not to move. In panic Jason concluded, superwoman or not he had enough testosterone to cope with her for the time being. At that moment she mercifully changed her pattern.

It was happening, he thought and heaved a sigh of relief as she knelt down beside him.

'At last', he thought as she positioned a slim leg either side of him. He shut his eyes as he imagined she would raise her bottom allowing her wet vagina to slide the full length of his rampant penis.

'My God,' she cried out. 'Quickly! Quickly!'

With that she nudged her knees forward until the muskiness and wetness of her vagina came into contact with his face. He grabbed her buttocks and dragged her pulsing clitoris onto his mouth. His tongue had only five seconds to explore, when she screamed out, drenched him in wetness and shook as if in an earthquake, before she flung herself clear and lay panting on the mattress.

'Holy shit!' gasped Jason unable to comprehend the dynamics of the last half minute.

She reached out for his hand and lightly squeezed it.

'You were great,' she said softly and then added in a whisper, 'I need three'.

'Holy shit!' gasped Jason again, quite audibly this time and before he could impose his own special needs, she had climbed back over him again, dragging her breasts across his face so that the erect nipples carved lines through his wet stubble. She wriggled forward and allowed him to lick up the hormonal juices of the previous encounter.

This time she purred like a cat as his tongue softly outlined the petals down the sides of her clitoris and savoured its salty sweetness. After a minute or so of rubbing her sprouting pubic hair against his cheek, the purr turned into a throaty moan. He felt her clitoris harden and expand and her thighs tighten against his body. She caught her breath and threw her head back and went into spasm for a second time, soaking his lips, chin and chest again.

Jason by now was out of control. So much seminal fluid had trickled down to the base of his penis that his pubic hair had become sticky and matted, and he was not in the mood to let his prize get off him and escape a second time.

He held her hips tightly and brought her face down on to his and kissed her incessantly. Without opening his eyes, he judged her open thighs to be perfectly positioned and pulled her lower body down on to his.

On reflection sometime afterwards, he recalled how he had marvelled at nature's resourcefulness, in that the female entry point lined up so perfectly with the male erection.

There was no need to readjust his phallus. It just slid inside. Once there she gripped it with a muscle like a soft vice and held it steady, while his breathing accelerated and she recovered from the orgasm that she had just had. He was lying in a lake of sweat when he became aware of the slackening of the vice and a rippling sensation of the innermost parts of her vagina.

It was too much. Jason arched his back and pumped endless semen deep inside her and cried out, matching her outpouring of profanities earlier.

He thought to wriggle out from under her and 'die' but she was having none of it.

'Wait!' she implored. She gripped him tightly with her thighs and lowered her lips on to his and sucked his tongue in a way he had not experienced before. She held her pubic bone tight against his and gently oscillated her hips. His erection would not surrender. The feeling of male instinct to be sure the job was done properly pulsed through his veins and he knew he would be able to orgasm again if she continued the way she was doing.

She must have felt the hardness of his penis extend deeper inside her and so she shut her eyes, in order to allow the rubbing of her clitoris against his bone to generate the orgasmic desire her body and head pleaded for. The desire suddenly overwhelmed her and she thrust her pelvis up and down in waves of uncontrolled supreme pleasure.

She exploded as did Jason. There was no timescale to measure how long and to what depth the explosion took place, only that when Jason became aware once again of his surroundings, he was lying naked on the mattress with the woman he loved, with their heads sharing the same pillow, with a glowing fire and starlit night for company. It mattered not to him that they may have been the only persons on the planet, as he knew he had in his arms the best that humanity could have possibly provided for him.

*

In a sand filled gully a mile or so from their cabin, after a week of tedious exertion and several futile attempts, Amanda and Jason had excavated a pit down to the water table. There the wet sand slowly produced a pool of fresh water. Their following days were spent carrying lava rocks to the site and constructing a rudimentary well-head, that did not cave in before they could draw water.

These were happy days working together, sometimes clothed, sometimes not, depending on the ferocity of the sun. On returning to their cabin each day, they feasted on coconuts, dried turtle and shark meat, supplemented by the remainder of Jason's in-house supplies. The diet was far from ideal but provided them with plenty of energy. The coconut milk and goose barnacle broth was a real winner and they looked forward to it each day.

En route daily to the well site, they picked their way through the flotsam at the water's edge, tossing potentially useful items above the tide line and all the coconuts that came into sight. Jason continually assessed the density of the foliage that had piled up along the shore, in the hope that there might be some sort of free channel to give him access to the deeper water to fish. They passed the aeroplane wing on these journeys and reckoned it was a bit nearer the shore but still jammed up with big, half submerged trees.

It had been Amanda's careful analysis of the terrain that had defined the spot to search for water, and in the area near the well-head, she had established her corn patch where she could daily water the potential crop. Within a few days the kernels had germinated. She had also moved her precious banana plant there and excavated a trench deep enough for the roots to reach down to the water table.

Jason had accompanied Amanda and supported her in all these activities, and was far sighted enough to realise that their future depended on a secure water supply and basic agronomy. During this period, he had suppressed his desire to venture wider and to try and re-establish their protein supplies. In his role as the strong male or 'alpha male' as she often called him in jest, he dragged wood up from the beach and competently built a rudimentary shelter by the well-head to rest under during the heat of the day.

Each day she climbed down into the well and filled up bowls and saucepans for watering, and he had seen her delight in pouring one over her head and down over her lithe tanned body as she walked delicately through her corn crop. Inevitably she reserved one for him and gave him a good scrub off, before taking his hand and leading him under the racuba, where they regularly made love before napping in the heat of the day.

Their idyllic days had to end. Both Amanda and Jason were fully aware of that. Their shark and tortoise supplies would soon be used up, besides which the quality was also deteriorating and might make them sick before too long. It was decided that Jason would again make the tricky swim out to the aeroplane wing and use it as a fishing platform, in the hope that deep water lay beneath it. Amanda decided that she would go with him, armed with the small saw from his tool kit and spend time clearing a route through the branches, to make a direct line and easier access.

They set off early in the morning, Amanda apprehensive and Jason excited. He had sorted through his tackle bag the night before and rounded up a spool of line and a selection of hooks and weights, all of which would fit into his shorts pockets. They stopped short of the wing at one of their tethered pallets and filled a plastic bag full of goose barnacles for bait.

Again it took Jason about twenty minutes to reach the wing, by partly swimming and partly clambering along logs and through a tangle of branches. He was glad he had not brought his rod.

The wing had its own strange motion, unlike any boat; it sort of hovered on the top of the slight oceanic swells, before grinding its way down into the next trough amongst the great trees alongside. He spent a minute or two peering down into the water at different positions along the wing, because he did not want his precious line to become foul of tree branches. The length of the interval between the swells made him hopeful that there was plenty of deep water beneath.

He baited a single hook with goose barnacles and gradually paid out the line. Fifty meters and still going down. He looked hesitantly at his one hundred meter spool. 'Volcanic island,' he muttered under his breath. 'No shelf...only a drop-off. Could be lucky.'

The line went slack at eighty meters. 'Wassal', he muttered again in an excited voice, using his favourite Arabic expression meaning, 'it has arrived'.

No sooner had he recovered the slack line, than he felt a ferocious tug. He yelled out to Amanda.

'Unbelievable! I've got something on the line already. It's giving a hell of a fight!!'

Amanda stopped her arduous job, sawing through a wet branch which kept jamming the saw blade, wiped the sweat off her face and grinned. 'The boy is on his home ground again,' she mused and, not wishing to miss out on the excitement, she hung the saw up on a decapitated branch stub and yelled to him.

'I'm coming out.'

Jason was too busy to reply and within a minute or two a wet and scratched Amanda was hauling herself aboard the wing, just in time to see the flapping spotted grouper being yanked out of the water and pounced on by her animated companion.

'Wow! Unbelievable! Who needs a boat? The ecosystem has recovered. Hey! Mind my line.' He waved in the direction of his eighty meters of monofilament line lying haphazardly over the wing. 'How did you get here so quickly anyway? Are you a monkey or something?'

He looked quickly at her shining dark skinned naked body, showing all her white teeth which presented a devastating smile, and grinned back at her. 'Silly question. Need I have asked?'

'I want a go!' she said forcefully, not wishing to miss out on the excitement.

He looked at her doubtfully as he took the hook out of the fish, but realised there was to be no compromise with this woman and passed her the hook and bait.

She squatted down on her haunches, while he showed her a technique to keep the bait securely on the hook.

My God, he commented to himself, while he briefly feasted his eyes on the wet petals of her labia minora. *She can be such an animal at times without even realising it.* He wanted to make love to her there and then, but his other love took over and he carefully paid out the line as Amanda let it slide through her fingers.

Another bite straight away and another grouper. Amanda was wild with excitement.

'I didn't know fishing could be so easy. I never saw you catch fish like this off the rig.'

'It was six miles deep,' Jason said defensively.

'Hmm.'

'Also, if this is where we think it is, it has been a conservation zone for more than fifty years and we are fishing illegally.'

'Hmm. Perhaps the conservation vessel will arrest us. That would be nice. I will go and find some vine to string these up or we cannot get them ashore.' With that she slipped back into the water and returned shortly afterwards trailing a vine.

They caught another six fish before Jason lost his hook and weight to a large predator. They spoke briefly of the loss, decided to quit while ahead and strung the fish onto the vine. Jason thought better than to worry his companion about sharks, but suggested that they stuck to the above water branches wherever they could, even if it was not the most direct route ashore.

Amanda registered the gravity in his tone of voice and chose not to respond. She behaved as the primate Jason had hinted at and skimmed through the branches with little trouble, often doubling back to relieve him of the bundle of fish.

Eventually they hauled up on to dry land, somewhat relieved that the expedition had not ended in disaster. Looking down at their catch, Jason shook his head in amazement.

'How incredible the ocean is,' he remarked, 'that it can return to a pristine state so quickly after so much trauma; massive tsunamis, days of acid rain and volcanic dust. Doesn't it give you hope that all is not lost, and the planet will soon recover?'

She hugged him, 'Yes sweet darling alpha male. It will recover. We know that for sure now,' and with that she wiped off the saw blade with coconut milk, while he gave her an enquiring look.

'Tomorrow we start to build a pontoon to reach the wing. We cannot afford to have you eaten by sharks, since there is no longer the possibility of *designer* babies to populate the planet.'

Jason found a nearby pole of wood, so that they could hang

the forty kilos of fish from it and carry it home between them on their shoulders. Her last sentence repeated several times in his head: 'populate the planet' and the combination of 'alpha male' and 'no more chance of designer babies'. What was she alluding to? Populate the planet with *normal* babies...... 'Shit, I'm not ready for this yet,' he thought, and chose to forget the remark.

They spent the rest of the day preserving their catch. Jason cleaned and gilled the fish and made enormous butterfly fillets, while Amanda gathered up enough salt to rub into them for preservation. Except for one side of one fish, they were strung between lava rocks to dry. The large unsalted fillet was reserved for roasting at the side of the fire later on.

They ate well that evening and luxuriated on the mattress outside by the light of the fire, congratulating themselves on the day's successes. In the short term, Amanda commented, they were well provided for. They had a fresh water supply and now a fresh fish supply and mountains of coconuts and mountains of wood.. Survival was no longer going to be a constant problem, providing there were no big changes.

'Like health issues, deluges of rain or further tsunamis,' Jason interposed. 'But what of the rest of the planet? There must surely be whole communities elsewhere that were able to escape the poisonous atmosphere, and were high enough not to be affected by the tsunami.'

He left the question hanging in the air and then added, 'Do you think there would have been massive earthquakes as well, from the tectonic activity that caused the Tsunami?'

Amanda replied, trying to be positive and snap him out of those depressing probabilities.

'Much of the Cordillera is above fifteen hundred meters, as are large parts of Africa and who knows, the tsunami may not have reached much of Africa anyway, though I imagine the poisonous volcanic atmosphere might have done. People must have had warning Jason. There must be pockets of survivors and enough infrastructure to get the World up and running again.'

'As a long shot,' said Jason. 'It will probably take a couple of years before we get to know, a couple of years before clever people are fascinated enough to venture away from their oasis of survival in order to colonise what is left of the planet.'

'Colonise!' She echoed, 'Will it be like that? Every man for himself?' She shuddered and groaned and suddenly wished that the rest of the planet had been totally wiped out. 'I don't want to be colonised. Can't we declare this as an independent state?'

'Hang on a minute,' Jason cut in. 'This place belongs to Ecuador or the UN trustees for World Heritage Sites. It would be an act of colonisation on our part to call it whatever.....'Amandaland' and hope the rest of the world accepted our ownership.' He chuckled, 'Hmm I like that 'Amandaland'!'

'Well if there is nobody else, we have to start naming places. What about the well-head and the nice shelter you built there? We could call it 'Jason Towers'!' She laughed and they slapped their hands together.

'Enough of this nonsense,' Jason said in a more serious tone. 'Tomorrow we have to find out what this island consists of. I suggest we hike a day's walk off to the south and attempt to gain as much height as we can and see what the size of the island is. Then we can plan further expeditions to at least define 'Amandaland'.'

Amanda purred like a cat on the mat in front of the fire and felt that she already had queendom and that she should start making plans for its infrastructure.

CHAPTER FIFTEEN

She slowed her pace and looked over her shoulder to see how far behind Jason was with the back pack of water and provisions. The sun was already well up in the sky, but their climb over the rough lava fields had taken them high enough to attract a breeze and cooler air.

'Must be a thousand meters above sea level now,' he remarked.

'I need to go back to classes,' she said apologetically after a while of gazing at the dry lava fields stretching off to the southern horizon.

'I wasn't going to say anything,' he responded, wiping the sweat off his brow and reminding her of the fifteen miles long, which she thought the high mountain island to be. He then laughed and poked her gently.

'Your territory is bigger than you thought. Let's get higher and see how wide it is, now we've got this far. Maybe you will need some help to govern it.'

She rushed on up and across the mountain's flank, eager to refresh her mind and recall the geography she had been taught. After a while she took another rest stop and waited for Jason. This time she estimated they had gained another three hundred or so meters. The air was definitely cooler and the breeze stronger. She stared desperately to the south, hoping to see the end of the island and concluded her domain must be fifty miles long, not fifteen. The volcanic plain and minor

hillocks went on and on. She shook her head in disgust at her oversight.

Jason caught up and put down the pack. He took out a bottle of water and offered it to her, while wiping more sweat off his face and concentrating his gaze on the land that stretched out before them.

'I remember now,' she said apologetically. 'I think it's more like fifty miles long, not fifteen! How far do you think we can see now?'

'Thirty or forty miles I should think.' His attention had wandered to the shore stretching out in front of them. 'Look at all that green. There must be millions of tons of vegetation piled along the whole length of the shore and as far to seaward as we can see, though I think I can vaguely make out an edge to it further off.'

'South America must be stripped of everything the tsunami came into contact with. The devastation there must be horrific,' she stated sombrely.

The magnitude of the planet's destruction was no longer a hypothesis for them. Its manifestation was clearly laid out. Choosing not to dwell on these depressing thoughts, Amanda rose to her feet and set off briskly towards the summit. After a while she paused to catch her breath and scanned the horizon above her.

'Jason! What's that?'

He quickly scrambled over the last few ridges of lava, eager to find out what sort of life form she had discovered this time.

She was not looking down but instead pointing upwards to the horizon in front of them.

'Jesus! They're structures. They're some sort of buildings that are above the tsunamis highest level. Look you can see a scouring line which must have been the highest point the wave reached. The flank of the mountain above it is more ash-like and undisturbed. Oh shit, I'm trembling. I didn't anticipate any buildings or life here.'

Amanda stared ahead and started to shake also and suddenly became aware of her half nakedness, with only Jason's oversized shorts on and one of his boots and the one jelly sandal she had found two weeks ago.

'Is it safe to continue?' she whispered. 'Do you think they've seen us yet?'

Jason reminded her that there was no need to whisper, as they were at least a mile away and that there was no reason to think there was anybody there anyway.

'The structures look very old and partly ruined to me, and could just be some early sacred site,' he suggested.

After ten minutes they crossed the line which the peak of the tsunami had reached. Here they had to clamber up recently formed screes to the firmer undisturbed flank of the mountain. Not too far off to their left hand side, there was an unmistakable pathway leading up to the buildings.

Amanda became exceedingly nervous about going the last half mile, and suggested that she lay down out of sight in a nearby gulley, while he got closer and checked things out. He shrugged his shoulders and let her do as she wanted, leaving her with the pack.

He crossed over to the pathway and slowly and apprehensively sauntered up to the gateway that lay ahead of the little cluster of primitive huts. It was as if he were on a tourist trip to some sacred site, he reflected. Gathering confidence, he passed by the freshly painted white stones that marked the way in.

He paused before entering the complex, to listen for sounds from within. There were none; only the breeze coming over the mountain top. Then he heard the sound of pattering feet and froze.

Wheeling round with clenched knuckles, half expecting to find some foe about to attack him, he saw a sweating Amanda trotting up the path to his side.

'I couldn't bear to lose you,' she panted. 'What's that awful smell?'

Jason sniffed deeply.

'You're right. There is a smell, like a dead dog or something.'

'What is this? No one can live here. It's mostly ruins; it's no observatory or anything scientific. But the stones are freshly painted so someone must come here from time to time, to offer prayers maybe.'

They moved a few paces nearer to the first hut. The smell became more intense.

'I don't like this at all,' whispered Jason softly to his companion, who by then was clutching his arm in fear. 'It's a sanctuary or some sort of religious retreat I think. Look over there. Isn't that a picture of the Virgin Mary? I can just make out her halo. The Catholic influence is still quite strong in certain Latino societies.' He was pointing to a white-washed wall with a poster attached to it and underneath was a small inscription.

They moved closer in order to read it.

The neatly inscribed words were in Spanish but Amanda was quick to translate.

'God blesses even the LBGT community.'

'So that's it,' murmured Jason. 'A retreat for non-traditionalists who feel ostracised by conventional society.' He felt less threatened by a seemingly peaceful group and decided it was safe to announce their presence.

He shouted out, 'Hello. Is there anybody there?'

They waited in the uncanny silence for a reply. Jason called out again, louder this time. He turned and looked at Amanda, shrugged his shoulders and went inside the first hut, expecting the worst.

The stench was appalling and before he even saw the first body he gagged. Amanda, who had pushed past him to see what was inside for herself, wretched and vomited, before she fled back outside, holding her hands over her mouth and nose. There was plenty enough light from the doorway and nearby windows for Jason to see the forms of four fully clothed men lying partly face down, each clutching a towel or item of clothing over their faces. Their bodies were grotesque, inflated with the gasses of decomposition, while at the same time their limbs were mummified with the effects of dehydration.

The macabre scene was unlike anything he had ever seen or imagined before. He wretched again then vomited, before rushing outside to join Amanda who was on her knees still being sick.

Reluctantly Jason said they had better check out the rest of the retreat before leaving, in case there were items of communication equipment or other useful things, of no benefit to the corpses.

Amanda staggered to her feet and took his arm before they went up to the only other hut that looked habitable. The smell was almost unbearable but, with their hands covering their mouths and nostrils, they entered what was obviously a shrine of some sort. It was immaculately clean with a rudimentary altar at its back and a withered bunch of flowers in a vase set at one side. An image of the Virgin Mary was set in a frame at the opposite end of the altar.

They choked at the lack of fresh air in the chamber and then stared down at the bodies of two naked females stretched out on a blanket before them. They were holding hands and not covering their faces as the men were. It somehow made the whole life-ending more dramatic and horrific. Their fetid bodies were also blown up with gasses yet their faces sunk into their skulls as dehydration had taken its toll over the past two weeks. Their eyelids were closed as if laid out by an undertaker.

Something caught Amanda's attention. She knelt down beside the nearest woman's body and picked up a hypodermic needle with an empty phial attached. Surprised, Jason noticed that there was a similar one beside the other woman. He crackled out an explanation.

'A suicide pact before they became asphyxiated.' Amanda nodded in agreement.

'Don't think they will need that lot now,' she stated with false bravado, pointing at their bundles of clothes neatly stacked off to one side.

'I guess not,' he said, and helped her gather them up and added, 'I expect they will be really happy to think their meagre belongings have helped the poor and needy!'

They left the shrine and for an unknown reason, Amanda turned her head and gave a discreet bow of respect before continuing out of the retreat. Clutching the possessions of the dead women, they turned off the path briefly, to get up-wind of the structures and away from its prevailing smell. There they sat together in the steady breeze for several minutes without saying anything, while the enormity of their experience sank in.

Finally and with a loud sob Amanda broke the silence.

'You know something? Those people were alive when we first arrived on the island. It's just that they didn't have an oxygen pipe to suck on as we did for several days. So that's it; there are no other people on the island but us. The tsunami wiped out the rest.'

There was some finality in the way she said it but they both knew it to be true.

'And that would have been the way for the rest of the World,' Jason added, 'so there are only a few clusters of survivors, I suppose. It was that toxic cloud of sulphurous gases that did the damage, probably more so than the tsunami. What will it have done to the plants, trees, crops and so forth?' he enquired of Amanda.

'It was only for a few days here,' she remarked, 'and the effects of acid rain are usually measured in terms of years, so I can imagine that a lot of hardy trees and shrubs will pull through, but as for plants and crops, they definitely don't like Sulphur dioxide or acid rain and probably perished. Their saving grace is that the seeds, on the plants, in the ground or in packets will more than likely be okay.'

He thought about that for a while and then light heartedly said, 'Your corn is doing alright anyway.' Then by squinting his eyes he pointed out to his right hand side.

'Look you can see the sea on the other side of the island now and, if my eyes are not fooling me, away in the distance is the other end of Amandaland. It is very faint but it looks like sea on the horizon.'

They made their way back to where she had ditched the back pack and washed the taste of vomit from their mouths with some of their precious water. Jason reckoned that the downhill trek of four or five miles could easily be made in daylight, so they stuffed the bundles of the women's clothing and belongings into the back pack and sombrely set off back to the cabin.

At Amanda's insistence they stopped off by the well-head. She drew up two bowls of fresh water and drenched each of their bodies while standing in the corn crop, in an attempt to rid them of the lingering smell of death. To some extent she succeeded and they raced off the remaining mile in lighter spirits as the evening closed in.

Jason fanned up the glowing charcoal and piled on fresh wood. He soon had enough flames to see and to cook the remaining side of grouper, that Amanda had lightly salted from the day before. They had collected a handful of goose barnacles from their trusted pallet, and the much appreciated coconut milk broth soon regenerated their spirits. The smell of barbequed fish replaced the smell of death in their nostrils, and a sense of balance was restored.

That night they held each other more tightly than usual, as they made love in an attempt to rid themselves of the images of the corpses up at the retreat. It was as if a heavy responsibility had descended on them. The confirmation of their previous assessment of the global catastrophe made their bonding even more relevant.

As he pulled her tightly against him with his penis deep inside her, they spoke of their resolve to give back to the planet the best of their joint resourcefulness, even if it took years. He tugged her hips down onto his body and allowed her little breasts to bury themselves in his hairy chest. He lay motionless under her and watched the full moon illuminating her shoulders, presenting them like polished steel. As she leant down and kissed his lips long and deeply, his eyes closed. His only conscious feeling was that of the slow rhythmic contractions of her inner vagina and his own surrender to orgasm. How long they stayed like that he could never recall, only that their joint surrender represented a turning point for the planet.

They slept outside the rest of the night and in the morning scavenged more meat off the bones of the roasted grouper before bathing in the sea near to Regina's empty pen. She had been set free to forage for prickly pear stems along the seashore. They had seen her occasionally as she scurried behind a rock and they felt reassured that this creature at least was ready to step into the next geological era.

Walking back to the cabin, Amanda suddenly remembered the pack full of the women's clothes and things from the retreat. As she carefully unpacked the bag, laying each item separately over adjacent rocks to air, it became clear to her that these women had just their day clothes with them, as if they had fled up to the retreat in haste, hoping to avoid the tsunami.

One set of clothes was a nurse's uniform. The symbolic Red Cross indicated that she had been a home help or district nurse or even a doctor. Amanda turned to Jason for guidance. He admitted that he knew little of the uniforms of remote Latino communities. Next came out the nurse's regulation hat, and folded up with it was a small zipped up day-bag which she probably carried with her on her rounds.

Undoing the zip nervously, she first pulled out a small

laminated I.D. card with the name 'Anna Maria Martez M.D.' embossed on it, followed by 'Isabella, Galapagos' and some national security and phone numbers.

Confirmation of their location was no longer relevant, but with a nod she passed the ID card to Jason. Also inside the bag were a number of medications, small first aid materials, phials and packets of pills. Lastly, as if a magician, she pulled out a small phone. She scrutinised it carefully before handing it to Jason.

'It's a sat-phone. I suppose persons of her importance needed phone links wherever they were, regardless of Earth stations. What possibility is there that it still works?'

He studied it carefully and checked out its functions.

'This phone belongs to the government agency she worked with and they would have been paying for her calls. It's partly charged and can be fully charged if we leave it outside. It has its own solar energy converter. She had to put her thumb print on the screen to give her access to the system. Only she could use it.'

'Do you think we are clever enough to open it up and bi-pass this function?' She enquired.

'We could try, but we might wreck it altogether if we did that. You're probably smarter at that sort of thing than I am.'

'I doubt that,' she said thoughtfully and took the phone back from Jason. 'Do you have any teeny weeny screw drivers in your tool kit?'

'I just happen to have some for overhauling the reels in my fishing tackle bag. I'll get them and see if they're any good.'

'Wait a minute!' She exclaimed jumping up. "Are we stupid or something? We know where the thumb is, don't we?"

Jason groaned a long, 'Ahh!' registering the significance of what she said.

'What are you suggesting? We take the phone up or bring the thumb down?' His face was screwed up in revulsion.

'I think we need to take the phone up because there are four thumbs to choose from. In any case, it might be an index finger that opens the phone.'

The concept of this grizzly task was grotesque but they knew that to get a sat phone working would be manna from heaven. Jason cast his eyes up to the mountain and declared that it was already too late to make the excursion that day. They had better prepare themselves for an early start the following morning and he would see what tools he would need.

'What tools?' she queried looking up at him for answers. He refused to say.

CHAPTER SIXTEEN

Janet thought she heard a crackle from outside the storeroom and leapt up, tugging her one piece all-weather suit tight against her body. She pushed open the emergency door and went over to the oxygen tank, where her satellite phone had been sat for over a week. Her skills were in communications and she had calculated that her best signal reception point was there.

Her heart raced as, despite numerous tries, there had been no response to any of her SOS cries for help. She dared not go any further outside than the shelter of the oxygen tank bunker to get a better signal.

Several meters of grey snow had piled up against the ruins of the observatory following the earthquakes and, despite her protestations, Yoshi, in an unbalanced state of mind, panicked and without adequate clothing, had left the bunker to find help.

His intention was to get down off the mountain. No sooner had he stepped out into the deep snow, than he set off a massive avalanche that rumbled down the mountainside for some minutes. That was the last she had seen of him.

She got to the phone, clasped it tightly in her gloved hands and excitedly transmitted her SOS again, repeating slowly.

'This is the Cerro Chajnantor Observatory in Chile. Please try again!'

There was an agonising pause while the sender got back to the phone and made a further transmission. The satellite signal strength was poor and Janet was cursing her position when the call display sensor lit up on her screen. The sender's phone number showed clearly in the top corner and, despite the crackling, Janet heard words spoken in English.

'We are the only two survivors on the island of Isabella in the Galapagos. What about you?'

Janet was hysterical and almost unable to reply.

'I don't know of any other survivors. I have been trying with SOS messages for over a week and you are the first to respond. The Observatory is wrecked by an earthquake and has no power. Two of us survived in the basement storeroom with the help of oxygen. I have enough food here for a year, but I'm afraid my colleague might be dead. He set off for help and got caught in an avalanche......Can you help me?'

Her words faded away as did the transmission.

Janet shuffled back inside and shut the door. She was elated, upset and angry all at the same time. Her solar powered battery had died and she knew there was nothing she could do until the next day.

Inside had become her home and by now she had explored every part of the store. Her all-weather suit had been her greatest discovery and, now that she knew where everything was stored, she planned her survival until rescued.

During the evening she gathered together half a dozen brooms. She unscrewed their handles and lashed them all together to make a pole about twenty feet long. She then taped her phone to the end, so that it would reach up into the sunlight the following day.

'Sunlight,' she kept repeating to herself. 'Thank God that has come back and that disgusting sulphurous air has passed by. Two other survivors! At least I'm not the only one left as I'd feared. There's hope. Maybe they'll find others with their sat phone. I can call them in the morning as soon as my phone charges up.'

She went back outside to the edge of the abyss where the avalanche had started and tipped out her latrine bucket, as if she might expect visitors and wanted her home to be spick and span. Complete nonsense, she admitted to herself, but the telephone link had changed her outlook.

*

Jason and Amanda looked at each other in total disbelief, hardly able to comprehend the reality of another person in communication with them. They both tried calling her number back several times but with no reply.

'Her battery failed,' Amanda suggested, because the strength of the signal had just faded away. 'She said her many SOS's had been unanswered. That's depressing. I thought that many of the high altitude observatories would be doing okay, once the sulphurous cloud abated, because of their ability to control their own atmosphere with additional oxygen.'

'Maybe her signal is obscured,' Jason suggested.

'In that case, why have we heard nothing back from any of the other observatories? I've been trying to make contact with every one for three days now.'

'She's in a situation as tough as ours,' commented Amanda. 'She's holed up in an underground storeroom which must be freezing cold. She has enough food for a year but if she leaves, she can only pack enough food for a few days on her back. By the sound of it, the descent off the mountain is extremely hazardous, if not impossible. There must be a track down I suppose, but more than likely it is blocked by earthquake debris and avalanches. No. I think if I was in her situation, I'd stay put as well, and hope to be rescued at some point.'

'If she gets her phone charged up tomorrow and we make contact with her again, we should pump her for as much information as we can. Find out how much she knew before the earthquake struck. It's important for us to have an idea about other parts of the mainland, if we are to make plans to sail there eventually.'

'Sail there?' Amanda raised her eyebrows.

'Well maybe, if we build a boat. If the conditions are right and if there is any community worth heading to.' He stopped there, realising he had spoken his thoughts... 'any community worth heading to.' It was as if a profound chasm was opening up between them and the rest of the remaining world.

'Having a phone almost makes matters worse than before because of the chilling truth about the mass destruction, the mass annihilation; it all becomes more apparent. What possible use can we be to her, or her to us, with three thousand miles of ocean and five and a half thousand meters of elevation between us?'

'Come on Amanda. Don't be so negative. Maybe these early communications might lead to others, and others to networking. It is like building a business. You've done plenty of that at high level meetings. One thing leads to another. Keep every door open.'

Amanda was sullen.

Finally she spoke out softly.

'You know Jason, I don't think I *want* to leave this island. I want to restore some of its beauty. I want to do things with you, build things, make a jetty, make electricity, and make a life here together. Why should we risk everything again, now we've come this far? What's out there across the ocean may not be worth having anyway.'

Jason looked at her for a moment, and then put an arm round her and held her petite body close to his chest. He choked on the next few words but finally got them out.

'I'm so glad to hear you say that. I've been hiding behind the fantasy of getting you back to civilisation, in the belief that that was what we should be doing, but all along I've known that these were only dreams. Waking up from these dreams now, at this moment, and making this decision, is the best decision we will ever make. Let the rest of the world take shape if it is able to, and someday some people will come to us. It is better that way.'

Amanda sighed with relief, as if to say, 'Okay, we will draw the start line here!'

Jason pulled away from her. 'I'm going to build us a house, up by the well on the hard ground at the side of the corn patch. If we deepen the well, we'll have plenty of water and I'll make a windmill to draw the water up and pipe it to the house. If we move the fittings from the cabin we can have cupboards. It'll be easy enough to make a table and chairs from all the drift wood. We could even make a smoker so that we'll have another way of preserving the fish.......'

Amanda stopped him. 'I've thought of another possibility for the fish. Block off one of the gullies with rocks and pebbles and contain a pond behind it and keep a few fish swimming, so we can eat fresh ones at will!'

'Brilliant idea!'

They went to their mattress and lay there holding each other for a long time, bouncing one idea after another off each another.

'We're no longer visitors to Isabella,' she said with finality. 'We're settlers,' and with that she climbed over him and rubbed her now softening pubic hair over his genitals until he slipped inside her. The moon climbed up over the mountain and they slept peacefully under just a sheet. Only the dawn disturbed their dreams. Jason's were about building a house and hers were about planting more seeds and developing a farm.

Janet's call came back to them soon after they had breakfasted and were about to initiate some of the schemes they had talked about the previous evening.

Her news and animated voice painted an even more depressing picture of the rest of the world than before. She said that the other high altitude observatories had evacuated hours before hers was shut down, so that their personnel could reach their families in the villages lower down. The earthquakes followed shortly afterwards and then two weeks of darkness, sulphurous air and incessant snow. She thought that it was unlikely that any of them had survived.

After Amanda briefly related their own encounter and present situation, she asked what news had reached Janet's ears before the earthquake.

She did her best to describe the satellite images of the massive tsunami crossing the isthmus of Panama and burying the low lands of America and the Caribbean islands. It was on its way across the Atlantic when their observatory was wrecked.

Land based communication had all failed hours before, she said, and airways jammed up with hysterical voices and static crackling. Since then, her phone had been silent for nearly three weeks.

Asked what her plans were, she burst into tears. Finally composing herself again, she sobbed that she desperately hoped her phone would last out. Day by day she planned to carefully clear snow, to access the highest remaining part of the observatory, where she should be able to see if there was a clear way down off the mountain. She said there was a small mining community at about two thousand meters and about twenty miles hike away. Perhaps they had taken shelter underground and might still be alive.

Amanda managed to catch most of her words and passionately advised her to be careful and not to rush into something when she had a year's provisions at hand.

They arranged that calls should be made early in the morning, as she and Jason were out of the cabin during the day, and that there were certain arduous procedures involved in opening their phone. Amanda had no wish to describe how it was necessary to extract Anna Maria's thumb from a small jar of gin and place it on the screen in order to activate the device.

*

Amanda's and Jason's resolve not to leave the island was strengthened after hearing Janet's report. The planet was unmistakably in a bad state and it was now obvious to them both that staying put was the best solution, at least until more information came to them about the European and Asiatic nations.

Amanda leapt to her feet, now comfortably clad in Anna Marie's sandals, or her girlfriend's , she cared not which, and declared she was off on a mission.

'What sort of mission?' enquired Jason.

'A mission to improve our agricultural prospects.'

'Like how?' he asked curiously.

'I'm going up to the retreat again to bring back the vase of flowers.'

'Whatever for?' Jason was mystified.

'I didn't want to watch the surgery and my eyes scanned the vase of flowers. I can picture them now. Amongst the dried out flowers were different grasses and tassels of what I think is sorghum.

I want to bring them down and plant the seeds. I'm sure Anna Marie and her mate would be very happy for me to do that.'

With no further comment, and before he could stop her, she hoisted on a blouse that had belonged to one of the women, put on his baggy shorts, grabbed a bottle of water and was about to leave.

'Hang on a minute. I can come with you as far as the well. Remember I have a house to build there!'

She relented and grinned back at him, then waited while he pulled on his boots and found his work gloves, before they set off together in great haste in the direction of *Jason Towers*.

Being her third trip to the retreat, she was familiar with the route and made the journey in half their original time. She held her breath through the formidable stench at the macabre scene, grabbed the vase and ran outside again, briefly nodding a discrete bow in reverence as she left.

Once upwind in the fresh air, she hauled a plastic bag out of her pocket and placed the vase and flowers inside, so as not to lose any of the seeds on the way back. Pausing for a moment, she sat and studied the endless lava plains that rolled out before her, and bit her lip hard to remind herself that this was to be their home; it would surely be a daunting task to change any of it. Finally, before getting to her feet and descending the mountain, she clutched the bag with the withered flowers, grasses and sorghum and hoped against hope that some of her trophies would one day germinate.

She could see her alpha male bobbing about in a white t-shirt, long before she got back down to him. He had been busy carrying lumps of lava rock to a site overlooking her corn patch and, from her vantage point on the mountain's flank, she could see a small cairn of the material.

'He has been busy!' She remarked to herself and smiled as she thought of the early settlers to the remote areas of the Americas.

Sweating and dusty, he greeted her with gusto.

'See those rocks propped up over there and behind us? They mark the cornerstones of the house.' He said it with authority, as if the building was half complete and could not be changed.

'Hmm,' she replied, scanning the marked out rectangle which enclosed deep gullies and hillocks of lava. 'Where will the kitchen be?'

He looked at her thoughtfully in order to come up with the right answer.

'Over there,' he said, pointing to a large hillock of lava, sliced down the middle by a deep gully. 'It's the nearest corner to the well.' He knew he was on dodgy ground planning a woman's kitchen, and added in his defence, 'I thought it would involve less pipe work.'

'She scrutinised the site and then jested, 'Well I should get a good view out of the window from atop of the lava ridge while I'm washing dishes!'

'Have you not heard of *cut and fill*,' responded Jason, again on the defensive.

'Wow!' she laughed. 'You mean it will have a level floor? I can help with that and I also thought it should be my task to sort the well out.

Look! I have all sorts of seeds from the flowers and grasses, and enough sorghum heads to get a cereal crop started.'

Jason peered sceptically into the plastic bag and felt glad he had brought his fishing line with him.

CHAPTER SEVENTEEN

Janet scanned the diary which she had started at the end of her third week in the storeroom. Writing it had kept her sane and occupied, and allowed her to keep track of the endless similar days. She was now approaching the end of the eighth week in that cold, over-familiar, dungeon-like place. She knew that the height of the southern hemisphere summer was approaching. If she was to take a chance in getting down off the mountain, she must do it soon.

It had been a messy business clearing a way up to the top of the ruined observatory, but in many places nature had done most of the work for her. The constant wind and daily sun had melted most of the snow, revealing great slabs of concrete and steel. Precarious as they were, she had clambered up over these until she had managed to get a panoramic view from what had been the canteen.

Much to her surprise, the snowline was less than a thousand meters below the observatory. Only the adjacent mountain peaks were capped with snow, like her own. It would have been a magical scene, she commented to herself, had the snow not been grey.

She could see rivulets emerging from the snow line below and snaking away down the valleys. All this was new to her. During the year she had worked at Cerro Chajnantor, there had never been any precipitation of any kind to occupy the water courses, and the tops of the mountains rarely had more than a dusting of snow on them.

Finally she decided it was safe enough to scramble down the thousand meters of decent, through the snow and patches of outcropping rock, to the rough track that served the observatory. She could see sections of it from her vantage point. The scar where the avalanche had taken place, carrying Yoshi with it, was now largely devoid of snow. That was to be her choice. It was steep and gravelly and she could make out sections of concrete that had come off the observatory. The track up to the observatory was a good mile off to one side of that scar, where it disappeared under the snow line. Nevertheless, Janet calculated that traversing rubble and scree at the bottom should be easier than trudging through deep and unstable slushy snow.

In her native New Zealand she had frequently hiked through similar alpine country on the South Island. She took note of the possibility of further avalanches using the same route as the scar. Indeed, there were unstable blocks of fairly deep snow quite close to the observatory which would use that track.

Remembering her previous excursions into the mountains at home, she recalled that avalanches took place once the sun melted some of the overnight frosts. Her mind was made up. At dawn the following day she would scramble down the avalanche route, avoiding most of the snow patches and get off the scree to the harder ground as soon as she could. Then she could take a rest before traversing the broken rocky area to the track. She reckoned that the whole decent to the snowline should take less than an hour.

Daily phone links to Jason and Amanda had long since ceased, due to lack of interesting conversation and often an inadequate connection, so by mutual agreement they transmitted voice mails of short messages to each other that could be accessed at any suitable time. This time, with some trepidation in her voice, Janet issued the statement that she intended getting down off the mountain the following day, and that she would take her phone with her.

Amanda responded by wishing her good luck and to be sure to take water, dehydration salts and first aid items with her, together with as much food as she could safely carry.

It was barely light when Janet slid down the steepest part of the mountain the next morning, before virtually skiing down the remaining scree. She avoided the concrete slabs and stopped only occasionally to glance back up to her starting point, hardly able to believe that her descent had been so rapid.

Towards the snowline she could sense the moisture amongst the gravel and pebbles, indicating she was out of the frost zone, and cautiously looked round for a route out of the gulley. The sun was already showing on the mountain tops across the valley, so she realised her safe window of opportunity was running out.

Scared of what might happen to her if another avalanche came down the gully, she made a mad scramble to traverse the wet and unstable flank off the route. She sunk up to her knees at some points in loose gravelly material, which impeded her progress greatly and absorbed all her energy, causing her to panic.

Slowly she gained better footing and eventually clambered out of the gully altogether onto firmer ground. She was sweating profusely in her all-in-one all weather suit. Regaining her breath, she cast her eyes back up the gulley to the ruined observatory. She could hardly believe that she had made it down off the mountaintop so comparatively easily, after all those weeks in the underground storeroom.

Her mind danced around in circles as she trudged across the broken rocky terrain towards the access track. At one moment she was euphoric in that she had reached freedom and the next moments were of dark and desperate fear that she had severed her life-line and was alone in a desolate world and would slowly perish.

By the time she reached the observatory's roadway, she had descended several hundred meters and had conceded it was undeniably warm. She sat on the low bank of gravel that had been routinely created by the grader that serviced this only route up to the observatory. There she peeled off her all-in-one suit and, before tucking it into the straps of her backpack, gulped in a mouthful of her precious water.

Looking down the damaged track in front of her, she realised that the smooth, well serviced road that she had been familiar with was no more. It had suffered from five days of rain and unprecedented snowmelt from higher up. This had removed all the fine material, so nicely rolled in by the grader and, in stretches, rivulets had gouged great ravines through it. Nevertheless it marked a route down to civilisation. She set off along it with growing confidence, meandering round the ruts and climbing down and up where the run off had cut the road too deeply to hop across.

The nature of road construction in those parts of the high Andes was to follow the contours wherever possible and cut through promontories with tunnels where necessary. Therein lay the problems for Janet. Where the mountains closely flanked the track, there had been numerous avalanches, created by the earthquake and excessive rain.

The minor ones had not been too much of a problem; she had been able to scramble up and over them to regain the track on the other side. However, the nearer she approached a ravine area where the track had made a fairly steep descent to avoid switchbacks, the avalanches became more numerous and difficult to climb over. In one place she felt she had lost the route altogether and began to panic, as she arduously negotiated slabs of rock and large boulders, before finally getting a glimpse of a tunnel opening ahead.

The tunnel entrance was half closed off by avalanche debris, but Janet could see the undisturbed track lying inside and made her way down to it. She stopped a few meters inside and put her pack down again. She was able to rest in relative safety, protected by the overhang and away from the direct sunlight which by then had made her sticky with sweat.

She took courage from the draught of air coming through the tunnel, which indicated that it was open at the other end at least. After fishing out a torch from her bag, she proceeded into the darkness. It gave her some comfort to see that the engineers had cased the whole tunnel in steel and wire mesh. Water ran freely down a ditch at the side, and frequently a dribble of drips wet her head and shoulders from above. She remembered this as the longest of the tunnels, but the half mile seemed an eternity as she sploshed along, accompanied only by eerie echoes.

Eventually she emerged from the lower end and sighted the next tunnel entrance only a short distance away. The mountainside in this area had clearly been too steep and avalanche prone for the engineers to construct a viable roadway round it, and so they had chosen to link a series of tunnels with short sections of concrete strips, with safety barricades on the outer edges.

To Janet's horror she found that an avalanche had swept away the concrete section of road linking the two tunnels, and created a very steep gulley in its place. The avalanche path was totally un-negotiable and looked to be dangerously unstable as well. Hanging in mid-air was the crash barrier, looking more like part of a suspension bridge than a roadway. She eyed it up with a mixture of suspicion and dread. Was this to be her only way of continuing down to the mining community?

Moving gingerly forward, she critically inspected the mechanisms that anchored the guard rail to the remaining concrete strip by her feet. It was only about ten meters, she kept telling herself, and the anchoring bolts looked intact. The alternative was to return to a point several hours back and try to find a route down the ravine or up over the mountains. This was an exceptionally gloomy prospect, she thought, and would probably end in failure anyway. It had to be the guard rail.

Scared stiff, she clutched the metal of the top rail of the barrier and placed her feet on the lower section, while only a foot or so over the precipice, and gave the whole structure a strong shake, as if to strengthen her resolve. It didn't move so, not daring to breathe or look down, she edged her way across the abyss, until gaining the remainder of the concrete strip on the other side.

Once on solid ground again, she took off her pack and looked back at her achievement. Her legs went to jelly, hardly believing what she had just done.

Finally she proceeded into the next tunnel and without further incident into the third and last one, from which she emerged into bright sunlight. Now she was faced with much gentler and kinder topography, as the road took wide sweeps across a mainly desolate terrain without further interruptions.

No longer absorbed with issues of her immediate safety, Janet hiked along at a good pace, mentally ticking off the miles as she passed mundane yet memorable landmarks: lay-bys, concrete culverts or peculiar rocky features. By midday, she reckoned the mining community to be only three or four miles ahead and it should be in sight once she rounded the next sweeping bend.

She distinctly remembered, with disapproval, that the village dump, although not actually visible itself, was always frequented by wheeling birds, some of the vulture family, that sought to scavenge an existence from the rubbish. These flocks of birds always marked the village before its buildings came into sight.

Eventually she rounded the bend that gave her the first glimpse of the buildings. There were no wheeling birds and the profile of the village looked quite different from the one she remembered. A sinking feeling of helplessness and loneliness descended on her. The silence that had accompanied her during the hike suddenly became more poignant.

It was true, she reflected miserably, she had seen no lizards or flies that might have bothered her. There had only been the ubiquitous desert-loving sage brush. As she approached the village, she could pick out the familiar acacias that the locals gathered under during the heat of the day. There had to be some life here she thought.

However, it soon became apparent that most of the buildings were in ruins, presumably as a consequence of the earthquake. Janet could see that some vehicles were crushed and inoperable due to falling masonry, but a large cluster were assembled at the mine site itself near to the portal.

Recalling her logic and hoping that the inhabitants would have taken shelter underground, she trudged up the slope to the mine entrance. On the way she also passed the stinking skeletal remains of a dog and held her breath until she got clear of it. She passed a dozen or so empty vehicles, some with their doors still open, as if the occupants had been in a serious hurry to get out. The scene reminded her of a horror movie and, to make matters worse, the daylight was beginning to fade and long shadows cast macabre shapes onto the remaining buildings.

To get near to the mine portal, she had to negotiate her way through the wreckage of several hangars that housed the mineral dressing machinery. Adjacent to these were the workshops and fitting shops that serviced the mine. A gentle breeze caused a thin sheet of aluminium to rattle against a steel post. She froze for an instant until she worked out what it was. She was petrified and despondent, not knowing whether to go on or go back.

It was getting dark. She would have to camp there anyway and sort things out in the morning. While she stood there motionless, deciding where to go, she detected a different noise and something caught her eye. She went ridged. Something had moved in a nearby workshop.

CHAPTER EIGHTEEN

'What do you think of that?' Jason announced proudly, pointing to his freshly constructed table, which consisted of a number of sawn planks of roughly the same thickness, selected from his pile of driftwood. They were held together on their underside with slats and supported on legs made from stout round poles he had foraged from the trees on the foreshore.

Amanda was mightily impressed. She had not dared to question all the banging and chopping that had been going on during the last few days and instead chose to be busy with her agricultural matters.

'I had to make mortise and tenon joints,' he announced proudly, 'because none of the nails I've managed to salvage from the driftwood were long enough.' The two chairs he had already made were a much simpler matter, the nails he had being adequate.

She pulled one up over the rough floor, sat down on it at the table and beamed up at her alpha male. She then sprang to her feet and disappeared outside. Shortly afterwards she came back with a bunch of flowers, went over to the recently installed shelves and picked up the vase from the retreat. Having filled it with water, she installed the flowers and plonked it down in the middle of the table.

Grinning back at Jason she said, 'Now we really have a home,' and then added tearfully, 'It's the first one ever for me.'

He looked at her thoughtfully and then at the rugged walls of lava blocks, the vacant windows, the uneven floor and considered it for a moment, then put a bronzed muscley arm round her.

'It's the same for me. I've never had my own place and guess what? No council taxes, no end of month bills, no mortgage payments!' He raised the palm of his hand and she heartily smacked it with hers.

'We have to say thanks to Anna Maria and her partner for the flowers. Many of the seeds germinated and this volcanic soil is so rich the growth rate has been phenomenal. Have you looked at the corn lately? It's already got cobs forming. I was so relieved to see them because many of the heavily farmed varieties are genetically modified and infertile.'

'I've noticed the corn getting taller every day. Sometimes it's difficult to tell whether you are there or not.'

'That's because I have to get to my knees to shake the pollen off the flowers onto the tassels of the cob trusses,' she explained. 'There are no insects, so we have to help nature a little bit,' she added grinning.

'That reminds me,' he said, excitedly following on from her theme, 'The last time I went out to the wing fishing, I had to move an old rotten branch out of the way and a whole bunch of small beetles came out of it and some actually flew away. Sorry, I meant to tell you but the fishing stories made me forget.'

'Wow! That's really significant. Life is emerging from the South American continent. I suspected that some seeds, and in this case pupae, would survive the sulphurous air. No llamas yet I suppose?' she jested with a laugh.

The following day was spent gathering volcanic ash to spread over the rough floor of the house. Once levelled off and doused with water it set like cement. It had been a particularly difficult task because, as Jason had remarked, the wind was uncommonly fresh that day.

By the following morning the weather pattern was definitely changing. The wind had become more north easterly and they no longer had the protection of the mountain. Wispy clouds flurried across the sun and a heavier swell caused the stranded trees to heave against one another, emitting sounds like grunting pigs.

Jason felt concerned, and he and Amanda went to their unused rubber dingy and hauled it well away from the shoreline. They then set about the task of pulling as much wood and tree debris up away from the shore as they could, in case the whole mass of trees suddenly moved away leaving them without fuel.

By midday, the clouds had thickened and squalls of wind picked up dust from the sandy basins. Amanda felt the need to rush back to her agricultural patch, basically the square of corn plants, in case there was a need to tie them up. When she got there, she was relieved to find that they were quite secure down in the gully, mostly out of the wind.

She was about to go back and help Jason haul some wood up for the fire and the smoker, when she felt the first raindrop. Within a minute or two, it was lashing down. She thrust some burning logs into the smoker and closed it off with a slab of rock to preserve the fire, then turned to see Jason dashing up towards her.

'Bloody hell!' He shouted as he turned into the house. 'This must be the rainy season you spoke about! How long does it last?'

'I don't remember, but at least we needn't worry about the falling water table anymore!'

She scurried round, putting bowls under the major cascades coming through the roof, which had already pitted their nice new floor.

'I thought there might be glitches with the design of the roof,' he confessed apologetically. 'It was designed for sun protection, not deluges of rain. Where is the pile of dried fish?'

'Ah!' she groaned. 'Still outside. It'll be fine but I'll have to re-salt it and dry it again when the rain stops. We still have half a dozen groupers swimming in the pond anyway.'

After a few minutes of pounding rain, Amanda decided to check that the rivulets running down the mountain side were not washing out her crops. She had only taken two steps outside the doorway when she gave out an agonising cry.

Jason rushed to her side fearing the worst; that all her agricultural efforts had been washed away. Even before she spoke he could see the corn was fine and probably enjoying the rain, and he worried what else could have alarmed her.

He followed her gaze in the opposite direction.

'My washing!' she cried in dismay. 'I washed all our clothes yesterday as they were caked in ash,' and then, putting on fake voice of concern, 'Now we have nothing to wear.'

'That didn't seem to worry you today,' he said over her shoulder as he pulled her wet back against his hairy chest and cupped her breasts. 'Oh you must be cold.'

'I'm not,' she giggled.

'Then why are your nipples sticking out between my fingers?'

'It's natural,' she said with a laugh and pulled away from him, shaking her hair like a dog before going back inside, to attend to the damage being done by the leaking roof.

He thought he was in for some spontaneous sex, but instead the alpha female ordered him to go over to the cabin and bring back the awning, so that the roof of their new home could be made waterproof. Jason wrestled with his disappointment but realised she was serious and, despite her erect nipples and the state of his penis, he would have to fix the roof before any further favours would be granted.

By the time he had retrieved the awning and hiked most of the way back, the rain had stopped and the wind had dropped to an eerie calm. The sun soon popped out and in no time the rocks were steaming and normality had returned, except for the sound of rivulets running off the mountain.

She was busy turning the washing over and attending to other wet items. He helped her drag the mattress out and place it over rocks to dry.

'Everything is so clean and fresh looking,' he remarked, and shooting her a seductive glance and patting the mattress hopefully said, 'I see your nipples are still sticking out.'

She snorted and pointed up at the roof.

While he was climbing up on to the roof, he turned and noted that she was discretely checking her breasts and formed the opinion that she did not want him to linger too long performing his task up aloft.

CHAPTER NINETEEN

Janet was unclear whether it was fear or excitement that caused her to slowly move behind a nearby wall to hide. She did not believe in ghosts or any other supernatural phenomena, but up until this point all her observations had hinted at death and destruction. She had already prepared herself to accept that that was all she would encounter here. This mining community appeared both destroyed and abandoned.

As she trembled behind the wall, she repeatedly scanned the building across the yard, almost believing that she had imagined the noise and movement there. She had never felt so scared in all her life. Crossing the ravine on that shaky guard rail earlier was nothing compared with the total vulnerability she was experiencing now.

It was getting darker adding to her wretchedness. Her thoughts of dying in this dreadful, isolated and abandoned place were suddenly interrupted by a more distinct and definite noise coming from the workshop.

She stiffened, startled at the continuation of some activity within the building. There was life there, she acknowledged, not a figment of her imagination. Her heart raced as she waited for more clues, not wishing to blow away her cover. The wait seemed endless. Periodically there were bursts of unidentifiable noises punctuated by tense silences. Maybe it was a ravenous dog that would attack her she thought, and shuddered.

There was another sequence of noises followed by a terrifying hiss. Janet was at the point of bolting back down the track, when suddenly the whole building in front of her became illuminated from inside, casting long beams of light into the rest of the yard. She involuntarily ducked down behind the wall and held her breath. Not only was there life within, it must be human life, she concluded.

Without warning, a thickset man plodded out of the open door and walked some distance away from the workshop in her direction. She ducked down and hid, hoping he had not seen her, remembering the motto used in battle: *surprise is the first element of attack*. He could be heard urinating on the other side of the very same wall she hid behind. At least the guy was well enough to do that, she reassured herself, not yet wanting to break her cover.

He had retraced his steps back inside, Janet reckoned, before she dared peep over the wall again. She wondered if there were any more people inside. What would he do if she just walked in? The question of rape surfaced in her mind. That was one thing, and man being man, she reasoned, this would be inevitable over time. Maybe there were more men. Gang rape? She shuddered. Maybe there were women inside and social norms would prevail.

She waited a while longer, trying to assess the situation further. She heard a sizzling noise and caught the smell of frying garlic. That was enough for her. There was a comforting sense of some sort of normality, whatever the social set up, and she walked boldly across the yard before her courage failed, shouted, 'Olla,' and walked through the doorway.

CHAPTER TWENTY

The periodic heavy downpours lasted for a month and the change in wind direction loosened up the mass of floating vegetation. Jason climbed up the mountain flank on several occasions, to check if there were any open stretches of water further down the island.

Their preoccupation with the status of the floating debris was well founded. He and Amanda realised how dependant they were on the trees and other vegetation, not only for fuel but also for building materials and compost.

Their progress had steadily reduced their knife edge existence to simple daily challenges. Jason had already expressed his view that they needed to capture large areas of the flotsam, in order to bridge the gap until foliage and wood established itself on the island. He had identified small inlets and bays further down the coast that could be pounded off with long ropes, so as to prevent the floating material from drifting away.

The scheme seemed possible, but it took over a week to string the hem rope, plus handmade extensions, across the first inlet. Amanda had done most of the monkey work, clambering through limbs of trees while dragging a thin vine behind her, while Jason fed the thicker rope on behind. It had been a technical nightmare with the vine breaking on several occasions and the trees moving their positions overnight. Amanda suffered many scrapes and cuts and ended up with makeshift bandages over knees and wrists.

By the time they had secured both ends of the rope to outcrops of lava on each side of the inlet, they concluded that the operation was too risky and difficult to repeat. They would have to rely on fate to leave other stranded trees where they were.

Meanwhile the regular showers had done miracles for land based operations. They had started to harvest the first of the corn cobs, the transplanted banana had developed a magnificent flower, with the beginning of minute fruit developing behind it, and the sorghum had established itself over a wide area next to the corn patch.

The other miracle of nature's rebound was the emergence of various green leafed plants from seeds, that had apparently survived the tsunami by being trapped in cavities within the lava. None of the little seedlings could be identified by either of them. Amanda's reliance on her CONSOL had not prepared her for Stone Age woman.

She had hiked up to the lava tube while Jason had been fishing one day, so as to locate the tortoise eggs buried under the marker stone they had left there. To her utter surprise she encountered several baby tortoises trying desperately to get out into the open. Not knowing whether to help or hinder them, she rounded up four individuals and wrapped them in her blouse, before carrying them back to the area near the cabin where Regina had lived. She considered that there was enough vegetation in the flotsam for them to forage, so she set them free.

In another development, they had both encountered baby lizards while moving about on the aa aa lava. Their eggs must also have been hidden in crevices within the lava rocks, and had survived there until the rainy season triggered hatching.

Daily it seemed they could see Isabella coming back to life.

The euphoric experience of witnessing the regeneration of life and its diversity excited both Jason and Amanda equally. As they moved around, occupied with their own various tasks, their paths frequently crossed. They usually kissed and caressed one another during these encounters and more often than not found a convenient spot to made love. The freedom offered to them by being scantily clad or wearing nothing other than footwear, made love making very natural and quite uninhibited. Her pubic mound, by this time, had become a major feature and the sight of it from some distance away excited Jason intensely.

They usually dived for cover inside the house if the downpours looked to be prolonged. On these occasions, they took delight in first washing each other under a deluge coming off the roof from a fold in the awning. Amanda behaved like an animal on heat when wet from head to toe, and would become high spirited, often tempting Jason by kneeling just inside the doorway, with her posterior waving around in his direction seeking attention.

These were golden days for the couple. They were very happy and very much in love. Their diet now included corn on the cob which, according to Jason, was rounding out some of the more bony bits of her slim body. He often told her she looked like a model; irresistible, tanned and nimble. In addition to her black pussy mound, he remarked on one occasion, as they ducked inside to avoid the rain, that he found the tangled bird's nest of hair on her head a similar attraction. He said there was something aboriginal and Eve-like about it that suited their primitive life.

'Urgh!' she responded. 'The next time I get hold of your scissors it's all coming off, and regarding your remarks about the corn diet, it will all come to an end in a month, so you'd better make the best of ogling my curves. I'm saving a quarter of the cobs for seeds, to plant a much larger crop.'

'I thought as much. Never mind. Soon it will be sorghum bread and bananas I suppose.'

'I had bread made from millet in India once. I think this is a type of sorghum. They called it 'roti'. It wasn't bad,' she said.

'They call bread 'rooti' in some of the Arab countries,' he interjected, 'but I thought it came from wheat flour.'

'It probably would have originally come from a common hot climate cereal like sorghum.' Then she shot a critical look at his shining biceps. 'What are your thrashing skills by the way?' She enquired, cocking an eyebrow mischievously, half knowing that it would provoke a reaction.

So saying she ducked away and retreated giggling into the darkened back corner of the house, making a false pretence at protecting herself, while he pinned her to the wattle matting of palm branches hanging down the wall.

Her pathetic struggle and cries for help soon gave way moans of sexual ecstasy, as he hauled one of her knees up to her chest and entered her whilst standing. The encounter was brief and wildly satisfying and they both quickly climaxed, before slithering down to the floor panting.

'Phew!' He gasped with a grin. 'It must be Friday!'

'Friday? Why Friday?' she enquired, wiping off the sweat that was running down between her breasts.

'The old men used to say Friday night was wife beating night, didn't they?'

'Hey! What's this about wives anyway? Has my status suddenly changed, or are you planning to make an honest woman out of me?' she enquired mischievously.

'Huh! Not much chance of that,' he laughed, and continued tweaking her engorged nipples while in deep thought. 'We could just have a long engagement and be faithful to each other,' he grinned.

'That's not much of a reassurance when there is nobody else in the world to offer any competition,' she said with feigned disappointment.

'Okay!' he responded leaping to his feet and with a flamboyant gesture got down onto one knee.

'Will you marry me?'

'Oh! You are getting romantic now. Yes please.' She kissed him. 'Where is the ring?'

'Huh! I thought I had found the perfect woman only to discover that she becomes materialistic the moment she has a marriage offer!'

'You might get fed up with me and go chasing after that other woman, so I *should* have a ring.'

'Other woman?' he asked curiously and then remembering; 'Ah, the one up a mountain four thousand miles away in Chile, you mean?'

'Yes, Janet, the New Zealand girl from the observatory. We've heard nothing from her since she told us she would try to get off the mountain. It's over a month ago now and I can only assume it went horribly wrong for her. I didn't want to dwell on it. So anyway, you are stuck with me ring or no ring, but I will love you through thick and thin.'

He leant against the wall beside her again and went back to caressing her breasts.

'It's a pity about the crop coming to an end. I like the new curves. Corn on the cob seems to suit you!'

She beamed at him and said nothing.

CHAPTER TWENTY ONE

The stocky, full bearded Chilean blacksmith wheeled round from his cooking stove, stared very briefly at Janet and, terror stricken, crumpled to his knees, genuflecting in front of her. Putting his hands together in prayer, with wide open brimming eyes, he looked up at her and spewed out long exaltations that referred to her as the mother of Jesus. Before she could say a word, he cried out to God, asking for his mercy and bent forward and kissed her dusty boots.

Janet was astounded by this unexpected emotional outburst. The Spanish she could deal with, but the reaction was totally unexpected. He had a strong South American accent but she understood most of the words, and the body language said the rest. Her fear had fled. She was completely disarmed.

Letting her arms flop down onto his mighty shoulders, she told him in broken Spanish and English that her name was Janet not Mary, and that she was neither holy nor a virgin; just a survivor from the observatory.

He sobbed and did not wish to believe her. In his confused mind, she had to be an earthly manifestation of the Virgin or, at the very least, one of her saints, acting as an envoy.

Her back pack suddenly felt very heavy in an earthly sense and her body felt weary from her long hike. She hooked a hand under one of his huge biceps and hauled him to his feet. Looking into his wet eyes, she could see for the first time that he was as harmless as a pet dog. He had a warm gentle giant look about him and she breathed a sigh of relief; a fellow survivor.

While he was regaining his posture, she had time to glance round the workshop. There were no obvious signs of other people, and the makeshift kitchen and camp bed indicated that he was alone, and surviving in the same way she had done.

The garlic was burning, so she instinctively walked over to the stove and pushed the pan off the heat. This simple act of human nature defused his initial panic, brought about by the imaginary visitation of some supernatural being. He lifted her pack from her back, pulled up a plastic chair and waved her to sit down. Every now and then he cast a glance in her direction, while he busied himself with a kettle. It was as if he half expected her to vaporise and not be there anymore.

He rounded up another plastic chair and shook the dust off it, before returning with two mugs of steaming yerba mate, while she unlaced her boots and yanked them off. Before he sat down, and without any words, he shot off into the back of the workshop and came back with a wad of hessian sacking and placed it under her aching feet. She thanked him and smiled to herself, thinking, *Saint or not, it's nice to be treated like one.*

Finally, speaking in broken English and with a tremble in his voice, hardly daring to look in her direction, 'Many more peoples coming?'

'No. I am the only one from the observatory......The earthquake......and the poisonous air...... The only other survivor tried to get off the mountain and died, I think. He was caught in an avalanche.....It's only me...'

All the horrors of the past month came back to her in a single sentence and she broke down. Putting her head in between her hands she wept. The bearded man was clearly disturbed and wanted to cry as well, but instead nervously put a hand on her shoulder, until she stopped sobbing. After she had made a great inhalation of breath, he hesitantly spoke.

'We have a lot of things to talk about. You rest. I get supper.' With that he went over to a fridge, took out a plate of chicken pieces and placed them in his pan with the fried garlic.

The aroma soon permeated the whole workshop again, which brought back a sense of comfort and reality, so that she quickly regained her composure and started to look about her. She scrutinised the man that thought she was a saint. He had wavy black hair and a heavy black beard that merged with the doormat hair of his chest. His grubby white vest did not quite cover the golden crucifix that hung round his neck. He was wearing welder's trousers and steel capped work boots, which looked strangely incongruous in his role as chef.

Against the hum of a distant generator, she pondered over the extraordinary situation: the violation of their own separate spaces, the removal of all other human beings and the randomness of the new association. While she was still assessing the enormity of the situation, he disturbed her thoughts by appearing from the corner of the workshop with a sack of potatoes.

'I'll do that,' she offered. 'Can I have a knife?'

He produced a long and very sharp knife from a tool box and licked it across his welder's trousers to clean it, before hesitantly offering her the handle. After hauling some utensils out of a wooden crate, which he pulled from under the bench, he unravelled a hose pipe, opened a valve and ran off some water.

Janet watched these actions in silence but his situation was becoming clear to her, in that he had had to move into his workshop for both shelter and security, and was surviving there in the same way she had done in the observatory storeroom. It had become his home since the disasters but, through his initiatives as the mine's blacksmith and fabricator, he had been able to replace the basic requirements of water, electricity and gas.

The stocky man shortly pulled up a steel fabricator's table, laid a clean piece of cardboard across it and they ate heartily, though mainly in silence, while each weighed up the strangeness of the new liaison. Finally, with refilled mugs of tea, they relaxed and their individual stories unravelled.

'My name Fidel,' he announced nervously, 'and your name is Ha.....' he broke off apologetically.

'Janet', she prompted.

'All people here dead. First come the earthquake and nearly all houses collapse. All people run to mine, because inside the tunnels are all protected with concrete and steel and safe from earthquakes. I shout to people to come into my workshop because it is safe, made of steel, but they not listen. They must go inside mine portal. Then come the poisonous air. The ventilation system of mine sucks in air at portal and pulls it out again from ventilation shaft at back of workings. All people die from poisonous air....'

His speech faltered as he recalled the trauma.

'And you,' she enquired sensitively. 'How did you survive?'

'I nearly die also. I choke for an hour or more and then had the idea about my welding gasses. I do some welding for some jobs the old way, with oxy-acetylene gas, so I open the valve of the oxygen cylinder just a little bit and lay on the floor of workshop, with valve open by my face. At first I think to die because it get dark forever, days maybe and the cylinder half empty anyway, but by my prayers there was enough oxygen to push the sulphurous air away from my face. It was a Hell. After some days, the rain stopped and it came light again and the air became okay to breathe. Then I looked for other people and for food.'

He heaved a great long sigh.

'You found nobody alive?'

'I found several bodies in the ruins of the village. Some died from falling walls caused by earthquake, others from gases in the atmosphere. Even dogs died. My house was small because I live single here and it was collapsed. I found some useful things in the mess which I bring to workshop. I have wife and children in another village near the coast. Last time I speak with them was that they rush up into hills to escape tsunami. I afraid they are dead because of gasses.'

He broke off and shuddered, wringing his hands.

It was her turn to lay a hand on a shoulder.

'Maybe they found shelter and oxygen like you,' she suggested sympathetically.

'No,' he replied with finality.

'Why are you so sure?'

'Because I drive quad bike down the road, to a place which is now blocked by an avalanche, but from there I see down to the coastal area and the hills where the villagers must shelter. There is nothing there now. No trees, no villages, no soil, nothing. All is scraped bare by the huge tsunami. No persons could have survived, even before the poisonous air.'

'My God!' exclaimed Janet, visibly shaken by the revelation of the undeniable truth.

Clearly Fidel had resigned himself to the catastrophic situation and had taken steps to continue his existence. He looked across at Janet for encouragement. Without hope during the previous few days, he had gradually been losing the will to survive, and now suddenly that hope had been rekindled.

'I can make a place for you to sleep in one of the less damaged houses. There is still some houses little bit ok,' he suggested in a voice of lifted spirits.

'No. Don't worry now. It's dark anyway. I will spread out the hessian sacks to lie on. I have a sleeping bag in my pack sack.'

'Thank you,' he said and continued to speak nervously in a sombre tone, 'The problem in village is some places still have terrible smell of death and also have unsafe walls and roofs.'

She screwed up her face and recalled the stench of the dead skeletal dog's remains that she had passed on the track up to the mine site.

'When air clear, I take mine excavating machine to the edge of town and dig hole. After I round up the dead bodies from village and bury them in mass grave. Because I know them all well, I make small crosses with names and put over mass grave. It was horrible job and I sick many times. There are some bodies still covered in rubble in the collapsed houses. What can I do?'

'And those in the mine?' she felt she needed to know all the details, so as to have no further assaults on her agonised brain.

'I drag each body out with a rocker-shovel and push them into another hole, near portal. After I cover all with waste rock from underground workings. Then I weld up forty more iron crosses and place them over new mass grave, each with name on. I knew them all. They my friends and work mates. I have nightmares about all this until now. All this business keep me busy for week.'

She stared at him in awe. This man was incredible. He was possessed not only with compassion but utter pragmatism. She felt her own ordeal was nothing in comparison.

'I could camp in one of the houses tomorrow,' she offered, wishing to sound helpful. 'That's if you consider it's safe,' she added cautiously.

'There is no water or electricity, until I fix something up for you.'

She detected an uplift in his mood. It was as if her presence represented a new and exciting challenge, that might enable him to regain his focus on living.

'We could do it together,' she suggested, echoing his renewed enthusiasm. 'How can we get electricity and water restored?'

'It's not easy,' he replied thoughtfully, 'The mine site has some diesel for my generator. There is enough here for me to run generator for maybe half year if I careful. We have many vehicles, tools, pumps, fridges and equipments at mine but they almost all work by electricity. The electricity is partly generated on site by solar power and partly from grid distribution, coming from hydro plant other side of mountains. Because of earthquakes or poison gas, I don't know, but this supply finished and network of solar panels now broken. Don't know if I can fix it.'

She studied his big gnarled hands, burned and battered by many years of blacksmithing, and wondered how those rough fingers would be able to manipulate the tiny wires associated with solar panels.

'I was the communication officer for the observatory and my training was in circuitry. There is nothing I like better than sorting out a confusion of broke wires to enable a system to be up and running again.'

He looked at her intensely, his eyes beaming back at her.

'I can manage the distribution network, if you can fix wires on all good panels I can find for you. One thing about this place,' he remarked with a smile, 'we have plenty sun!'

Her thoughts and enthusiasm were running before her, in her mission to start a new life and not just survive.

'What about food?' She asked, remembering the chicken legs and garlic.

'The mine has own cold store and village shop. Food security now very important because no help coming, everybody dead. The cold store has automatic shut-down system, so doors stay shut when no electric. Cold store underground, so not damaged by earthquake. Also, it has lithium battery bank, to give electric for about a week, so no defrost. I know this because part my job is to look after cold room.

Before I bury all dead bodies, I take small mobile generator down to cold store and recharge batteries. I do that every four or five days ever since.'

'You are incredible.' She could not hide her admiration. 'How much food is in there?'

'If the electric is fixed, there is enough for seventy families for two months! Also many dried products like rice and pasta and also tins in ruins of village shop. I take out pasta and potatoes and not look for other things.'

'You found the garlic!' she laughed.

'Priority!' he joked, and then continued more seriously, 'Is important now to fix electric supply, so that my precious diesel is not finished. We can look at everything tomorrow. I fetch you bedding.' With that, and despite her protestations, he went off with a torch into the night.

Calculating that he would be gone for several minutes, going backwards and forwards to the village, she went outside to the wall, made her ablutions, came back in, ran off some water into a plastic bowl and had a good wash, slipped her underwear back on, located her sleeping bag, laid it on top of the hessian sacks and climbed into it.

Minutes later he returned clutching a bundle of sheets, a blanket and a camping mattress.

He looked a bit crestfallen, seeing her already tucked up in her sleeping bag.

Janet immediately felt a flush of embarrassment at her mistake.

'Where did you get those?' She enquired looking up at him from the sleeping bag, while resting on her elbows. She was aware that her ample cleavage must have been well displayed and wriggled deeper into the bag.

'From remains of my little house,' he said in a pathetic almost apologetic voice, pretending not to have noticed her perfectly formed breasts.

She did not wish to offend him or diminish his efforts to make her more comfortable, so she reassured him that what he had in his hands looked infinitely better than what she had.

Without further ado, she slid out of her sleeping bag and brazenly stood before him in her bra and pants, while reaching out for the camping mattress. She saw him gulp in a large volume of air before he discretely averted his eyes. At that moment Janet knew that she was safe with this man. He could have easily used his superior power and position to take advantage of her, yet he did not.

Sometime later she lay on her back, gazing at the stars through the open door and window frame. She realised she was more comfortable there than at any time in the previous weeks, while alone in that cold storeroom up at the observatory. She considered how lucky she had been that long day. First it had been her rapid descent from the mountain and then the guard rail episode and finally the meeting up with Fidel, the kind and gentle giant of almost Greek mythological proportions.

She could hear him just a few metres away on his camp bed gently breathing. It was not a snore so much as a purr and very comforting and reassuring. She knew already in her heart it could not be long before she would be encouraging those mighty arms with their bulging biceps to hold her as tightly as child with a doll. How could it be any other way? There was she, a twenty nine year old woman with a slender hourglass figure, an attraction to almost any man and blessed with a libido which she found difficult to contain within social norms.

Neither her fellow technicians nor scientists had tempted her to form a relationship up at the observatory, and the few days she had spent confined with Yoshi in the storeroom had been less than conducive to love making, it being bitterly cold and she wrapped up with a chest infection. Now the situation was totally different and her body was sending her different messages.

As she lay there she considered both her own situation and that of the new hero of her life, Fidel. There was no way of knowing the fate of her family in New Zealand, or that of her Texan boyfriend, or for that matter any chance of finding out. It was also clear that Fidel no longer had any family to consider, and so she decided her only route was to draw a line under her life to date and start a new and completely different one.

Fidel offered her a chance to live on. He may not have been an obvious partner in her former life, but from what she had learnt of this man that day, she could only hold admiration for him. Despite his swarthy, hairy appearance there was an almost child-like softness and innocence to him. His religious beliefs, and dedication to proper burials and the crosses of remembrance, indicated he had a genuine high regard for others and his concerns for her welfare had been so wonderful. She felt her life had changed completely and that she, like Amanda far away, must lead the way into a new era.

Profound as her thoughts may have been, she still had the overtly passionate drive for thrill and adventure. The purring blacksmith two meters away had already ignited a fantasy that would not go away. She allowed her legs to spread inside the sleeping bag and her pelvis to offer itself upwards. Janet sucked hard on a finger and dreamt of being entered by the hairiest, most muscular man she had ever encountered.

CHAPTER TWENTY TWO

'You are surely the most gorgeous, delightful and sexy person I have ever come across in my life,' Jason moaned, as he rolled her off him for the second time that morning. 'How are we ever going to make a farm, build a boat or extend the house if you keep me penned down like this until the sun gets up? Is this honeymoon going to last forever? Your curves are just like those of a pharaoh's princess. You said that they would disappear once the corn crop finished but they haven't. Look at your boobs; they are magnificent, like those of a model,' he said, slipping the nearest one of Amanda's nipples in between his lips.

She laughed and pulled away. Standing in the doorway, she silhouetted her long, beautifully formed body against the early morning sun and stretched. He shook his head as he looked at her in disbelief before she disappeared round the corner to tend to the fire box.

Stirring the charcoal up and shoving an iron plate over the embers, she pasted a dob of sorghum doe, which had been left to rise overnight, on to its hot surface. The result was slightly bitter tasting flat bread. They had been eating it for several days by then and were getting used to its roughness. The first of the bananas had just turned from green to yellow and she mashed one up and spread it over the flatbread, declaring the new breakfast to be the best ever.

He stretched and joined in the feed, sitting on the log opposite her. She wore nothing, not even her sharkskin slippers and un-ashamedly did little to hide the wetness of her inner thighs. Jason sighed and grinned up at her.

'You are such an animal and I love you so very much it hurts. The flatbread is delicious. Is there any more?'

'The way to a man's heart is through his stomach, they say, and you just proved the point.' She laughed and passed him another piece before she set off with a bowl to the well, saying over her shoulder, 'How is the windmill progressing?' Not waiting for an answer she disappeared from view.

He studied her nubile form as she strode away from him. She was no longer the skinny and somewhat fragile woman that came to visit him the night of the rig break-up. Now she was tanned and muscular, curvaceous in the extreme, a couple of kilos heavier than before perhaps but the extra spread nicely over her breasts and posterior. The diet of fish, coconut milk and corn cobs and now sorghum was obviously suiting her.

He gave a heavy sigh and went over to the side of the house, where he had been shaving driftwood planks into windmill blades. They were almost complete and, after a week's laborious shaving, all three were just about identical. His plan was to fabricate a wooden hub and socket the blades into it. He considered that, within the limits of his available tools, this was all possible. The next step, of locating or fabricating some sort of shaft and keying it into the hub, was taxing his imagination. He could think of several options, but none would satisfy his desire to make the windmill function in the long term.

There was also the added complication that its intended use was to pump water to the land surface only when needed, otherwise the well could be pumped dry and that would be a disaster. Therefore there had to be some kind of brake to stop the blades from rotating when not needed. Again Jason could visualise several options but focusing on the best one was preoccupying his thoughts.

After a while he imagined that by visiting the well site again he might bring some solutions into focus. He encountered Amanda sitting on a rock close to the well-head with a bowl of water, looking very sorry for herself. She looked pale and lethargic.

On seeing him, she rose unsteadily to her feet and shook herself in an attempt to appear normal and, picking up the bowl, made a move towards the house. He deliberately blocked her way and bombarded her with questions concerning her pallid looks. She shrugged them off until he convinced her of his concern.

'It's nothing,' she muttered.

'But you look pasty. I've never seen you like this before. I hope you're not sick. We only have Anna Marie's first aid box,' and then panicking spluttered, 'but you were fine just an hour ago!'

'I know. It came on while I was bending over to get the water. I thought I was going to be sick but it has passed now. Are *you* alright? Maybe it's the sorghum. I don't fancy it anymore. Perhaps it was the under ripe bananas.'

'I feel absolutely fine. I don't feel anything coming on either and I have been bent over the windmill blades, so the breakfast was perfectly okay in my opinion.'

She shrugged her shoulders again and stepped past him and then sauntered back to the house.

He let his gaze follow her beautiful tanned and curvy body. Her back view was as perfect as any woman could be. Her bottom had the curves of a beauty queen and he commented to himself that their regular cereal diet had softened the emphasis of the underlying pelvic bone structures.

He allowed his thoughts to luxuriate in the images of her padded pelvis, when suddenly he jolted into sober reality. 'My God......I reckon she is preg.......She can't be. She said her menstrual cycle was in hibernation mode. What now? What can we do?'

Panic set in. His thoughts raced.

'I'll have to do all the housework. ...and fetch water....Better get the windmill finished quickly. What are we going to do about nappies? Do I cut the cord straight away? Do I tie it or what? Can't google anything here. It's a lash up. Maybe it's not happening anyway. He tried to calm himself and promised that he would not make love to her for a month until everything became clear. He re-thought the promise instantly. 'Won't make any difference anyway now....silly idea. I will make her eat more cereal and fish, wrap the fish in sourdough, yes that is the solution. She must eat more to build up her reserves and get plenty of milk ready....there is no powder stuff here. She has to go on light duties and rest a lot.....'

With that resolve he marched back to the house and immediately took charge, ordering Amanda to lie down and rest while he made her some lemon-grass tea.

She glanced up at him unprepared for such a commanding tone of voice.

'I'm not ill.'

'No. But you might be. We are taking precautions.'

'Precautions? We are taking precautions?' she repeated with the emphasis on the '*we*'.

Yes... precautions. *We* don't want you to overdo it.'

'Overdo what?'

'Anything...Everything,' he stuttered and proceeded to puff up the mattress and pillows.

She looked up from her task of washing the salt out of a fish completely puzzled.

'Are you crazy? I have jobs to do. I can't lie down now. It's the middle of the day and I'm not ill.

'Yes you are. I can see it all over you. You have that look about you. Sit in this nice chair I made for you while I make the lemon tea.'

Amanda continued to look puzzled and carried on washing the salt out of the fish. Jason muttered something about her being stubborn and grabbed up a bunch of lemon grass and put it in a saucepan to boil.

'You know you will have to rest everyday while you are in this condition,' he stated wagging his finger at her.

'Rest every day? You must be joking! We have crops out there that we depend on for our survival. I have nothing wrong with me and I don't know what you're on about. Thanks for the lemon tea anyway. I'm off to do the watering when I've drunk it.'

'Arr!' He growled, 'I'm only trying to look after you. You'd better look out; I'm going to monitor you!'

'Oh that will be nice,' she grinned up at him, 'Like you did this morning,' she teased, while provocatively widening her thighs as he glanced at her.

He groaned and went back to shaving his windmill blades.

*

Many vivid and unfinished dreams flashed through Janet's mind before she finally awoke the following morning. The scenes were like a series of unrelated movie trailers that had no beginnings or endings.

Finally reality clicked in with the sound of Fidel's heavy work boots, sometimes near and sometimes far away from her camp bed. She had needed her sleep after the long hike the day before and her state of mind had not yet come to terms with the enormity of the situation. Out of all the chaotic dreams that charged around her head, came one reoccurring obsession. It was that of the refurbishment of the solar panels. It was as if it was the one thing and the one only useful contribution she could make in the otherwise endless list of tasks.

Her mind cleared as the smell of bacon frying and the aroma of steaming tea drifted into her senses. She beamed up at Fidel and wriggled out of her sleeping bag. This time she clung to a towel, a little more aware of her extreme curves that might have been construed as provocative.

Returning the, 'Buenos Dias,' she fled outside to the 'wall' and as she squatted down, the hazy sun of the early dawn brought back the reality of the trek down the mountain, and how the unknowns and horrors of the apparent mass destruction had unfolded. Nobody she had ever known had ever had to deal with the annihilation of humanity on such a scale. The thought instantly depressed her. She no longer had friends, no longer a Texan boyfriend and no hope of seeing her family again, even if they were alive. Neither would there be any planes or vacations, nor targets to strive for. Where was life to take her now?

Chile was never meant to be her home. It was a place of work, exhilarating, high up in the mountains, with top level academics from many nations. It was the preserve of eagles and a million stars in totally dark skies. She had never meant to live there. After her year-long contract, she had intended meeting up and travelling with her boyfriend, having much needed and overdue, passionate sex while savouring the natural beauty of the continent.

She paused in her thoughts, as she caught sight of the cairn outside the mine portal decorated with neat lines of little crosses. Instead I have a decimated planet to deal with; onewith no detectable life further than the dusty planes of the high Atacama.

......And then, her thoughts ran on, *there's Fidel. Not my type*, she mused, *yet on the other hand*, she grinned shaking her head, *I am so eternally grateful for his presence and I know in my heart I can and will learn to love him.*

She stretched and shook the tussles out of her curly hair, then hugged the towel closer to her body against the chill of the early morning air, as she strolled back to the workshop.

Fidel plonked a mug of yerba mate on the steel table in front of her and enquired how her sleep had been. He had on his blacksmith's apron and heavy work trousers. His neck and upper chest were bare. The open-necked shirt had the top buttons undone or missing. Thick black hairs on his chest continued relentlessly up his neck and into his beard. She had never encountered such a hairy man.

He reminded her of some Greek mythological character of Herculean proportions. The delicate slices of toast and thin rashers of bacon seemed almost incompatible with Fidel's stature and strength.

She tugged on her jeans and blouse, then dived into her packsack and off-loaded on to the table all the food, drink and consumables that she had carried down the mountain.

'Not much to offer from my side,' she said apologetically in broken Spanish. 'There's much more if we need it up at the observatory.'

He smiled back at her nervously, noting her reservations about the observatory.

'If we have wings, we bring it down,' he laughed. 'Anyway, here is enough for a year.'

Lowering his voice in a serious manner and catching her eyes he addressed her in soft tones.

'You very brave to do it. I saw broken road and hanging guard rail.'

'Really?' she replied astounded.

'I take the quad bike up to find out if any people survived in observatory. I discover not possible because road destroyed by avalanches in this place.'

Janet detected Fidel's growing respect for her and she began to feel more comfortable about crashing into his world.

'Let's see what we can do about the solar panels,' she suggested enthusiastically, getting up from the breakfast table, wishing to be more of an equal partner.

Fidel looked at her curiously, then briefly rested a heavy hand on her shoulder and smiled a fatherly grin at her.

'This is Chile you know, not New York. In my country we do things without rushing, but we do them all the same!'

He laughed and made her sit back down while he poured her another mug of tea. She noticed the hair on the back of his hands when he offered her the mug. Even the backs of his fingers had hairy tufts between the joints, making them look more like the paws of a bear and quite unlike the delicate hands of the astronomers she had known. She caught the sparkle in his eyes and instantly felt an unaccountable surge of oestrogen that probably showed as a flush on her face. She hoped he hadn't noticed.

'We start with the panels on workshop roof,' he suggested. 'The roof still good after earthquakes and maybe wires still good too. I fetch ladders after breakfast.'

She nodded and cast her eyes round the workshop, searching for useful tools. As if reading her mind, Fidel reached under the bench and presented her with a leather case of electrician's tools and a box of testing instruments.

'Sorry about dirt and grease,' he said apologetically. 'I take them round site with me.'

'Seems like you don't need any help to fix anything,' she noted despondently, assuming his practical skills far exceeded her own.

'I do! I do!' he exclaimed, trying to reassure her. 'I know steel, wood and concrete. I cannot do copper.' He laughed, hoping the simple admission would restore her confidence.

As he laughed, the sparkle of a golden eye tooth glinted through his bushy beard and a hint of his mischievous nature emanated from his eyes, but it was gone as quickly as it appeared.

Walking over to the tool rack, he reached down what she took to be an embossing device. He fiddled with the digital mechanisms for a while which pre-set the letters, before casting a worrying glance in her direction.

'So you say you are not the mother of Jesus,' and muttered under his breath that he was not sure about that. 'Then shall I call you Maria or what?'

Realising that her name had never become apparent, she stumbled out her name.

'Janet.'

'Ah, Hanet!'

He busied himself briefly with the instrument and then held it to the electrician's bag and with a loud click embossed the letters 'Janet' and proudly returned it to her.

'It's yours.'

She looked at the name proudly, then grinned back at the blacksmith and realised she had stepped into a new role. She thanked him for his kindness and took a deep breath, feeling that the transition was now much simpler than she had previously imagined.

CHAPTER TWENTY THREE

Two weeks had passed with seemingly endless glitches in progress, but finally a supply of 110v AC had been re-established at the workshop and at Fidel's former home, plus a feed into the underground cable that supplied the cold store.

Each day the pair had combined their skills and by sheer determination had engineered the solar energy into usable power. Their previous reliance on diesel fuel had diminished to the point where they could relax and allow their own social needs to surface.

Hanet, her new adopted name, now slept, washed and rested alone in what had been Fidel's little house. The roof and structure had been restored to a usable state and within the two short weeks her life had been transformed. Starting as a refugee on a workshop camp bed, she now resided in a house with water, electricity and sanitation. Meanwhile Fidel, having resolved not to become attached to her, wandered back to the workshop after their evening meal together.

He had been uncontrollable in his almost super-human attempts to establish these norms of existence. Janet could think of no other person that could summon up so much energy and hands-on skills. Her heart went out to him, yet she understood his fear of unveiling his own pent up emotions.

She had observed him on some occasions with his eyes shut in prayer, and knew this was a territory out of bounds to her, and that she had to stand back from his private thoughts in case it broke the bond of respect that had grown between them. The loss of his entire family and their village was only too apparent, whereas the fate of her own folks in faraway New Zealand was far less certain, and without evidence she would not allow herself to dwell on it.

However, she did dwell occasionally on the probable loss of her Texan boyfriend. At night, alone in Fidel's little house she was acutely aware of the needs of her body; she even allowed herself to drift into her favourite fantasy. The one where his bronzed body laid over her while she forcefully raised her pelvis upwards. On these occasions she furiously masturbated, yet her orgasm came flooding with confused images of both the Texan and the blacksmith. In its own way, this confusion helped her to respect and sympathise with Fidel's situation and to preserve the status quo.

The solemn moments Fidel spent daily were surely his way of mourning, and coming to terms with the grief at the loss of his wife and entire family. There was no way he was going to enter into a relationship until these matters had been concluded. Janet respected this, despite her own carnal longings.

As if on cue, on their first day of rest Janet was awoken by the sound of the quad bike outside the house. Fidel was there with a full set of clothing on and a spare helmet dangling from the handle bars. There were extra fuel cans strapped to the panniers and a steel box full of food supplies at the rear. She had never seen him in all this gear before and realised he had a serious mission in mind.

'Hanet,' he shouted excitedly. 'Bring many clothes. We go long way!'

His excitement was infectious.

'Holy crows!' she mulled to herself, and rushed to the bathroom for a quick pee before she quickly scurried around and donned her all-weather suit and walking boots, at the same time stuffing a few odds and ends into a small backpack.

He handed her the second helmet as she climbed up behind him, and they quickly set off down the track leading away from the mine site. Janet felt her pulse racing as she clasped her hands round his waist and experienced the mountain air rushing past her face. She felt sure a new chapter was about to open.

The track meandered across the open plain, and for the first half hour there seemed little evidence of the catastrophic upheavals that had befallen the route down from the observatory. She was familiar with this terrain and noted the small gravel airstrip where she and her colleagues were dropped off and collected, on their way in and out of contracts up at the observatory. From there on down, the countryside was new to her, as the flights had always come from the opposite direction, passing first close by the observatory.

Fidel confidently negotiated the gravelly wash-outs that interrupted the track, where small streamlets had crossed it. These were fairly insignificant compared to those further up the mountain and he hardly needed to reduce speed. Janet noted the increasing number of acacia trees and their attendant sage brush, yet there was none of the normally abundant birds and butterflies, nor was there anything green. As they progressed downwards, lichen covered rocks started to appear jutting out of the gravel like erratic teeth, yet there were none of the usual predating birds perched on any of them.

Fidel slowed the quad bike and dropped a gear as they approached a section of more rapid descent, strewn with rocks and gnarled acacias and now the odd taller tree. These trees, she noted, had brown shrivelled up leaves as if they had been hit by an airborne defoliant. The whole countryside displayed the depressing signs of poisoning and death.

'Sulphur dioxide and acid rain,' she whispered to herself. Fidel showed no surprise, as he had been this far on his previous excursion. As the route descended further, with a zig-zag of switchbacks, there was the development of a substantial valley below them on the right hand side. It became the dominant feature with precipitous drop-offs and they had to be more careful. The quad bike climbed over gravel piles formed by local avalanches, which would have barred access to conventional transport. They also had to negotiate trenches through the track caused by the violent rain storms. Janet had never experienced anything like it before and clung on to Fidel's waist in the blind hope that he knew what he was doing.

Without warning the track veered to the left and levelled off. They cruised on for another five minutes on a relatively flat and obstacle-free section, until they reached a wide sweeping corner on the shoulder of the mountain. Here there was a lay-by and passing point for vehicles. It also commanded a striking view of the terrain below and a vista that stretched way beyond the canyon mouth and away to the distant coast of the Pacific Ocean.

Fidel pulled into the lay-by and switched the engine off. As he dismounted he removed his helmet and indicated that she do the same. They could speak now for the first time, without the roar of the bike's exhaust and the clatter of wheels on gravel. The silence at first was uncanny and the increase in temperature un-nerving, as if they had come into another world.

He spoke first, his voice emotional and cracked.

'I come only to here before,' he stuttered in broken English with his back to the open view behind. She could see the tears welling up in his dust strewn face before he swung around to avoid her gaze and, with a sweeping gesture that encompassed the entire area below and in front of them, he slurred out the words, 'Down   there were   houses of my village. My friends, all my family, the farms, the gardens!'

That was as much as he could say and he sank to his knees sobbing with his hands clasped together, most probably in prayer. She could no longer see his face and it seemed so strange to see that mighty body wracked with despair and grief. Words from her would have been useless, so she just rested a hand on his shoulder and gripped it tightly until his rocking body was still again.

Janet used those moments to look over his shoulders and survey the scene beyond. She was aghast at the image of complete devastation. Nothing could be clearer. Like a contour line drawn on a topographical map, a horizontal distinct margin followed the mountain flanks on either side below them. Above the line was the natural mountain vegetation of mixed trees and bushes, all of which had adopted sickly brown hews, and below the line was nothing other than bare rocks and wash outs that had come from the avalanches higher up.

The appalling devastation caused by the tsunami as it had scoured the west coast of the Americas could not have been more apparent. Suddenly it occurred to Janet that their little bubble of normalised existence at the mine, and all the energy they had put into it, might actually all be in vain in the context of a planet that had been struck a deathly blow. Her mind flipped back, recalling all the doomsday scenarios screamed over the airways in the moments following the unprecedented plate movements in the Northern Pacific; those animated voices that predicted the end of a geological era and eradication of most forms of life .

Could this really be the case? She questioned herself. How come she and Fidel plus the two others in the Galapagos had been spared? Is it up to us to restart the planet? Who knows if there are others?

So many unanswered questions. She considered resorting to prayer and recalled her distant Catholic family roots. Within seconds she dismissed the idea. Feeling Fidel's rugged shoulder muscles under her hand, she considered there was probably enough spirituality in him for both of them.

Fidel must have registered her feeling of alarm and despair and prepared himself to comfort her, because when eventually he got back onto his feet and wiped his face, he took hold of the hand that had rested on his shoulder and squeezed it but did not let it go. Instead he led her to the edge of the road where they could look right down into the valley.

'See where the valley enters the plain. Here used to be farms,' he explained. 'Soil good and wells down to bedrock. Here stream hiding in summer, always plenty water for crops. This why our village stay here hundreds years.'

She nodded in sympathy, but was too choked with emotion to allow any words to come out.

'We go bit more down,' he whispered, as he led her away and back to the quad bike.

As if in foreign territory they gingerly crept down the broken track. They continued for twenty minutes until the route was abruptly cut short at the tsunami line. The road had completely disappeared and ended in a dangerous overhang. Below them were boulder fields interspersed with sandy screes, that filtered off into the distance under a glaring sun. Janet commented to herself that it was not unlike the pictures of Mars sent back from various Martian rovers.

Despite the inhospitable nature of the landscape, Fidel was

determined to see more. He turned the motor round and backtracked to the first avalanche site, where he was able to ease the vehicle downwards and avoid the tsunami induced drop-off.

'Hanet,' he called over his shoulder, 'Hold tight and have faith in me!'

She recalled that mischievous nature in him which she had glimpsed before and held him more tightly, until they came off the avalanche path and onto the firmer and smoother scree below. The scree stretched like a tentacle away into the distance and they followed it almost to the sea. There were gullies on each side which developed into small valleys the further they went. Eventually the scree petered out and gave way to a sandy delta, that finally merged into the sea a mile or so away.

The ocean's waves had penetrated the delta where the valleys had developed, making little salt water creeks.

There was little point in going any further. They had descended at least three thousand metres from the mine site and would need a fair bit of their reserve fuel to get back, besides which it was oppressively hot there on the open coastal plain. Fidel got off and checked the tank and declared that they would top up again once back on the mountain road.

Casting his eye off to the north, he told her that the site of Porta Maria was close to where they stood. They could see that the coast was now devoid of any structure or any vestige of civilisation. Shrugging his shoulders in disbelief, he turned to her, but found her gaze fixed on what appeared to be an anomaly on their south side where the valley entered the salt water.

He followed her gaze.

'What's that?' She exclaimed excitedly. 'It's not a rock is it?'

He did not answer, but leapt onto the quad bike and fired it up and sped over the dusty scree to the edge of the valley, with her perched behind him still holding on to his helmet.

By the time they had dismounted, the discovery needed no explanation. It was the battered hull of a steel vessel lying on its side. It was perhaps twenty metres long and appeared wedged between the rocks at the mouth of the valley. The topside had two open deck hatches, displaying fully flooded hold areas inside. The water was level with the hatch combing.

Fidel rubbed his chin and turned to her and grinned.

'Well at least it not leak!'

She raised her eyebrows, not knowing what to expect next.

'When tsunami come, it fill with water straight away. Made from iron, it never move. The engines, must be two,' he added with authority, 'because two propellers. Boat not rust in seawater like in hot air.'

He was as excited as a boy with a new present for Christmas. Janet could see where this was going and started to share some of his enthusiasm, but with a great deal of apprehension.

They clambered down for a closer inspection. The tide was lapping the stern. The rudder was intact along with both propellers.

'Engines I can fix', he declared enthusiastically.

'How can you move it into the sea?' she queried.

He scratched his head. 'Drill hole and let water out, then block hole. Then it float again when tide come.'

She seemed sceptical. 'Maybe there is no tide here, or perhaps it is already high tide,' and then not wishing to dampen the enthusiasm, 'Why don't we just syphon the water out then you don't have to fix the hole'.

'Brilliant! We are in business. I get this beauty in water one way or other. Don't worry.'

He peered into the murky water of the flooded holds. The water within was black and oily, with only a tangle of severed electrical wiring visible through the gloom. Janet mentally wrote it off as a wreck, though it was obvious that Fidel had his restoration project lined up, and she wondered what sort of miracles he could possibly conjure up.

After surveying the whole craft, back, sides, top and all exposed surfaces, Fidel concluded that the hull was intact. The wheelhouse and all super structure appeared to have been guillotined off at deck level.

'I think boat ready for scrapping when tsunami come, he commented, pointing out the stumps of deck fittings that had obviously been burned off with cutting equipment.

'Engines in boat still. This why boat very heavy and not move far. Engines always last to come out after deck clear. We see better when all water out.'

Casting a last look at the hulk, he grinned back at her perplexed face and caught hold of her hand, dragging her back up the bank to their bike.

'If we have boat, one thing we can do we can do is catch fresh food. Before, I go with brother many times from Porta Maria. I have fishing gear in workshop and here is plenty of fish. God willing fish still there.' He drew in a deep breath, realising that this was something he had no control over.

He let go of Janet's hand when they reached the flat ground ahead of the quad bike. She had a notion that there was a sense of hesitation and reluctance for him to do it. She instantly knew his period of mourning was nearing an end. There was no doubt anymore that their lives together had become inevitable and that all life on the coastal plain had been obliterated. Survival together was now their main way foreward.

CHAPTER TWENTY FOUR

For the third day running, Jason hauled Amanda to her feet from where she had been sitting close to the well, looking sick. The Galapagos sun had not faltered for over a week and the crops certainly had to be watered. It seemed that the rainy season was over and so she had taken her duties seriously.

He led her by the hand gently back to the house and insisted once again that she rested.

Putting his head on one side, and waiting for the right moment when she was looking straight at him, he addressed her as softly and knowledgeably as a mother might have done.

'Amanda.' He paused, while making sure she was still looking at him. 'It's no use continuing to be in denial. You are pregnant!'

She flinched while acknowledging the truth.

'I had assumed so.'

She shuddered and looked pale.

'My periods are supposed to be in hibernation mode.'

'For how long?'

'My CONSOL told me two months.'

'Amanda... Two months... How long is it since the break-up of the rig? Four months?...six months? I've lost track of time.'

'But I haven't had any periods', she whined in protest.

'Perhaps it's an immaculate conception then,' he jested, giving her a big loving smile.

'Some hope of that,' she said nodding in the direction of his already half erect penis. 'What am I to do? I don't know anything about babies.'

'It's a fine time to announce that. I don't know anything either. I was an only child.'

'It's alight for you to talk; I don't even have a mother or father. All I know was that I came from an egg donated by a Balkan athlete.'

'Then you should be fine. Look at the gene pool we have between us!'

'Ahh!' she groaned. 'How is that going to help us when there are complications; not enough milk, and God knows what else.'

'Listen Amanda,' he commanded, 'There won't be any complications, there will be loads of milk, especially if you keep devouring coconuts the way you do, and you don't need to worry. Another thing, our child will not need all those inoculations they seem to be so keen on these days, as the sulphurous cloud must have taken care of loads of bacteria.'

She remained sullen and unsure of herself.

He turned and stoked the fire box, encouraging the saucepan of hot water to come to the boil. Shortly afterwards he brought her a mug of lemongrass tea.

'You will be absolutely fine,' he reassured her, 'and by the way I finished the windmill mechanisms yesterday. Today I plan installing them and hopefully we will have a test run by this evening and water pumped to the crops tomorrow.'

'That would be miraculous,' she said cheering up. 'Can I help? I feel better now.'

'No. Rest awhile,' he said sensitively. 'Let's forget the watering today, in the hope the crops will get plenty tomorrow. They surely won't hurt for one day and if my systems fail I will carry water myself tomorrow.'

She was about to get up when he rested a heavy hand on her shoulder.

'You stay there while I fetch a fish from the pound, and from now on in you are on light duties. Okay? We can't have you miscarrying.'

Jason felt quite proud and self-confident using the word for the first time in his life, yet actually having no idea of its full meaning, only that it could be associated with a pregnant woman lifting heavy items.

She beamed back at him and he felt he had gained some brownie points.

In the late afternoon, when the fish smelt good on the barbeque, Amanda heard a squeal of delight coming from the direction of the well-head.

She had observed Jason's bronzed figure bobbing up and down endless times, as he clambered in and out of the well, accompanied by a number of irritated curses, and decided she had better leave him to it rather than intervene.

At one point he tore off back to their old cabin and returned carrying a length of plastic pipe scavenged from the bathroom. The windmill had been turning intermittently and emitting a dreadful squeak. This noise almost disappeared once Jason had scraped the insides of several coconuts on to the moving parts of the hub. She had looked on with approval without saying anything. Now he was shouting for her to come and look.

'Wow! Look at that!' she exclaimed seeing a little stream of water running into the improvised gully, made from the material of the old methane collector. The trickle of water was making its way slowly over to the sorghum patch.

She kept a safe distance back from the windmill, which seemed to have an oscillating motion all of its own.

'It's only a test run to see if the pumping idea works,' he said defensively, while keeping a steadying hand on the wobbling windmill pole. 'I will sort out the details tomorrow.....'

Keeping her head down in fear of being struck by the windmill blades, she rushed over to him and gave him an almighty hug, kissing him passionately on the lips at the same time.

The seeds of success triggered a massive libido response and the inevitable impulses, as she raised a knee into his groin. With one hand he put the brake on the windmill blades and with the other hand he cupped her pubic mound and slid a finger down beside her wetting clitoris.

He led her back to the house, pushing the cooked fish to one side as they passed the fire box.

She wasn't waiting to be asked. She had already thrown herself onto the mattress and lay provocatively on her back with splayed legs, propping her pelvis up with her hands.

He could have just sunk into her there and then but he hesitated, savouring the moment. Carefully, he knelt down on the floor between her legs and pulled her buttocks to the edge of the mattress where the level and pose was perfect. He then pulled her vulva towards his waiting lips.

She moaned and threw her head backwards, as he expertly ran his tongue gently from side to side of her erect clitoris, not rushing but not teasing her soaking wet vagina, until her moans turned into a guttural slur and she utterly lost control and erupted into spasms of intense orgasm.

While she was still squirming and uttering nonsensical profanities, he floated his manhood deep inside her and, with just a few thrusts of his hips, delivered his sperm in surges of total pleasure and relief.

Shortly afterwards, Amanda dragged herself on top of his collapsed body, which by then was on the mattress and let her thighs straddle his chest. She leant forward and caressed his lips and closed eyes as only a person deeply in love can do. Their tongues entwined as he drew his arms round her back.

He sensed her wet vagina rubbing into the hairs of his belly and felt the muscles of her lower body contract. She ran her pouted lips down over his chest, teasing one nipple and then the other, before she went lower and arrived at the pool of semen and hormonal juices that had run out of her on to his belly. There she dramatically lapped them up like a cat awarded with a saucer of milk, and purred as she did so.

It occurred to Jason, as he lay there while she busied herself setting out the fish supper, that those previous moments of total intimate bliss could only be born out of instinct, nothing could have been rehearsed and so it would be with the birth of their child. It was with those reassuring thoughts that he roused himself and with a beaming, confident smile, joined her outside by the barbeque.

In the weeks that followed, he attended to the refinements of the windmill and also engineered a second gully down to their house, where they had a storage tank fabricated from bits of their old cabin. This held enough water for their domestic needs for up to a week. On the agricultural front, the second corn crop was well on its way and Amanda was having some success experimenting with seedlings of rice. She had germinated a few plants from a bag of organic rice, kept by Jason for curries, which had survived intact in one of the bolted cupboards in the cabin.

As for Isabella, she had sprouted minute residues of weeds and cacti during the rainy season. These colonies, despite the heat of the sun and lack of further moisture, had continued a perilous existence. These little oases of life brought inspiration to Jason and Amanda each time they noticed them, during their own daily tasks of scurrying round gathering coconuts, fish and other sea products.

The volcano had settled down into a quiescent phase, much to Amanda's relief. While gathering goose barnacles, they had each spotted Regina on several occasions, but seen no other reptile or land creature, other than a couple of sightings of small green lizards amongst the lava piles. The fate of the small turtles which she had carried down from the mountain was unknown.

They had long since given up on hearing from Janet in Chile, ever since the last message from her that stated she was going to come down off the mountain. They had sadly concluded that she hadn't made it.

After several weeks of painstakingly opening the sat-phone with Maria's preserved thumb print and finding no further responses, Amanda had given up hope of there being another survivor, and had put the phone away.

She periodically patted the bulge in her stomach and concluded with some pride that she was destined to be a mother, a hitherto unimaginable scenario. While at the same time, Jason only seemed to be able to imagine that it would be a boy and would be born at six years old, because he had become obsessed with constructing a tiny boat and a second set of fishing gear in readiness. Amanda could only smile and shake her head in disbelief.

She and Jason had spent many evenings together, weaving a carpet for the house out of strips taken from the canvas of the methane collector. It was quite a bonding process for them both, working together and creating something of a luxury and an appropriate softening of their floor area in readiness for a baby.

The morning sickness went away after a few weeks and, despite Amanda's rapidly changing profile, she still busied herself all day with the crops and preservation of fish. Jason had come across a salt pan during his wanderings down the coast and so he had been able to carry back copious quantities for preservation, which had saved them the time consuming operation of scraping small quantities out from cracks and crannies nearby, which inconveniently often contained some sand.

Neither of them had any idea how long it would take coconuts to grow into palms, nor when they would eventually produce coconuts. There were certainly many nuts now germinated along the coast and, well fertilised by the decomposing vegetation, they were showing green quite rapidly. Their main concern was to prevent their stockpiles of un-germinating coconuts from suddenly leaping into life and becoming useless as food. Their answer to this was to spread the stock piles out and keep them away from moisture. This occupied Jason in several days of hard labour.

One evening, after they had been squatting down for an hour or so weaving the new carpet, Amanda, who had obviously been uncomfortable, took a break and leaned back against a wall with her hands resting on the bulge in front of her. Suddenly she gave out a delighted squeal.

'Look, Look!' She shouted excitedly pointing to the bulge. A distinctive commotion was going on inside while the baby turned over or around or made some readjustment to its cramped surroundings. They both looked on in amazement.

'Holy Jesus!' exclaimed Jason in panic. 'Is it going to be born?'

'No, I hope not,' she said excitedly. 'Just letting us know it's there and wants to have a change of scenery.'

'Change of scenery,' echoed Jason. 'Can it see anything in there?'

She chuckled and scanned her naked belly. There was a little lump right in the middle of the bulge.

He looked at it with great interest.

'It's a boy,' he declared with seeming authority.

'How do you know?' she said sceptically.

'That is his penis.'

She threw her head back in laughter.

'YOU being the father of the baby, you are probably right.'

They both laughed.

*

Janet realised that some of the pressure was off Fidel's daily life, now that the house was usable and electricity had been restored to the cold store. She allowed him his private time, busying himself in his precious workshop, without too many questions about his activities there.

She perceived a notable change in him. He would turn up for no apparent reason at the ruins of the mine shop where she spent her days, extracting non-perishable goods to take back to the house. He would keep asking her if she was okay or if she needed anything. This would happen several times a day and each time he would almost loiter around looking for some excuse to stay longer, before he reluctantly returned to the workshop to carry on with the projects he was engaged in.

She understood this to be his transitional period between mourning and a new life, and it was not up to her to precipitate a liaison. However, after more than a week of this cat and mouse game, she concluded that she had to break the impasse.

This thought occurred to her after three consecutive nights of more and deeper indulgencies in eroticism and extravaganzas of sexual positions and of contrived dreams while she furiously masturbated. Never before had she felt the desire for a sexual relationship more strongly. She even imagined her breasts to be bigger and firmer than they used to be. She caressed them endlessly in every private moment, as soon as Fidel left the supper table and returned to his bed in the workshop.

Finally she concocted a plan. She would tell him about a leak in the bathroom and then hide behind the door. When he was kneeling down looking for the problem, she intended leaping out, naked, from her hiding place, declaring the leak to be between her legs and suggesting he fixed it.

She dwelt on this plan for a while before dismissing it as one of her fantasies. No. The approach had to be more subtle, otherwise he could be scared off.

Perhaps she could bar the door so he could not leave after supper. No. That would not work either. He would suspect her motives.

She racked her brain as to what would seduce him to the point where his desires overtook his reservations.

Suddenly she remembered one of the oldest aphrodisiacs in the history of civilisation: a woman's perfume. She had none of her own but she had seen cosmetics in the dust down at the mine shop. She would investigate. That and a white blouse with no bra underneath would provoke a reaction. She could leave the top two buttons undone perhaps. There would be no need to orchestrate any more. She would see what happens.

The following day they breakfasted together early. He had arrived on the quad bike wearing more than just his shirt and shorts and she enquired what he was up to.

'Moving things around,' had been his reply.

She suspected he did not wish to divulge his entire programme, so she questioned him no more. In any case she had her own secret plan for the day, so was happy he would be occupied with his own tasks.

When he was gone she undressed and checked through her pitiful wardrobe, holding up various items against her naked body to see how they looked. Catching sight of her full rounded breasts in the piece of mirror glass she had propped up on the dressing table, it was as much as she could do to resist another round of fantasies and prolonged masturbation.

'Phew,' she sighed under her breath, as she dragged her hands away from the already erect nipples, 'another day of this and I'll go mad'.

She pulled out the blouse she had in mind and a pair of black leggings and threw them into the sink. She washed each of them furiously, before finally wringing them out and hanging them outside to dry. She then gathered up her empty back pack and went off to the derelict mine shop again.

During the previous days she had systematically been dismantling broken walls, shelves and counters, so that she could examine and retrieve the stocked items safely. This day was exceptional in that she had reached a section of grocery preserves, many of which would be fine. There were jars of olives and pickles, tins of fruit and various types of beans and, under a collapsed shelf, an array of toothpastes, hand creams and cosmetics.

Some of these she had spotted the previous day, lying in the dust. This time she carefully cleaned them off and registered their names. She nodded with approval as she recognised some brand names sought after by women who wanted to project an aura of opulence at weddings or special occasions.

With her packsack loaded, she made several trips back to the house and set up a fairly comprehensive pantry. Having chosen an assortment from the new array of preserves and opened a tin of wild salmon, she set the table with the most seductive food she could lay her hands upon. It was four o'clock and he should be home soon. She had not seen him all day.

She showered and made sure that every possible contour and fold of her body was immaculate and that her hair was dancing and tantalising, following the experiments she had performed with the hair curlers she had found under the cosmetic shelves.

The blouse needed ironing and there was no iron, so she shook it furiously until the ruffles dropped out, and then pulled on her sexy leggings without underwear. She slid into her white blouse, which nestled neatly over her full breasts, just covering them with the top two buttons undone. She was satisfied that the simplicity of the outfit was effective enough, yet somehow she felt she lacked confidence, then suddenly remembered the perfume.

Sensitively she removed the wrapper and exposed the spray nozzle, fondling it with the reverence it deserved. She doused herself from head to foot, almost becoming intoxicated in the alcoholic vapour.

Five o'clock and still no sign of Fidel. He was always back at the house by then and she started to worry.

Six o'clock and she thought she detected the sound of the quad bike in the distance.

She went quickly into the bedroom and checked her hair again and gave herself a renewed spray of perfume. Another hour of daylight. Surely he would walk through the door any minute. She shook in anticipation, her confidence on a knife edge.

Half an hour later she heard his footsteps approaching and the door rattled.

Her heart pounded in her chest as his reaction to her clearly registered in his face. His muscular bulk filled the doorway and his freshly showered hair and face lit up, gleaming in the last of the evening's sun as he turned to close the door.

Fidel stuttered out apologies for being late and held out a present for her with one hand, whilst keeping the other hand concealed behind his back. She took it from him and as she drew closer he made an exaggerated sniff and then looked a little crestfallen.

'It seems I'm a little late.'

Her heart went out to him. It was an identical bottle of perfume to the one she had found.

'You are never too late. In any case it is the thought that counts. It's wonderful. Thank you.'

With that she broke new ground and put her arms round him and gave him a reassuring hug. The contact was only a few brief seconds long, but it was new and different from anything that had gone before. She did not want to let go. Her breasts had come into contact with that mighty chest, all be it through two layers of clothing, just as she had imagined so often during the preceding evenings.

'Come sit down and have supper. It's rather special tonight. Tell me what you have been doing all day.'

She waved him over to the table, deliberately ensuring that her erect nipples profiled in front of him through her blouse.

As she lowered her arm she stared in horror at the sleeve. The white blouse was smeared in fresh blood.

Aghast, she swung him round in order to see the concealed arm.

'What the fuck have you done?' She exclaimed while shaking in alarm.

Withdrawing his arm, he said calmly, 'Don't worry. Is nothing. No time to fix properly because I already late.'

He pointed to the rough towelling bandage oozing blood and bound on with insulation tape.

'Is just few scrapes. My shower make bleed again. Supper looks exciting,' and taking a step backwards gave her an admiring look. 'You too!'

'I'll give you a few scrapes!' she yelled at him and ordered him to the bathroom. 'You can't go around like that. You'll get infections and God knows what else. I've done courses in first aid and I'm going to clean that up,' she told him forcefully. 'What happened anyway?'

'I run chain out from pannier on quad bike. My wrist catch underneath.'

'Ugh!' she exclaimed in horror. 'Rusty chain as well I suppose!'

'Well..... Not new,' he replied defensively, resigned to whatever she had in store for him.

Off came the towelling and out came the nail brush, which she doused several times in boiling water to sterilise. He clenched his fists and teeth and looked away, while she screwed up her face and scrubbed the raw muscle, until there were no signs of rust or foreign particles in the various wounds, all the while with the tap water washing away the freshly released blood. Finally she got a clean towel and made him hold it tightly against the wounds until the bleeding stopped.

While he was holding the towel still, she went out to the pantry, found a bottle of brandy and poured him a generous glass.

'You probably need this,' she said with a grin. He downed it in one and returned the glass, giving her a broad smile without saying a word.

She went back out, poured a modest glass for herself and took back a similar shot for Fidel. Finally she took out sterilised dressings and bandages from her own first aid box that she had brought down from the observatory. Twenty minutes later Fidel was fixed up. He had become extremely quiet, barely saying a word all the time she was dressing his wounds. At first she thought it was delayed shock and then she realised he became particularly attentive each time she leaned forward to dip the bandage round his outstretched arm.

Until then, all her pent up sexual feelings had completely evaporated. She was so concerned about the poor man in front of her, who must have been in desperate pain, that she had forgotten the image she projected.

Whether it was the brandy or the return of her body instincts, she was never clear, but her gaze fell onto the distinctive bulge in Fidel's shorts. The one that appeared to pulse each time she leaned forward.

'This fucking guy has got the hard on despite all this,' she breathed to herself and there she was concerning herself about the pain he was bearing and how cruel her scrubbing must have been.

'That's it!.....' she murmured to herself allowing a surge of desire to flood through her body as she directed the mighty man back into the living room.

The air was electrified. She looked down at her blood stained blouse and then onward to his obvious erection. He came close to her and took in a deep breath of her perfume.

'What about blouse?' he stuttered. 'I make big mess of it.'

'I could take it off and put it to soak,' she suggested softly and mischievously and then, stepping even closer while exploring his nervous expression, added, 'Perhaps you would like to do that for me'.

She waited while he comprehended the invitation, half afraid she had gone a step too far.

He looked at her with wild passionate eyes for a couple of seconds, before gently undoing the remaining three buttons of her blouse and sliding it off her shoulders. It fell to the floor but neither looked down at it.

Her heart raced and her face flushed. Could she really believe this was happening, after all those confused dreams and aborted plans of the past week; after nearly four weeks of restrained affection and suppression of natural desires?

He didn't immediately caress her breasts as she had expected, while her head was back and her eyes were closed; instead he surveyed their beauty, their generous size, the large tan-coloured aureoles and puckered nipples. As she opened her eyes not knowing what to expect, he was peeling off his t-shirt, exposing his gigantic chest, totally covered in thick black hair, complimented by massive bulging biceps. He resembled a bear.

The t-shirt dropped down beside her blouse. Neither of them looked. His arms had found their way round her back and his lips fell gently onto hers. She felt entirely electrocuted; privileged to be the subject of his attention, the richest girl on the planet, undressed by the strongest gentlest giant of them all, a flower in the hands of a herculean blacksmith and the envy of any female anywhere and everywhere.

His manhood rolled relentlessly against her pubic bone for the entire duration of their first passionate kiss. She cared not what would happen next and knew nothing could hide the developing wet patch in the crotch of her leggings. In abandonment, she thrust her pelvis hard against his upper leg so that he could register the dampness and the true meaning of a woman out of control.

The salmon and special supper faded from memory as she dragged him to the bedroom and yanked his shorts down and frantically kicked off her leggings.

CHAPTER TWENTY FIVE

It must have been ten in the morning. Jason had been out on the wing fishing since they had had an early breakfast, when Amanda, now with a huge bump and feeling particularly uncomfortable, decided she would have another attempt at making some kind of contact with the outside world. For weeks they had not bothered with Anna Maria's sat-phone and it remained perched up on a ledge at the back of their new house.

Dragging herself to her feet, away from the meal preparation, she waddled over to get the phone and took it outside where the sun would recharge its solar panel.

Returning to her corncob preparation, she cupped her hands beneath her belly to lessen the weight of the overhang and reflected for a long time on her condition. She could only guess how long she had been pregnant. It seemed forever. They had been particularly bad at accounting for days, let alone weeks and months. Their only marker had been the rainy season, which seemed to have passed by months ago. The days had become almost unbearably hot for her. During the afternoons, she had taken to bathing semi submerged in the shallows near the wing, often while Jason was out there fishing.

Before she ventured down there on this occasion, she decided she would open the phone with Anna Maria's thumb print and make a broadcast to the world, announcing that she was expecting a baby and for the world to wish her all the best. She realised it was a nonsensical notion but felt desperate to share her news with somebody, almost as an instinct. Since there had been no news from Janet the 'world' seemed the best solution. 'Who knows?' she thought. 'Maybe everything was alright again out there!'

An hour later she had painstakingly offered up the preserved thumb to the phone and waited for it to receive satellite reception. Wiping the screen off and hiding it in the darkest corner outside the house, so she could see it properly, she watched the reception bars at the top as they registered one satellite after another. She took a moment to marvel that these clever little bits of engineering still continued to orbit the planet, doing their job despite the fact the world below them was in great trouble.

Before she transmitted her plea to the world, she scanned all the media channels for broadcasts. As she anticipated there were no transmissions, so she depressingly switched to 'messages' and scanned down the serious of text messages she had received from Janet months ago, before her announcement that she was coming down off the mountain, and the follow up unanswered messages from her own side, for several weeks before she had given up.

Curiosity prompted Amanda to touch the 'refresh' button, in case there was a 'timed out' function to the phone.

Incredulously she stared at the phone as a text message spun across the screen.

'Sorry, Sorry, Sorry. I have had no phone for several months but Fidel has fixed it for me now.

Are you still there?

Love, Love, Love Janet.'

Amanda studied the text several times in disbelief, before bursting into tears and with trembling fingers replied.

'We are here, we are here.

I am expecting a baby.

Love Amanda and Jason.'

She visibly shook as she pressed the transmission button, hoping it would work before any time-out or transmission failure foiled her elation.

Clasping the phone tightly, she ran as best as she could down to the shoreline, close to the wing where Jason was fishing. Even though she was panting, she managed to yell across the water at the top of her voice for him to come in.

He stood up and could be seen frantically rounding up his fish, before hopping from one plank to another on the makeshift pontoon, as he hastily made his way back to the shore.

'What's up?' he shouted nervously as he approached. 'Are you having the baby?' There was an air of panic in his voice.

'No! No!' she exclaimed. 'Janet has texted us. Her phone is working at last and she has a man!'

'What?' shouted Jason, as he splashed back into the shallows, dragging his fish on a bit of string.

She showed him the text by cupping the phone in her hands

to shade it. He had trouble to see the script because of the sun, so she handed it to him. Almost in disbelief, he rushed off to a nearby coconut palm that had just displayed its first spreading leaves, so he could find enough shade to read the screen properly.

'Holy shit,' he muttered strolling back to her. 'We are not alone after all! She must have found people and this guy Fidel is smart enough to get her phone working again. Wow! What shall we do now? Request rescue service and find out if they have a maternity hospital up and running yet?'

Amanda stared at him in disbelief.

'I scanned all media stations and there is nothing, not even a crackle, so I think you're dreaming if you think of hospitals and rescue services.' Then defensively she added, 'Anyway this is my home and I don't want to be rescued.'

He looked down at her huge bump and distraught face and concluded she was right, and he had to face up to the fact that he was going to have to be midwife, doctor, father and provider all in one.

She lay back against a flat rock, obviously upset by both her run down to the beach and his statement about being rescued. The bump stuck up like a mountain, making her breasts look tiny by comparison, despite their doubling in normal size.

He knelt down beside her and held a hand. She was sweating profusely and looked haggard and uncomfortable. 'You are right,' he said softly. 'This is our home and you are the queen. We will find out more about the mainland from Janet in the coming days.'

He leant forward and kissed her wet lips, holding her shoulders tightly as he did so. The moment was somehow magical. The wavelets were barely lapping on the shore and the very light breeze was just enough to dry off the perspiration. Her panting slowly abated, though there seemed no position offering her any comfort, so she periodically raised her weight from one buttock to another, sat up and then lay back again.

Jason felt useless and could only feel sorry for her. He offered to walk her slowly back to the house, where she could be more comfortable on the mattress. She argued that she had work to do and that supper was only half prepared. She rested a while longer with him at her side and then in a moment of silence there was a rush of water.

She sat up sharply and stared helplessly at the stream running down the rock face and emanating from between her legs.

'My God something has happened!' She shouted in panic and at the same time she grimaced as there was a contraction low in her stomach.

'Help! Help!' she wailed. 'What do I do? What's happening?'

Jason completed his third random circle, trying to get a grip on his role.

'That must mean the placenta or something has broken and the baby comes next,' he stammered with no certain authority.

She had another contraction and a minute or two later a third one.

'Your bump has definitely moved lower,' he informed her, as if it was of great importance. Amanda had no interest in the position of the bump and was bravely dealing with the pain of the contractions.

In a moment of inspiration, Jason dashed off to the nearby young banana ferns, which Amanda had been nurturing, and within a minute or so was back with a couple of broad young leaves, like extended soft green doormats, which he laid down on the gravel at the base of the rock.

'That's thoughtful of you,' she said, as she winced her way through a fourth contraction. Her statement did little to restore his vanishing self-confidence and he just looked on pitifully.

Each time she had a contraction, she groaned as her pelvis automatically widened. This went on for what must have been nearly an hour. All discussions about returning to the house were abandoned as it became obvious she was going nowhere. By this time she had slithered down onto the banana leaves.

'Can you see anything yet?' She squealed.

For the first time in their relationship, he *modestly* peered up between her legs, feeling a little uncertain and definitely not sure what he was supposed to be looking for.

'Can you see anything?' She repeated yelling at him.

'Yes!' He exclaimed screwing up his face. 'I can see something'.

'For Christ's sake Jason!' she screamed at him while pushing hard, 'Can't you tell if it's a head or a foot?'

'It's a.... the..... head, I think,' he informed her with a degree of uncertainty.

She was not waiting for any further deliberations and with an almighty push and a guttural roar she gave birth.

The baby almost shot out from her body and Jason by some paternal instinct or other moved in and cradled the little wet thing perfectly, before it tumbled onto the banana leaves. It was no bigger than his two hands together and, with its tiny screwed up face and minute digits, he found it hard to believe it could possibly be another human like them.

Amanda peered down at the tiny infant and managed a mother's smile through the rivers of sweat running down her face.

Jason passed her the child with the most exaggerated care imaginable. The little girl's genitalia were almost inside out and Jason was not prepared to announce whether it was a boy or a girl. Amanda held her proudly and told him that the baby was a girl and sometimes at birth it was not always clear at first.

Jason was so elated, he momentarily forgot he was not just the father but the midwife. The umbilical cord was as round as a sausage and obviously attached to the baby. He had no wish to investigate where the other end was and was rummaging through his bag of fishing tackle for some twine.

Amanda cried out to him for help in a panic. The little child in her arms was breathing and kicking her little legs but Amanda was in deep trouble. She was crying out in pain and her hips were still in spasmodic contractions. Water and blood, together with the trailing umbilical cord, was adding to the confusion between her legs.

Believing Amanda was about to die Jason yelled at her imploring her to tell him what to do.

She could not answer him and instead almost forced the baby into his hands, while throwing her hips upwards, groaning through tightly grated teeth and pushing down on the rock with both hands.

Jason was in panic mode, now holding a baby still with umbilical cord trailing and his precious Amanda seemingly in the throes of death, with blood and water emanating from her body. He could barely bring himself to look at her but when he did so he almost had a fit. A second baby's head was appearing through the mayhem.

He felt a surge of urgency and, holding the little girl to his chest, he reached forward and cupped the new arrival in one hand and pulled it clear of the tangle of cords, membranes and fluids.

'It's another one!' He shouted as if he was witnessing a production line.

He was in absolute panic, standing there for a second or two with two tiny babies, one in each hand with their attendant umbilical cords hanging down, the second with the cord well wrapped round its neck.

Instinctively he handed the first child back to Amanda, who was lying back exhausted against the flat rock, with rivers of sweat running off her, while he freed the cord from around the neck of the second baby. He prayed feverously for the survival of the child, as he opened the tiny mouth with a finger and blew very gently into it, all the while massaging the little creature's back.

To his utter delight, a tiny leg kicked and a spluttering little cry came from the wet bundle in his hand. He looked up to see Amanda courageously propping herself up on one arm, beaming admiringly at him through her tears and holding the first baby to her chest.

It looked like they were both surviving he thought, so with regaining confidence he handed her the second baby for her inspection.

Without saying a word and with trembling hands, he found his twine and tied off each of the babies' cords close to their stomachs. With their food supplies cut off, the tiny girls instinctively made sucking noises and, when offered up to Amanda's breasts, attempted to feed.

During the following three hours Jason became the midwife, taking his duties very seriously. He rushed back to the house and within minutes returned with towels, clean and long since rescued from the debris of the cabin. He also brought containers of fresh water. He bathed Amanda and gave her fresh water to drink. Satisfied that the two placentas on the banana leaves had no further use, he cleared them up along with the cords, which he had snipped off with scissors, and put them in the sea, believing they would benefit some other forms of life.

Amanda was desperately tired and obviously very sore but, being the strong woman that she was, found a way to deal with each problem as it arose. One breast was issuing some sort of watered down milk while the other was reluctant to give more than a watery fluid. She moved the babies from one nipple to another in the hope they would get some nourishment.

Jason had rigged up a temporary sun shade with poles and canvas and brought her a snack from their remaining precious supply of tinned food.

Her dilated cervix had stopped bleeding and she became conscious for the first time that she had survived giving birth not just to one baby, but two.

She met Jason's beaming smile as he stood back watching her in silence, barely able to comprehend the enormity of the last four hours.

With one baby on each breast she grinned up at him and joked softly.

'What the fuck have we done to deserve this lot?'

He thought about it for a minute before giving her a proud smile.

'You probably used the right verb!'

They both laughed.

The sun was setting as he helped Amanda nervously to her feet and with a baby each, cradled in towels, they set off slowly back to their house. The scene could not have been more like a documentary on the evolution of mankind if had been totally stage managed, reflected Jason.

The only oddity must have been his jelly sandals and her sharkskin slippers, yet the tribal group, plodding off to their hut on an otherwise uninhabited island in the middle of nowhere, seemed to define its place in history.

*

Janet clambered stiffly off the back of the quad bike for the umpteenth evening in succession, after spending the day down on the coast, helping Fidel with the restoration of the steel boat. Their daily work had been hard, at first outside the hull, then in the depths of the interior. They had cleared debris, assessed the requirements for the rebuild of the engines and gradually introduced spares and equipment from the workshop.

Fidel's enthusiasm never wavered, nor did his energy, despite the fact that the demands of their honeymoon were keeping him up half the nights.

It had taken Janet a while to understand the almost feverish nature of his rush to rebuild the wreck. During the days, travelling up and down the track to the coast, she had noted that the devastation to the forest, the grasses and all life forms was total. Nothing, absolutely nothing was showing any signs of revival. She began to realise, with a sinking admission, that the reality was that there had been a total poisoning of all life forms, as a result of the noxious atmosphere that resulted from the simultaneous eruptions of hundreds of volcanoes. It had only been their oxygen supplies that had allowed Fidel and her to live through the weeks of that hell. The planet had not been so lucky. She and Fidel had concluded that the poisonous clouds in the atmosphere had hung on over the great land masses for much longer than the remote oceanic islands of the Galapagos.

She conceded that, although Fidel had had a much simpler and shorter education than herself, he had grasped the dire situation and, looking at the long term, had recognised that they must find a food supply from the ocean, and probably move to somewhere that had escaped the total devastation of the western Cordillera.

After showering, she prepared a supper for them. The evenings were cool and pleasant at that altitude and during that time Fidel routinely cleared out the panniers of the quad bike, refuelled it and packed tools and useful pieces of equipment from the workshop, ready for the following day. After that he showered at the workshop to remove all the grease and grime of the engine overhauls, so that when he arrived back at the house he was restored to honeymoon mode.

There were usually enough moments for her to check her phone during the intervening time. It had been more of a ritual than anything else, since Fidel had changed its battery and revitalised its solar panel, but there had been no response to any of her outgoing messages, or any transmission signals from terrestrial stations.

Doubtful that it was actually working, Fidel made the point that the satellite strengths and signal receptions were all quite normal.....It was simply that there was no one there to answer.

It was well into her second week of phone checking when Amanda's text message showed up on her screen.

'We are here......

I am expecting a baby.....'

Janet stared at the screen again and again, hardly daring to believe that they had re-established contact.

She typed in a quick paragraph, describing what had happened to her in the intervening months, followed it with hearty congratulations on the pregnancy, with good luck wishes for their future, and signed it off Janet and Fidel.

Two minutes later she decided that the message was not enough, and wrote a paragraph about her love for Fidel, the hero of her life. She transmitted it just as he walked through the door. Caught unawares, she felt a bit shy about the openness of her second text, and decided to read out loud the transmission from Amanda and paraphrase her reply.

Fidel was as excited as she was. Now they knew that the two other survivors had not only worked out a way to feed themselves, but were able to communicate. This was sensational and unprecedented news and a total encouragement for him.

Fidel bombarded Janet with a list of questions to transmit in the coming days.

They did not have long to wait for a reply. It came two days later.

It simply read:

'Had twin girls yesterday.

We all seem to be ok so far.

Jason is being wonderful.

Catch up with you later

Lots of love

Jason, Amanda and girls'

Janet held up the phone for Fidel to read as soon as he got back from the workshop.

'My God!' he exclaimed. 'How far away are the Galapagos Islands?'

'Don't know...Two or three thousand miles I suppose. You don't think we have to go there do you?' she enquired concernedly.

'Look Hanet, number one, we look here at all things. If no good, number two, we go north and look to see if new life there, else we starve.'

These were truths that Janet had been avoiding. Until then, the euphoria of the honeymoon had blocked out the realities of what lay ahead of them. She looked upon Fidel as the knight in shining armour, that had plucked her from obscurity and made her a queen. Now it would seem that their only hope, in the long term, was to rebuild the steel vessel and sail off on voyages of discovery, as did the great seafarers of the sixteenth century. She shuddered at the enormity of the prospect.

It took Fidel and Janet a further six weeks to right the vessel onto an even keel and winch it down to a floating position in the saltwater creek. Fidel made light of the task of getting the many tons of steel vessel down the narrow canyon to the water. Used to moving huge and heavy pieces of equipment in narrow places at the mine, he rock bolted anchoring devices to the canyon sides and used pulleys and chains to edge it cautiously down to the water.

Janet marvelled at this feat of engineering, which she had previously considered an impossible task, and cheered each time the giant hull scraped an inch or two forwards. Once afloat and secured with ropes, their task of fitting out the bare hulk commenced in earnest. It was agreed that the engines, which both fired up reluctantly following several days of frustrating adjustments, would only be their docking and emergency power because of the limited supply of diesel.

Sail power had to be their first option but neither had any experience at all in the world of sailing. They talked endlessly in the evenings back at the house about the rig of sails, what to make them out of, what to do for a mast and boom, what to do about stays and how to navigate.

The weeks went on, with several overnight stays down at the coast. They slept together inside the boat which they had named 'Hope'. Their main concern was their dwindling supply of gasoline for the quad bike.

Janet's health was beginning to suffer also. She had lost weight and had a hard job summoning up energy for the tasks she undertook. Her skin was also taking a hammering under the relentless, coastal, desert sun. Despite this, she pushed herself to equal the effort Fidel put in. She did her best to work in the shade inside the vessel, but it was extremely hot there for the latter half of the day and she sweated profusely.

Dehydration headaches had become a regular feature and late one afternoon, while she was resting against the side of the hull between jobs, Fidel took a long look at her and then put his hammer down, wiped his brow and slid down to sit beside her.

'Hanet,' Fidel said softly, 'Here very hot for you. I can finish here. Better you stay at mine and make sails. This good work for you and we need sails.'

Until then they had never been apart and had grown incredibly dependent upon each other. Janet looked crestfallen.

'I'm okay really. I don't like to think of you here on your own. Let's talk about it at home when it's cooler and I can think straight!'

In her heart, she knew her body had reached an undefined limit. The opportunity to work back at the mine in the cool was a concession she was reluctant to make, but understood it to be the most sensible thing.

On the trip back up the track to the mine on the quad bike that evening, she hugged Fidel's back tighter than ever before.

Three days later, before going down to the coast again, Fidel called back at the house with the quad bike towing a trailer with the mobile generator lashed on to it. He explained that most of the fabrication of fittings had already been done in his workshop, and that now he needed welding gear down at the boat. He also gave her the dimensions of the mast and boom which he had already made from aluminium tubing at the mine site.

During the previous day, they had rummaged through the mine stores and located several sheets of heavy duty synthetic canvas, which were used as temporary ventilation doors underground. The sheets were of various sizes up to three metres square, and striped with high-viz yellow and black bands for safety reasons. These were to be the raw material for the sails. Janet had been shown some basic tools and equipment for cutting and sewing the sheets in the workshop.

After Fidel had gone, Janet sat down in the house and shuddered, holding her head in her hands. She wanted to cry but held the tears back. Her stomach hurt, her face, arms and shoulders were burned by the sun and her brain kept regurgitating the many issues they yet had to confront.

It was the first time in months she had been left alone and a feeling of utter hopelessness haunted her. Two themes kept recurring in her thoughts: firstly the fear that all their efforts to leave the area and find a new enclave of life somewhere would eventually fail, and secondly the thought that her own mental and physical state would collapse before they got anywhere.

She held her stomach again and wondered if she had strained it, pulling the heavy canvas sheets around the day before. Her periods had been unpredictable ever since the events which overtook the planet and her lock-in up at the observatory. The prevailing heat and tough life, going up and down to the coast, had caused them to cease altogether. That morning she had had a small bleed and considered it to be the start of a period but nothing had come of it.

Her thoughts wandered off to Fidel, who would be well on his way down to the coast by then, and she tried to imagine how he would be able to negotiate some of the avalanches and ditches while towing the trailer. She had every confidence in him but realised that he was also pushing himself to the brink.

In an effort to restore her confidence and recapture her enthusiasm, she dragged herself to her feet and poured the remainder of Fidel's breakfast yerbe mate into a mug. Before she could drink it, her stomach turned over and she rushed to the toilet and was sick. She felt terrible and at the end of her tether, and imagined that when Fidel returned he would find her dead on the floor.

While she was kneeling on the floor, with her head poised over the pan, she blearily registered the first aid box up above and the thought occurred to her that there was probably something suitable in there to prevent further nausea.

'Seasick pills, no,' she considered, then cheering up slightly, 'might be useful later on though.'

Apart from some opioid derivatives, which she considered too strong, there was nothing in the box to alleviate nausea. She was pondering what to do while she read down the list of contents. It was the first time she had been near the first aid box since she bound up Fidel's wrist with bandages, following his accident with chains.

Reflections of that first night together came flooding back: the euphoria, the passion and seduction and unleashing of primeval desires, all the wildness of falling in love...it cannot be wasted she told herself. Her body started to feel better as she dwelt on their love for each other and inevitable bonding. She started to replace the contents of the box, sparked by a resurgence of energy. Before closing the lid her eyes ran down the last few items on the contents list. The very last one seemed incongruous and caught her eye.

'Pregnancy testing kit'

After a few moments pondering, and with shaking hands, she un-packed the box again until the little package was found. Almost daring herself to do it, she read the instructions and then carried out the act.

'My God!' she cried out loud, 'What shall I do? What shall I tell Fidel?'

The sickness, the tiredness and lack of energy all made sense now, she was not dying after all she told herself....she was pregnant.

CHAPTER TWENTY SIX

Isabella, the island that is, not the first born twin, had not been the most welcoming host during the family's initial half year. Wolf Volcano had smoked heavily for three weeks and there had been minor earth tremors, which had sent moments of terror into the nursing mother and periods of intense anxiety into the Island's only male. Jason made it his business to scan the volcano's flanks on foot, in an effort to ascertain the most likely path of a future lava flow. He realised that they were in the lap of the Gods but concluded that at least their own local lava field was one of the oldest.

Mercifully the nerve-racking period of the volcano's murmuring was brief and it settled into a quiescent state again. The other major concern facing the new world's first family was that the continuous off shore breeze seemed to be causing the break-up of the mass of trees and vegetation that had amassed along their shoreline. Although this didn't threaten them directly, they had become reliant on the debris for fuel, fishing opportunities, coconuts and organic fertiliser.

The second and smaller twin, Anna Marie, named after the last female occupant of the island, had presented Amanda with numerous difficulties in getting her to feed consistently. She had to be nursed continuously. Isabella on the other hand would lunge at Amanda's available breast, drain its resources and go straight back to sleep.

Jason did his best to maintain Amanda's agricultural projects, fertilising the maize cobs by shaking the flower buds so that the pollen arrived at the awaiting tassels and also harvesting the sorghum. He even created a minute paddy field for the dozen or so rice plants that had germinated from the vac-pack. The banana ferns were looking particularly sad as a result of the prolonged drought and were in danger of dying. He laboriously carried the odd bowl of water to the nearest plants in the hope that they would survive.

In desperation to maintain their water supply, he spent several days deepening the well, until he finally reached bedrock and could go no further. A mere trickle of water ran over the old lava flow at the bottom and Jason had to make a dam there to create a pool that could be sucked up periodically by the windmill pump.

So precarious was their existence that Amanda went to work with the two tiny infants carried around in slings. She re-built the solar stills in the hope they would have enough fresh water to drink until the rains came. During this period they all drank copious quantities of coconut milk from their stockpiles of husks salvaged from the shoreline; even the children had been encouraged to suck coconut milk from beakers. Life was hard, and again their long term survival frequently became a subject of depressing conversation.

'We need luck,' Jason would say and then, looking across their humble home and catching sight of the two pairs of tiny dark brown eyes looking up at him and the smiling, beautiful, now skinny mother behind them, 'and we will have it, like we did when the rig broke up,' he said reassuringly.

'I reckon it is nine or ten months since the last rainy season so any day now things will change.'

He tried to sound confident but both he and Amanda knew

that the global climate could have altered, due to the dramatic consequences of the tsunami and air pollution. The sun beat down relentlessly on the sea, day in and day out. With all this evaporation, the moisture had to come down from the sky somewhere, they reasoned.

*

Far away, in the mountain mine site in Chile, another baby was born. He was dark and had curly hair like his father. Even at birth the similarities were striking. Fidel had used all his former experience as a father and had delivered the little boy with skill. Although Janet was almost half a day in labour and very frightened, he had lovingly attended to all her needs and encouraged her constantly.

He shouted to her to push and push once the baby's head appeared, until he was able to hold the tiny infant in his great hands. With the trailing umbilical cord he presented the boy to his mother, where he nestled between her huge breasts.

Janet and Fidel had made plenty of preparations for the new born baby. A little crib had been made and placed beside their bed. Bottles and bathing facilities had been salvaged from various derelict houses and sanitised. Fidel prided himself on the efficiencies of his midwifery duties. Janet could do no more that shake her head in wonder and adoration. Clearly he had had some practice with his former children.

During the last stages of Janet's pregnancy, she had rarely gone down to the coast with Fidel to work on the boat. Instead she had busied herself amassing suitable, non-perishable pieces of domestic equipment, tools and materials, all salvaged from the mine stores and derelict houses. These items had all been packed in wooden boxes and plastic crates ready to be transferred down to the boat.

They had decided that the voyage away from the creek would have to wait until Jose was at least three months old and Janet felt strong again. She had plenty of milk and the baby fed aggressively, so there were no immediate concerns in that direction. She had adopted a sling to carry the child while rounding up the items for the voyage.

During these months, she had contacted Amanda on several occasions. They had concluded that the poisonous air had hung around on the large land masses for months, and that was why no other signals had been picked up by either of their phones. The westerly ocean winds had mercifully cleared the atmosphere of Galapagos in a week or so, yet it would seem that the mainland must have suffered months of devastating pollution.

Janet and Fidel had commented that nothing, absolutely nothing, had sprung back to life in their area, and had assumed that the acid rain and poisonous air had killed every living thing.

'Surely areas to north, where forest come down to coast, we find more chance of life,' Fidel would frequently say, in the hope that these words would keep Janet's morale up.

CHAPTER TWENTY SEVEN

Jason came bounding back from his routine early-morning fishing trip, to find Amanda busy rearranging and securing all of their outside loose items, in the face of an unusually blustery wind.

'Change of direction of wind to onshore!' Jason shouted as a wisp of spiralling dust rattled through the sorghum patch.

'It got too difficult to fish with all the heaving of tree trunks near the wing. I hope it doesn't last too long. How much dried fish is left?'

'I thought as much,' she replied, looking at her towels flapping in the wind and nervously casting her eyes inside the house at the little twins sprawled on the handmade rug. 'A week or two's supply, more if we ration ourselves and then there are half a dozen groupers swimming down in the fish pound.'

Jason took a long look up at the sky. It was oppressively hot and had become very humid.

'It's going to rain!' he declared, as solemnly as if he had just had a prayer answered.

The noise of the tree trunks jostling amongst each other intensified as the day went by, so much so that in the afternoon they went down to the shore, carrying the twins with them, to watch the effects of the onshore wind.

As the ground swell continued to develop, it compacted the great mass of floating vegetation tighter against the shoreline and, although no waves could reach the beaches, the froth and surges brought in a host of new fragments of rotting wood and plant stems, and left them stranded higher up the island slopes than anything previously.

They checked the fish pound and decided that it would be alright for a while longer and placed a few more rocks on the barricade on the seaward side.

The wind made Amanda's now long hair dance around her shoulders, causing the twins to peer out from their slings, intrigued by the new sounds and smells. It was obvious to them all that changes were about to happen. The sun had not shone all day and the sky had darkened ominously. A squall raced across the heaving tree trunks, bringing with it the stench of rotting vegetation. The first rain drop splattered over Amanda's face, followed by another on a breast. She squealed in a mixture of delight and horror and made off directly towards the house. Jason followed briskly and, before diving into their home, he secured the windmill in the brake-on position and gathered up the dried fish.

Not long afterwards the rain lashed down in sheets. Torrents poured off the roof as never before in the previous rainy season. The babies cried as the temperature fell and they instinctively sought to cuddle up close to Amanda for protection.

Jason covered the firebox and brought a section in to the doorway to preserve the flame, then banked it well down with heavy wood so that it would take days to burn out. They could only gaze out through the deluge in the direction of their crops and hope that no streams coming off the mountain would wash them away.

'The ground is parched,' commented Jason, 'so hopefully the water will soak into the dusty soil before surface streams develop.' After an hour or so of torrential rain, his curiosity got the better of him. He put his jelly sandals on and ran out naked into the storm to examine the crops.

The rain lashed onto his bare body. He found it cool but somehow refreshing, and inwardly rejoiced in the fact that it had to happen, otherwise they would eventually perish. The wind had abated but the rain still came down in sheets. The corn and sorghum were still standing but the little rice paddy field had disappeared under a foot of water, it being deliberately planted in a depression. Jason organised some lava rocks to divert the torrents away to the side of the paddy field, so that the precious soil and vegetation compost did not wash away.

He went up to the well-head and windmill site. There was no sign of the well by then. It was in a stream path and completely filled with water so as to become a lake. Again Jason manoeuvred some rocks to divert the main torrents off to one side, in the hope the well itself did not fill with debris and require digging out again.

Satisfied he could do no more, and shivering for the first time since they were on the rig, he returned to the house and, grabbing up a towel, reported everything to the anxious

Amanda, who was propped up against the wall nursing both girls, one on each breast. Anna Marie, the more mischievous of the two twins, turned her head away from the breast and pointed to the door, waving her tiny fingers at the rain. He smiled back at her, shaking the mane of his sun-bleached hair so that droplets flew in her direction.

'It's bloody wet out there also!' he jested as she wrinkled her tiny face.

'Don't swear in front of the children!' commanded Amanda with a laugh.

'How will they know it's swearing, when there are no other kids or people to compare with?' he queried.

The reality of what he had just said lead on to a lengthy debate about bringing up children in the right way. It was a light-hearted conversation that explored all kinds of possibilities of child rearing in the absence of any surrounding markers. Eventually the rain eased off and they went out before it got dark to see how their agricultural projects had fared.

Streamlets still poured off the mountainside and deposits of fresh silt lodged behind blocking rocks, otherwise all seemed to have survived the weather onslaught.

Amanda cast her eyes up to the darkening skies of nightfall, commenting that no stars had appeared, suggesting more rain was yet to come.

It was totally dark when the next burst of rain spattered down on the roof. The temperature had fallen by several degrees, prompting Amanda to taunt Jason about the omission of a fireplace and chimney in the grand layout of their mansion. He responded by dragging the firebox further into the house with its attending smoke and odours of smouldering coconut husks.

'Thought it might help dry the washing!' he quipped, nodding aloft at the string of cloth fragments used as the twins' nappies.

She snorted and made a fake cough.

'I wonder how Janet and Fidel are getting on. Their baby is due anytime now and she said that they were going to postpone their boat trip up the coast until the new baby is a few months old. Does the rainy season stretch down to Chile?'

'How do you expect a 'failed architect' to answer such a complicated question? I only know that the Atacama Desert is supposed to be the driest spot on the planet, so therefore the answer should definitely be, *No*.'

Amanda snorted again, in a vote of no confidence in Jason's geographical knowledge. Putting the babies down on to the floor she commented, 'When I went to Lima there were loads of trees and forests down to the shore line, so they must get plenty of rain there at least. That's why Janet and Fidel are planning to travel North up the coast after the baby is born.'

'Have you heard from her lately?'

'No, but when the sun comes back out I'll charge up the phone and try to contact her again. She is busy packing all the stores she can put together at the moment, from the mine shop and derelict homes. They plan to take as much as they can on their voyage, and Fidel is going to empty the mine workshop of all the tools and equipment that he can possibly get down to their boat.'

'He sounds like a sensible chap,' commented Jason. 'The single biggest obstacle to many of my projects is lack of tools, and since the saw broke a couple of months back even the most elementary tasks have become difficult.'

An awkward silence followed while Amanda considered what to say to break his depression.

It was Isabella who came to the rescue. She, like her sister, had been lying on her back on the canvas rug while their parents talked and as normal had been kicking her little legs frantically in the air. In the process, the twin had rolled onto her side for the first time and then onto her stomach, and instinctively raised herself to her knees.

This action provoked cheers from Amanda and Jason and broke the impasse. Isabella, amazed at her own achievement, gurgled and rocked to and fro on her knees, while little Anna Marie did her best to copy.

Within days the two babies were crawling all over the canvas rug and Amanda had had to erect barricades to stop them leaving the soft surface. The additional exertion caused little Anna Marie to feed ferociously in an effort to rapidly catch up with her sister. Coconut milk, supplemented by breast milk and sorghum porridge, became their establish diet. They both seemed to be growing up fit and healthy, much to the relief of the parents.

Jason dwelt on the information relayed to him by Amanda regarding Fidel and his equipment, and his frustration intensified each time his daily tasks were thwarted or delayed by lack of tools. The torrents of rain returned on a daily basis, and there were numerous occasions when Jason's fire axe from the cabin was a hopeless substitute for a simple shovel, when it came to making levees and diversions for the streams pouring off the mountainside.

After about ten days, the sun spluttered through racing clouds long enough for Amanda to charge the solar panel on the phone.

 She messaged Janet and got an almost immediate response.

Had baby boy two weeks ago.

 Jose.

Doing fine.

Voyage preparation nearly complete.

Will wait a few weeks.

How are you both and the twins?

Love Janet and Fidel.

Amanda gave a cheer and read it out loud to the excited Jason who also cheered and shouted out, raising his fist into the air.

'Now there are seven of us!'

She laughed.

'You had better be careful as those numbers could easily go up if my periods start again. Breast feeding is only a temporary reprieve for your amorous advances and I can't imagine increasing the burden of the family we have already!'

'Hmm,' he replied, considering the consequences of lack of contraceptives, then changed the subject.

'Ask Janet if there have been any changes in their knowledge of other survivors or vegetation recovery. I noticed today all kinds of stuff greening up the cavities and ditches which had shown a brief flurry of life after the previous rains. The planet seems to be bouncing back. Surely there must be life elsewhere.'

Amanda tapped in a phone message for a minute or two, congratulating them on the arrival of Jose, then adding Jason's question before transmitting.

While the phone was kept open awaiting a reply, they both marvelled that the tiny satellites orbiting the Earth continued functioning in their normal way, despite what had happened at ground level.

Janet replied.

Ground water still too acid to support life here and have no clues of any other survivors. Hope for better news up the coast.

Janet

Jason heaved a great sigh of resignation. Glimmers of hope of other pockets of civilisation were fading. Finally he spoke out.

'They have the tools and we have the life. Neither one can work without the other,' he sighed, 'and,' he paused, 'unless they navigate further up the coast and find life we are all basically knackered.'

'I can at least remember something of my oceanography,' chirped Amanda cheerfully.

'The sea current sweeps up the coast from the tip of South America to about latitude four degrees south, and then follows the equator to way past the Galapagos, so their voyage could theoretically bring them close to us. If they have enough sail and engine power to slice their way across the equatorial current they could definitely make it here.'

'Hmm ...and then what?' Jason said thoughtfully.

'With tools and equipment we could civilise our lives to the point where we are no longer clinging to survival instincts, to just stay alive,' she said excitedly.

'You're right. That Fidel sounds like a brilliant technical guy. I think I could get along fine with him.'

'And we have the children in common,' interrupted Amanda. 'We now have basic crops established and with more help we could expand and make a little farm where there is more soil.'

'I was thinking just that,' Jason continued. 'When I was looking round the mountain to select an area less vulnerable to lava flows, I identified a large shallow sloping area four or five miles from here, that could well be a future agriculture area. There was a silty soil there which had accumulated during the last rainy season. If I have to build another house, I will,' he jested.

'Your adventure into the architectural world might even incorporate a hearth and chimney?' She teased.

He groaned and stoked up the firebox so that a belch of smoke made them both cough.

The rain started again and they turned the phone off.

CHAPTER TWENTY EIGHT

'Hanet,' remarked Fidel, as he peeled off his boiler suit in the doorway and cast a loving smile at sleeping Jose in his crib, 'Today I checked all fuel at mine site.'

Janet looked up at him nervously, expecting bad news.

'We have enough gasoline for maybe dozen trips to coast with quad bike. I must keep half for generator.'

'What about getting all of the kit down that we have packaged up?' She enquired panic stricken.

'Three of old mine trucks still use diesel and I think still good. God willing they take all heavy things to coast but not possible to come back again.'

'How are you going to do that with only one driver?' She asked hastily, half knowing what was coming next.

'Don't worry. I teach you to drive here at mine site until you good. Where track is bad, I drive trucks. You not worry. Quad bike too hard to teach you. It very old and have strange things with it, which only I know.'

'My God', she shuddered, realising that the moment of reality was approaching and it would overtake her cocooned existence as mother in their comfortable house. She knew there was no alternative, unless she was prepared to stay there and starve. In any case, she had complete confidence in Fidel to manage the exodus from the mine site.

Pondering the challenge of driving one of those enormous mine tipper trucks completely occupied her thoughts in the coming days. She had only ever driven a small electric car before and the very idea of climbing up six steps to just get in the cab was an awesome conception.

Five days after Fidel had introduced the subject, he arrived with a roar outside the house with a battered green and yellow ex–army lorry with high sides, and declared it to be the smallest and easiest to drive. He beckoned her round to the side door, saying she should bring young Jose with her in a travelling basket.

Putting on a brave face, she handed up the baby and basket to Fidel and then clambered up three steps, before slumping down nervously beside him with the baby between them.

The following three hours were hours Janet wished to forget forever. After a short test drive around the mine site with Fidel at the wheel, they changed seats. Mercifully she could reach the pedals on the floor but, having only driven cars with automatic gearboxes, she crashed the gears most of the time, stalled the engine on numerous occasions and used the wrong gears and the wrong speeds.

To make matters worse Jose wailed continuously above the roar of the un-silenced engine.

Fidel remained calm throughout and, when not sorting out Janet's mistakes, he unconcernedly held the baby as if they were only out on a family picnic. Janet's frustration turned into flares of anger and she started to drive the truck quite confidently amid her continuous string of profanities. Fidel did his best to conceal his smiles and just let her get on with it.

Finally she was directed to take the truck back to the house, which she did, bringing it to a halt in a swirl of dust. Fidel got down with the baby and went round to help her shaking body down the steps.

'Jesus wept!' she spluttered, wiping the grime of dust off her face and taking possession of the baby, who was now quietly sucking his thumb and looking thirsty.

'You now medium sized truck driver!' he laughed. 'Tomorrow I bring you big truck to play with!'

'You can't do that!'

'Why not? You qualified now!'

'Holy shit,' she muttered to herself, with an adrenaline flush and somewhat restored confidence. 'I'm going in to feed Jose and will talk about trucks at supper time.'

Fidel drove the vehicle away laughing, and said out loud, 'I know she make it!' Shaking a fist in the air, he went on to prepare the bigger tipper truck for the following day.

That night their love making was as passionate as ever. Janet felt that the truck driving episode had once again restored the balance in their joint venture, and the challenge to survive in a new life somewhere else. She moaned under his great hairy chest and clenched him with her thighs, refusing to let his erection go until he had a second orgasm while her own climax continued.

*

In a scene reminiscent of other historic migrations, the steel vessel *Hope* nestled quietly at the side of the creek, while three cargo trucks stood by, waiting to unload.

The preparations had been long and arduous as, piece by piece, the equipment and boxes had been loaded at the mine site, along with tanks of diesel fuel, gas bottles and cans of gasoline. The journey of the convoy down from the mine had taken two days, with an overnight sleep at the side of the track. Fidel had taken charge of each vehicle where skill and experience had been needed to negotiate ditches and avalanche debris. The ultimate challenge had been to get the convoy down the scree from the truncated track end.

Fidel had each truck in turn wired to a rock anchorage on the last of the track and had winched it slowly down the scree in a controlled decent, until it had enough traction to continue on its own. Janet had stood by and marvelled at this engineering skill, as she had done when Fidel winched the boat down the canyon to its floating berth.

When the third truck was safely down, Fidel clambered up the scree for the last time and took the baby and Janet down on the quad bike. From there she drove each vehicle down to the creek side after which Fidel ferried her back to the next vehicle with the quad bike.

Young Jose was not yet two months old and required frequent breast milk but mercifully accommodated the move by sleeping heavily and unattended between feeds.

Loading the boat took them ages. Boxes were slid down planks to the edge of the water where a hand operated derrick on the boat swung them, one by one, into a position where they could be lowered into the hold of the *Hope*. Fidel had rigged a pulley system from the top of the mast, with enough mechanical advantage that even heavy equipment could be hoisted and lowered by Janet who took charge of that side of the operation.

After some time Fidel became concerned about the displacement of the boat, and whether or not it would bottom out before the loading was complete. He strolled down the creek to see if deeper water was available close enough to the shore to load with the derrick. He concluded that there was no better place than the position they had. It depressed him and he had to confess that boats were outside his comfort zone. This made Janet anxious and she sought to find out how much more weight still remained to be loaded.

'Five or six tons,' was the reply. 'Space no problem, only weight here in creek. All heavy stuff now loaded to keep stability good.'

'What's left?'

'House and food stuff and fuel tanks. Fuel tanks go on deck.'

'Let's just carry on loading and see what happens,' Janet suggested with a shrug of the shoulders.

Fidel reluctantly agreed and by nightfall all three trucks were emptied of their goods and stood like the pyramids of Giza against the setting sun, stark reminders of their previous life.

Hope was firmly aground but expected to float at high tide.

High tide came and went. There had been less than a metre of tide anyway and it was agreed that the following morning would be the best time to assess their position, so uneasily they pulled out the bed sheet and settled into their new home.

It was hot and smelt vaguely of fuel. Janet climbed up on the deck to feed Jose in the middle of the night while an exhausted Fidel snored deeply below.

The air was cooler and fresher and, although they were still marooned in the creek, Janet experienced a surge of hope. She felt sure Fidel would find a solution once he had slept and regained his energy.

She looked into the night sky while Jose suckled and spotted two and then a third satellite slowly crossing the sky and uttered a prayer for their continued operation. Had the half-moon been less bright, she considered she would have had more sightings.

The morning high tide came and went and they remained hard aground. Fidel, after a long period of consideration, came up with a plan. They would tether the fuel drums and push them over the side where they would float and lessen the weight by a couple of tons at least. They could then proceed down the creek towing them into deeper water, before hoisting the drums back on board.

The plan was put into action, though Janet remained sceptical that they would ever be able to board them again. *Hope* rose in the water by an inch or two and at high tide she could be felt bouncing on the bottom, but not floating.

Fidel became depressed and was pondering what else they could afford to jettison when Janet suddenly thought of a solution.

'Last night I was up on deck feeding Jose when I noticed the moon was just half.'

'So....What that mean?' enquired Fidel, gazing at her half expecting some mystical solution to their problem.

'Well, when the moon is half there is a neap tide and when it is full or just a slither there is a spring tide.'

'Hmm,' he said 'I forget you work with astronomers,' and then added innocently, 'but how that help us?'

'When the moon becomes full again, the tide rise and fall will be much greater and we will float, I think.'

'Really!' he exclaimed. 'I not know about tides. We don't have them in mines! So, full moon in four days.'

Five days later, they were gently chugging down the creek towing the barrels behind them, though Fidel had reluctantly decided the quad bike would have to stay ashore. It took them two more hours to winch the fuel drums back on board and chock them down so they were totally safe from rolling round.

Another half mile and they could feel the first gentle motion of the not too distant open sea and, with darkness approaching, they anchored and sat on deck holding hands, each preoccupied with their own thoughts, both scared in their own way of the approaching unknown.

*

For three days, Janet was seasick and miserable. The roll of the Pacific Ocean was on their beam all the time, as they clawed their way northwards. To make matters worse, her phone satellite images of the coastal map barely showed any changes in their position. She began to be aware of the immense distances involved.

Fidel tried to keep her spirits up and, after moving various boxes around in the hold, found the one which held Janet's first aid kit and the seasick pills.

She reluctantly agreed to take them for a couple of days, in an effort to eat something and be able to feed Jose properly. Shortly afterwards she was tugging on ropes and commanding Fidel to prepare this and that food, not to mention tidying up the deck area. He laughed and actually started to enjoy life on board.

While searching for the seasick pills, he had come across the fishing gear that he and his brother used to use when he came down to visit him on the coast. Although they had not seen any signs of fish or birds, he thought they had nothing to lose by having a line behind. He selected what he remembered to be his favourite lure and let it trail fifty meters astern.

The action helped Janet's recovery greatly and took her mind off the never ending gentle roll of the vessel. All through the daylight hours, the spectacular high-viz sails she had sewn kept the boat on a steady reach without much attention. Not wishing to break anything, they kept the mainsail tightly reefed so it was only at half capacity. Sometimes the phone image told them they were doing five knots.

The wind dropped to nothing during the night and the *Hope* drifted on, maintaining the same course at two knots on the ocean current. During this time they were able to sleep and only periodically needed to check their position on the phone.

Five days into their voyage, and four hundred miles up the coast, the sea conditions started to change. There was noticeably more current and choppy swirls in the surface of the sea and also the odd scudding cloud in the sky, the first they had seen for months.

They were just beginning to become excited about the changes when a fish took Fidel's line. He leapt onto his rod and arrested the clutch on the reel. Janet unceremoniously dumped poor Jose, who was in the middle of a feed, into his secure basket in a pound and ran to Fidel's side. He was shrieking in animated tones as a dolphin fish jumped completely clear of the water at the end of the line. He yelled at Janet to slacken off the mainsheet in order to slow the boat down, so he could play the fish in to the stern over the following ten minutes.

Finally they yanked it aboard where it flapped violently. Its brilliant green, slim body, with gold and vividly blue spots, mesmerised them for a while. It was the first life form they had seen for a year. The impact on them was one of incredulity. It meant the sea had not died, or at least was beginning to recover on this side of the Pacific. The dolphin fish was a predator and, as Fidel reasoned as he de-hooked it and cast the lure back overboard, there must also be smaller fish for it to feed on.

All along their passage northwards they had hugged the coast, keeping within a mile of the shore in the hope they would spot some form of life or vegetation. The Andes were always a stark backdrop behind the narrow coastal strip. As at their starting point, a totally visible line defined the scour of the tsunami. Nothing green showed above or below that line, so the presence of a fish in the sea became an incredible surprise and a massive boost to their morale.

'Watch line,' Fidel shouted to Janet enthusiastically, as if another fish was imminent. 'I fetch stove.'

'Stove?' she repeated, 'What stove?'

Until then they had only eaten dried and cold, tinned rations. Cooking had never been a consideration with all the other new tasks to focus on, and in any case the roll of the boat and Janet's seasickness made it seem undesirable.

Minutes later, Fidel's curly, dark hair appeared above the combing of the hatchway.

'More fish?' he demanded hopefully.

'One a year is your ration!' she replied with a laugh and then, regarding the sack he plonked on the deck, 'What the hell's that?'

'That is solar power stove,' he announced proudly, as he unfolded an array of solar panels that stretched out for a meter on both sides of a little hot plate.

'I use with brother family on picnics. Work good in plenty sun.'

During the next few minutes, he occupied himself lashing the little stove down in a sheltered position inside a pound, where it benefited from being out of the wind and getting the most out of the early morning sun. While Janet restored the grizzling Jose to his interrupted feed, Fidel cleaned and sliced up their new trophy, before diving down below to find garlic and cooking oil.

Their situation became more intense as the day progressed. The sea became more restless as the coastline swung out in a more north-westerly direction. They had to tighten in the sails as the wind came more on their bow. *Hope* moved along faster and with less rolling motion but they had to be careful not to get any closer to the coast. Fidel became preoccupied with how they would manage the night-time sailing, and avoid the possibility of being shipwrecked while sleeping, and told Janet that he would have to stay up all night to keep watch.

She expected as much but did not like the idea of being responsible for everything during the day while he slept. By mid-afternoon the squally wind was parallel to the coast which left them with two options: one was to beat out into the open ocean, and the other was to get closer to the shore and either anchor or motor.

Janet scanned her phone's GPS map of the shoreline, and eventually directed Fidel's attention to a feature which resembled a peninsula jutting out a mile or so, that would offer shelter from the north-west wind. Maybe they could anchor there. This became their plan.

When they got within sight of the peninsula against its backdrop of massive mountains, Fidel became nervous about possible rocks running out from the near shore, so he went below and after some difficulty started one of the engines and then came up and dropped the sails.

He was sweating profusely and cursing about the lack of cooperation of the engine which had taken him ages to start. He muttered something about dirty fuel and blocked filters which went over Janet's head. However on sighting the calm water ahead he cheered up immensely and grinned at her. She smiled back, obviously relieved about the lessening of motion and pleased with her achievements with the phone.

'How close in can we get?' she enquired. 'I know that there is very little continental shelf and that deep water exists almost to the coast.' She said it with such authority that Fidel allowed her to take the helm while he went up into the bow area.

Not wishing to waste time trying to get an anchorage in deep water, Fidel rigged up a sounding line, as did the ships of olden days, and periodically tested the depth. They had reached a position no more than a few hundred meters from the rugged shore before he even touched bottom with his line. They then crept in a little more, until the depth was about forty meters, and dropped the anchor.

It was so peaceful and calm in the lee of the mountains, it was possible to stop the engine and relax for the first time. The solar stove had enough heat to sear the sliced up dolphin fish on both sides with its garlic dressing, so they ate hungrily, tossing the skin and bones over the side with the abandonment of a conventional family boat picnic. Even the warm yerbe mate seemed luxurious after days of bottled water.

By late afternoon, the sun cast long shadows along the shoreline, making it possible to detect un-natural features, and it was Fidel who first spotted what appeared to be piles of huge angular shaped rocks, each one the size of a family car. They were incongruous beside the beaches of randomly piled banks of pebbles and gravel.

'There was port here,' he said gravely. 'Big rocks before was breakwater, too heavy for tsunami to move.'

'Totally destroyed!' gasped Janet, as she scanned the hinterland and the mountainous area above the tsunami line.

It was no more than they expected, and the greyness of the distant vegetation higher up confirmed their belief that the poisonous air had caused the same catastrophic consequences here, as it had done near the mine site.

Depressing as it was, Janet still held out hope that, as they moved north into the hitherto wetter regions where forests came down to the coast, there would be pockets of resurgent life, like Amanda had reported from the Galapagos Islands.

They slept well that night, spread out on a mattress on deck in the fresh air under the stars and the lunar half disc. They made love as if it were their honeymoon and enjoyed the gurgles of Jose close by in his basket.

Fidel proposed that, on the following day, they should go to seaward on the other tack for at least a day until they were well clear of the coast, adding that they would not expect to find anything but devastation along the shore for many days, and at least if they were well out to sea, they would not have to worry about being shipwrecked.

'Then what?' enquired Janet with a hint of alarm in her voice.

'Then we turn in to coast again. Find land two hundred mile more north and hope we find life there. It rainy season. Maybe find good harbour and go search for life on land.'

She let out a great sigh, while contemplating sailing out into the open ocean, before replying reluctantly. She began to wish she was still back at the mine site.

'Yes. We had better do that. Let's try to make it three hundred miles further up the coast. I cannot see any point in exploring the nothingness close by here.'

They left soon after sunrise. Janet was anxious to charge the solar panel on the phone so she could plot their course. She was also concerned that, during their entire voyage, Amanda had not acknowledged any of her messages. When the phone panel illuminated she typed in a brief note and ended it by giving their position.

After she transmitted it, the thought occurred to her that not just Amanda but the rest of the world should know of their whereabouts, so she broadcast the message on the general airways. It seemed silly immediately afterwards so she shrugged her shoulders and went back to feeding Jose.

*

'I can't believe all this rain. It's barely stopped for over a week now. There's a lake formed at the bottom of the shallow slope I mentioned to you last week, the place I said we should make a farm.'

Jason shivered as he stood in the doorway, while coaxing the fire box to produce some more heat. A shower of sparks cascaded into the air and fell harmlessly back onto the floor.

'At least your agricultural projects seem to be enjoying their bath, though I've given up hope of ever seeing the rice again. It's under several inches of water most of the time.'

'It's the way of rice,' Amanda said cheerily. 'I expect it will be fine.' She tossed him a towel. 'You could try putting on some clothes next time you go out on your round of inspections!' she teased, while assessing his gleaming muscular torso. 'No don't do that,' she quipped as an afterthought. 'There's no drying space for clothes in here. You just have to run round naked as you normally do,' then rising to her feet, 'and I will be forced to warm you up when you come in.'

The last sentence descended into a guttural slur as she pulled her breasts tightly against his back and slipped her hands round his waist and down over his stomach.

They snuggled down together on the mattress briefly while the twins slept. Jason finally rolled over on to his back and spoke in a serious tone.

'You know, I think there's a patch of open water further down the coast. Some rafts of trees are breaking up and drifting seaward because of the new wind direction. There's white water touching the rocks down there, it appears. As soon as the rain clears, I'll make an excursion to see what's happening.'

They had not experienced the open sea with an onshore wind, since being deposited on the beach over a year and a half earlier. The raft of vegetation had cushioned all the effects of the ocean, besides providing wood and nutrients for their use. A change in the status quo would present them with certain difficulties for fuel and fertiliser, but with other opportunities for fishing.

'The onshore wind only lasted for the rainy season last year,' responded Amanda, detecting the seriousness of his statement. 'We've had a couple of breaks in the weather now, so maybe the worst of the wind and rain is over.'

Her last words were lost as another downpour crashed onto the roof and sprayed into the doorway.

Two days later, they had three or four hours of sunshine and the solar panel of Anna-Maria's phone charged up, so that later it responded reluctantly to the pickled thumbprint.

Down came a dozen or more of Janet's text messages. The final one read:-

'We finally arrived at what was Lima according to my sat map. Found sheltered anchorage and Fidel swam ashore to check for any signs of life. When he came back he reported no sign of the city, only a few slabs of concrete, no forests, just desolation. Totally depressing. Tomorrow we head north to Ecuador.

Our total love and hope goes out to you

Janet, Fidel and Jose.'

Amanda read out the string of texts to Jason concerning their journey from Chile and then emotionally spluttered out the last communication.

'They're tough people Jason, and pioneers in their own right, but from what they've seen it seems the continent is wrecked. I guess they have enough food and water to reach here if they can make the journey. What do you think?'

'They have the tools and equipment and we have live plants and fish. It makes complete sense to encourage them to make the journey. In fact it is the only way we can progress out of what will become our Stone Age.'

She texted Janet back.

'Please try to make it here if you find nothing in Ecuador. We all need each other to survive. We have had nearly 3 weeks rain here and the mountainside is starting to show green. We are optimistic.

Please try to get here

Love

Jason, Amanda and twins.'

CHAPTER TWENTY NINE

Janet cheered and showed Fidel the message.

'They finally got my messages. I think they must have had no sun to charge the phone. What shall I say?'

'Tell them one fish only in three weeks. Now we go Guayaquil. Maybe five hundred mile more. If no find food, we go to you.'

'OK, and the wind is on our beam now so we should reach Guayaquil in about a week.'

She transmitted a short message and asked which island they considered they were on.

Shortly afterwards they up-anchored and headed out to sea. The conditions there had become choppy and restless, with brief, squally showers that caused them to shelter behind deck pounds. Jose grizzled, not being accustomed to splashes of rain on his face. As darkness fell, they ploughed on regardless, into the darkness northwards and away from the coast.

That night seemed endless. They pitched and rolled with the sails creaking incessantly, even with a new reef, bringing the mainsail down to about a third of its size. The tiny slit of the new moon vanished soon after sunset and the stars frequently disappeared behind scudding clouds.

Fidel kept watch all night and Janet intermittently dozed, wedged into a deck pound with tiny Jose. This was their worst night of the voyage. The following morning was no better and they considered abandoning the plan to go directly to

Guayaquil, and instead seek shelter and await better weather.

Janet traced the coastal map on her phone in detail and could offer no better alternative than to keep going. The wind was too much onshore to allow them a close passage, so for safety's sake their best plan was to head out and northwards. Fidel tried to cat-nap during the daylight hours while Janet kept the *Hope* on a steady, though bumpy, course through the choppy seas that occasionally threw a cloud of spray over the deck.

They only managed to eat a tin of ham and some dried fruit during the whole day. In the following hours of darkness the wind abated a little and they both alternately cat-napped. By morning, only a heavy swell persisted, and according to Fidel it looked a bit fishy and so he resumed his trailing of a fishing line.

Janet checked their position on the phone and was astounded to find they were now a hundred miles off-shore. After checking their heading, it was agreed that they had encountered the equatorial current which ran directly westwards away from the continent. To reach Guayaquil they could run before the wind in a north easterly direction.

They immediately enjoyed a more comfortable motion and to make matters even better Fidel caught another dolphin fish.

Once they had hauled it on board and congratulated themselves, Fidel set about preparing it to eat. He had barely put a knife to it before he paused and turned to Janet while tapping the side of the fish.

She knew there was something wrong.

'It's emaciated!' she declared. 'I thought it was thin and it had no energy to flap like the other one. Is it sick or what?'

'It starving,' he said as he slit the underside open then added, 'Belly empty. No small fish for eating.'

'You know what I think?' she said after a pause. 'The big rivers that come down off the Andes are in flood because of the rainy season and are bringing down acid water which is polluting the near-shore and driving the small fish away.'

'Maybe you right,' he said soberly. 'Dolphin fish we catched off Chile okay because no rainy season and no rivers.'

They were silent for a while as he threw the lure back over the side.

She checked her phone. No messages from Galapagos. She downloaded the GPS map of the coastline again and checked their position and speed.

'You know we're barely making three knots headway,' she stated depressingly. 'It's the strong current against us that is slowing our progress.'

In the next couple of minutes two things happened simultaneously. A sudden puff of wind and following squall sent them surfing ahead at a greatly increased speed and a message came through on the screen of the phone from Amanda.

'Our location is at the foot of the Wolf volcano so the island

is Isabella and we are on the east side.

Love Amanda Jason and twins'

Janet scrolled across the screen and located the Galapagos Islands.

CHAPTER THIRTY

'If we make it to Guayaquil and find nothing, it's more or less a straight westerly course to the Galapagos. It'll be against the wind but we'll have the current behind us.' Then the wind drowned out their conversation.

The squall increased in ferocity and the *Hope* lifted on each swell and plunged forwards at a terrifying speed. Janet became frightened having never experienced such massive waves. Their twenty meter craft seemed suddenly tiny and insignificant in the great open ocean. Jose sensed his mother's alarm and wailed incessantly. Fidel tried to remain calm while grasping the tiller with his iron grip. Then the rain came. It cut across the vessel in white sheets soaking every part of the deck and those on board.

Fidel wiped his eyes many times trying to maintain the course and not make a catastrophic jibe which would put the *Hope* broadside to the cresting waves.

As quickly as it came the squall passed on ahead of them. The wind dropped to an eerie calm as the rain stopped. They looked at each other's bedraggled appearance while the sails flapped aimlessly and the *Hope* rolled without any propulsion to move it forwards.

A few minutes later the westerly breeze kicked in again and they regained their course at four knots.

This same sequence of events plagued their progress for over a week and by the time they expected to sight the coast, just south of Guayaquil, they were both exhausted. Their temporary plastic sheet shelter, erected to keep them dry, had blown down several times, and they had only slept intermittently while being subjected to frequent drenching from the passing squalls. In the daytime it had become hot and humid, yet there had only been enough continuous sun to barely recharge the phone. This was a continuous worry to them, as they had come to rely on it for their daily position.

On the tenth day since leaving the shelter of the Lima inlet, Janet stated confidently that the great bay of Guayaquil lay ahead of them and within that bay were islands which would provide a wind- free safe anchorage.

They had expected to see the backdrop of the Andes first, but nothing could be spotted in the fading light. Janet became alarmed, suggesting her phone might have been giving out false information. She could not recheck their position as the charge in the phone had died and, with less than the predicted ten miles to the coast, it could be dangerous to move in closer during the night.

Wearily they set a more northerly course parallel to the coast and hunkered down for the night. Janet gave Jose a long feed while Fidel did his best to put together another meal of tinned ham and dried fruit. The northerly course across wind and current caused them to roll so violently that Fidel decided that a return to their former north easterly tack was less hazardous. He decided to stay up all night and listen and watch out for the coast. He argued that the on-shore wind would at least provide surf and white water enough to warn him of any shallows ahead.

At Janet's insistence, he did go below and start an engine

briefly, to be sure they could motor back out of trouble should they encounter shallow water. The night wore on and by daylight they were still unable to sight land.

Janet suggested that they must by then be deep in the Bay of Guayaquil. Knowing that at least two mighty rivers flowed into that bay, it was unlikely that mountains would be close at hand, and more than likely the coastline was low with flood plains. She wished she had paid more attention to her geography lessons.

Finally the sun came up and as Fidel peered into the distance he made a quick comment.

'Water is really dirty. I think you are right about rivers coming into the sea in this place.'

'I should be able to get a map soon, if the sun keeps shining,' she said after a pause, while holding the phone aloft.

Fidel tied a bucket on a piece of rope and pointed the *Hope* downwind in an easterly direction with the sails slackened right out on the beam. As he hoisted a bucket of water aboard, Janet let out a cry while examining her phone.

'We are right here!' she cheered, 'Right in the middle of Guayaquil Bay. If we go a bit more north again, we should see an island about five miles ahead. We can shelter behind it out of the wind! That would be heaven!'

'You are fantastic!' declared Fidel tightening the sail in again with renewed energy and regained enthusiasm, while peering into the hazy sunrise ahead on their original course, 'You are right. I can see land on the horizon. That must be it', he exclaimed.

'The bucket of water? What's that for?' she asked curiously.
'Ah,' he replied, 'I want to taste. Water from big rivers is not salty, I think.'

She laughed. 'I think we have had enough water to drink over the last week!'

Fidel put the bucket to his lips and imbibed a full mouthful in order to prove his point. She looked on in wonder at the simplicity of this navigational act. Soon her face turned to horror as Fidel gagged, spewed out the water and coughed furiously for a few seconds.

After regaining his composure and wiping off his streaming eyes, he offered her the bucket, indicating she should just sniff the water.

She did so and wrinkled up her nose.

'Sulphur!' She exclaimed. 'The water is acidic.'

*

Jason returned to the house late the next afternoon, having completed his hike down the Island to inspect the white water.

'Big changes down there,' he announced. 'The mass of dead trees and branches has broken up. Some have been cast up high on the shore while the rest have edged their way southwards, embedding themselves in the next endless mass of floating vegetation.'

'You're saying the shoreline is free? Are there any creeks or sheltered gullies that would provide access to the open water?'

It was obvious that she had been concealing her private thoughts on the supplies of fish. They had almost gone over the previous three weeks, and with them their sustainable future.

'The open stretch of water must be about two miles and there's one deep gully, like a creek, with its head jammed full of debris that could provide a way out. At the moment a heavy swell is thundering in, making it look quite hostile, but if the wind drops'......his words were cut off by an interruption from Amanda, who had a well-rehearsed statement which she could not wait to get out.

'I checked my rubber dingy today.'

'I'd almost forgotten about that. It's over a year since we pulled it high above the water line. Is it still okay?' he asked nervously.

'Yes. Full of rain water but still inflated. I told you it was a good one,' she announced confidently.

'The fact still remains that we can't use it unless there is access to open water close by', he concluded wearily.

'I know. I've considered that. The foreshore is too jammed up with trees to attempt floating it down to your patch of open water, but we could make up some sort of skids or mount it on a sledge and we could harness ourselves up like huskies and pull it down there.'

He gave her an incredulous look before realising she was serious.

'We need fish Jason. I'll make you a long rope so that you are always tethered to the shore. Then if the wind blows offshore again, you're not in danger of drifting away from us. The fishing might be good with a change of site.'

The last sentence engaged Jason completely, making him forget all the immediate obstacles of getting the dingy there and the present ugly onshore wind.

'Hmm,' he nodded thoughtfully. 'This gully continues inland for quite a way and ends up in the flat area I suggested could be a future agricultural site for us. There's a freshwater lake there now after all this rain. I suppose it'll disappear once the rainy season passes.'

'Sounds very interesting to me,' she declared excitedly. 'I want to see all this myself. I'll prepare the twins for a long hike tomorrow and we'll backpack one each.'

He stared at her and reminded himself that this was the woman he loved, and that nothing limited her enthusiasm and desire to improve their lives together.

The following morning had an air of spring. The skies had cleared during the night and, with the cooling temperature, dew had formed. It sparkled in the early rays of the sun. Jason was returning from a survey of the beach, where he had been monitoring the swell each day, when something unusual caught his eye. In a crevice, and lit up by fine droplets of dew, was a spider's web.

He got down to his knees for a closer inspection and spotted the spider scuttling away into a hole. He hurried back to the house to tell Amanda, counting on his fingers as he went. The spider was now number six in the island's life forms and he wondered if the web would trap a fly sooner or later.

Later as they meandered through the lava flows, with the twins in backpacks made from the canvas umbrella material, they encountered more little spider's webs and several little green lizards. Gullies were sprouting shoots of several different species of plants. At last, after the severe rain storms, the eco system was emerging from eighteen months of hibernation.

'This is like witnessing the miracle of creation,' Amanda commented, as she pointed out new things to the arm-waving twins.

By mid-morning, they had arrived at the fresh water lake. It was as Jason had described, a depression lying at the foot of soft, silty slopes. Much to her amusement, they had left their foot-print tracks behind them.

Jason jested, 'There's something wrong. We are wearing sandals. When Leaky uncovered the first hominid footprints in the volcanic ash of the Rift Valley, they were bare feet!'

'True,' she said and spontaneously kicked off her sandals and giggled with some satisfaction, as she squelched on through the soft silt towards the lake, leaving behind a distinctly hominid set of footprints.

Jason chose to trail behind and take in the full spectacle of Amanda's utter nakedness. The simple act of taking off her sandals was somehow symbolic of the purity and naturalness of her near perfect body. She turned round to face him, making sure he was following and in so doing rested on one leg, thrusting her hips forward to counterbalance the weight of the baby on her back. The sun caught the sparkles of perspiration on her thighs and belly and highlighted her massive black pubic mound.

She noted the effect this was having on Jason's genitals and sensed where these images were taking them, so in a flirtatious manner she turned and scampered off at high speed to the lake edge, quickly sniffing and tasting the water before removing her backpack. She hoisted out an excited Isabella and waded off into the water with her under an arm. The other half of the family were soon alongside, kicking and splashing each other in a truly euphoric manner.

'This is it!' declared Amanda. 'The perfect location for our farm. Even when the lake dries up, there should be plenty of ground water for the crops and at the foot of the slope, where there's still enough lava rock available, we can build a house.' She was elated and bubbling with enthusiasm.

'The creek down there,' he pointed, 'is certainly the best site I've seen for an anchorage. The wind has gone today and I think when it returns in a day or two it will be the normal offshore direction. We can plan our move, but let's first look at the creek and then survey the mountain flank together, before we decide on a suitable house building location.'

They sauntered off down to the creek side, where the waves were still funnelling up from the open sea and lifting the rafts of floating debris. The ocean had removed the silt and ash in this area, exposing the old lava flows. The black rocks were warm, smooth and comforting, as they sat and ate a picnic of sourdough biscuits and smoked fish, washed down by the ubiquitous coconut milk. Amanda fed the two girls, both of whom enthusiastically suckled following their vigorous exploits in the lake.

By the time they arrived back at their house, the sun was going down quickly and Amanda had a compelling desire to relate the day's events to Janet, while the phone was charged up.

After she had gone through the routine with the thumb print, she eventually got a clear screen and then found a long message from Janet.

'Dear Amanda, Jason and twins.

We have just undergone the most horrible part of our journey. It took ten days to get from what was Lima to what was Guayaquil. We had bad weather and squalls that nearly rolled the boat over and as we drew near to an island in Guayaquil Bay to take shelter we went aground on a sand bar. It took nearly six hours with both engines going astern to chew our way off again and all the time the rain lashed down in sheets.

Jose is crying a lot and I hardly have the energy to feed him but the most depressing thing is the water. It stinks of sulphur and is very acidic. Nothing can live in such conditions. We have abandoned the idea of finding life here. As I write this message we are slowly motoring out from the bay into the wind and in the direction of the Galapagos Islands. Fidel is praying a lot and mostly silent. I think he is scared of what is ahead of us though he does not say so. We can only hope that as we leave this Hell-pit things improve to the westward.

Janet, Fidel and Jose'

Amanda drew in a deep breath and handed the phone to Jason to read.

'What can I say?' Amanda spluttered with her eyes watering. 'It seems wrong to be euphoric about our lake and the hope we have for our island, when they are daily facing life threatening events.'

'Do your best to encourage them; give them hope and reassurance,' Jason responded solemnly.

Amanda stared blankly at her phone for a minute and then frantically tapped in her message.

Dear Janet, Fidel and Jose,

Today we found a suitable place for you to moor your boat.

The rainy season seems to have come to an end now and the island is spouting life here and there.

We will think about you every day and will prepare for your arrival.

We all need each other, good luck.

Love

Amanda, Jason Isabella and Anna-Marie xxxx'

Amanda glanced once more at the text and, not daring to let her emotion show any further, pressed the transmission button.